SARAH SLATE WAS IN [...] A WEALTHY HEIRESS FROM PROVIDENCE, RHODE ISLAND.

She was well-educated and extraordinarily intuitive—and she knew about CURE. But how much did she know about Mark Howard?

"Dr. Smith, what does this mean?" she asked.

"How can I know without knowing—what he experienced?"

"When these experiences affect him to this level, it means something is reaching for Mark, specifically, right?" she demanded.

"Maybe that this place is being targeted," Smith replied. "Mark's is the most receptive mind to receive the communiqué."

"Attack, you mean."

"We can't assume that."

She glared at him. "Sure we can."

CREATED BY MURPHY & SAPIR

# THE DESTROYER

## DREAM THING

A GOLD EAGLE BOOK FROM

# WORLDWIDE®

TORONTO • NEW YORK • LONDON
AMSTERDAM • PARIS • SYDNEY • HAMBURG
STOCKHOLM • ATHENS • TOKYO • MILAN
MADRID • WARSAW • BUDAPEST • AUCKLAND

If you purchased this book without a cover you should be aware
that this book is stolen property. It was reported as "unsold and
destroyed" to the publisher, and neither the author nor the
publisher has received any payment for this "stripped book."

First edition April 2005

ISBN 0-373-63254-1

Special thanks and acknowledgment to
Tim Somheil for his contribution to this work.

DREAM THING

Copyright © 2005 by Warren Murphy.

All rights reserved. Except for use in any review, the
reproduction or utilization of this work in whole or in part
in any form by any electronic, mechanical or other means,
now known or hereafter invented, including xerography,
photocopying and recording, or in any information storage
or retrieval system, is forbidden without the written permission
of the publisher, Worldwide Library, 225 Duncan Mill Road,
Don Mills, Ontario, Canada M3B 3K9.

All characters in this book have no existence outside the
imagination of the author and have no relation whatsoever to
anyone bearing the same name or names. They are not even
distantly inspired by any individual known or unknown to the
author, and all incidents are pure invention.

® and TM are trademarks of the publisher. Trademarks indicated
with ® are registered in the United States Patent and Trademark
Office, the Canadian Trade Marks Office and in other countries.

**Printed in U.S.A.**

And for the Glorious House of Sinanju,
sinanjucentral@hotmail.com

# Prologue

The man cradled the gangly girl in his arms as if she were a baby, but she wasn't aware the way an infant was. Her mind was consumed by her need to fend off sleep.

"What else could be behind such dreams?" her father demanded.

The father had married into his second cousin's bloodline, which was the most sensitive branch of all the Peoples. Now he alone was free of the dream torment, while his wife, daughters and son suffered terribly.

The daughter in his arms was catatonic, her body half-dead from need of sleep.

The Caretaker of the People pondered this pathetic young victim as she tensed and slackened rhythmically, fighting to stay awake. She succumbed to her need, and became limp in her father's arms as sleep overcame her.

They held their breath, the father and the Caretaker. Maybe this time there would be no dreams....

The girl screamed, her eyes opening wide and her hands clawing at her father's chest. Her mind told her that she was falling from a great height, burning in boiling rain, sinking into water so deep that all light was erased.

Her moment of terror faded, but her reality was just as bad. She didn't see her father or the Caretaker, but focused again on fighting to stay awake.

"She is like this always now. For two days it has been thus," her father said. "I'm afraid she is already mad."

Okyek Meh Thih, the Caretaker of the People, felt sad and helpless. He stood up.

"What will you do?" the father asked.

"I will seek out wisdom," Okyek Meh Thih announced.

The girl's father showed a sign of faint hope, but Okyek Meh Thih felt no hope.

It was his duty. His grandfather's instructions were quite clear. If a time came when the dreams disrupted the lives of the People, then Okyek Meh Thih must go into the mountain again and meditate on the message in the cave. Every fiber of his being told him to stay and offer comfort to the suffering People, and yet he did his duty and walked away from them.

What wisdom could there be in those old mountains and the faded inscription of a people long dead?

## 1

Being insane makes it hard to keep track of the time.

How many days had it been? How far had he crawled? How close was he now to the surface of the world? How much water was left and how much air?

Only as an afterthought did he realize that the gnawing had stopped below his feet. The alien rock eaters were no longer chewing. This explained why the madness had left him; the insane chewing of the alien rock eaters had gone away at last.

His mind turned to his own rock eaters. Were they still eating? Well, of course they were. He could see, couldn't he? The yellow glow of their light was the only light he had seen in weeks. He wriggled until his face was close to the viscous trickle of yellow matter, and inspected it. Were the machines still fully functional?

He couldn't tell without a microscope. The fact that the carrier fluid still glowed was a good sign. The nanotech machines wouldn't glow if they weren't also digging. He had programmed them that way.

Once, a lifetime ago, he produced the machines

from a nanotechnological experiment that he never thought would succeed—but it did. He created functioning devices the size of gnats, and he programmed them to perform a few simple functions. He encapsulated the tiny machines in a tiny vial of silver and had the vial placed on his person, where it would always be with him. The dentist had balked at taking out a perfectly healthy molar to replace it with the silver vial, but a brick of twenty-dollar bills convinced him to do the deed.

The vial was intended to remain with him even after an intense search by law enforcement, and the nanotech machines were intended to be used to free him from a prison cell. Now his prison cell was the earth itself, and the nanotech machines had been put to work to perform a function for which they were not designed.

They chewed away the blockage in fragments smaller than the footprint of an ant, whether the blockage was steel security plates, reinforced concrete walls or solid limestone. Each machine transported its tiny fragment of material to the farthest possible point away from the excavation, and then traveled to the front of the excavation to chew off another fragment. For energy, they fermented small grains of whatever organic matter was provided for them to serve and, when they had energy enough, they provided a phosphorescent output. This was the sum total of their functionality.

The young man could control the direction and size of their excavation by manipulating the pool of excavating machines—this boiled down to smearing the creatures on the rocks that they should excavate. The smaller the cavity they formed, the faster they worked. In the interest of speed, he kept the cavity narrow. It was just six feet long, a foot high and not two feet in diameter. A coffin provided more elbowroom. It was made even tighter by the extra equipment: the air tanks, the small compressor and the canteen.

He had been in this enclosed space for at least forty days. No wonder he was starting to loose his marbles.

He pulled out his pocket notebook and squinted as he read. Depending on how many days he had lost to madness, he ought to be nearing another air chamber. His oxygen tanks were almost depleted.

Still, he was more afraid of what would be waiting for him in the cavern than of suffocation.

He must have slept, because he regained consciousness with cold, fresh air filling his lungs painfully. The nanotech machines had chewed through the wall of the air chamber. The young man scooted forward and pushed his eyes close to the tiny opening.

His angle of ascent had been precise. He was just outside the cavern at exactly the right place—within a few feet of the trickle of the water.

Fifteen minutes later, the opening was large enough for him to wiggle through, but first he scooped up the goo that contained the nanotech machines and applied it to the walls in a new place, redirecting the angle of ascent. A mile above them at an eighty-one-degree angle was another cavern and their next scheduled pit stop.

The young man stifled the pain. Touching the goo provided the machines with organic matter, which they chewed right off of his fingers. Leave them on too long and the machines would remove his skin as effectively as dipping them in a caustic acid.

He listened, but not for long. He was so used to the silence of the earth that the trickle of the water was loud to him. Every once in a while he heard a spatter, which startled him until he was sure it was just the stream.

When he emerged from the rock, his legs wouldn't hold him upright, so he crawled to the trickle and filled his canteens. He groped in the pool and found his emergency pack, stowed there many months ago.

Water splashed on his neck and he almost cried out. What was dripping on him?

Then he heard the sound of water splashing against stone far above, and he remembered the layout of the cavern. Some sort of intersecting vein of hard stone formed a wall alongside the tall shaft where the trickle had eaten away the limestone. It was like a bent and arthritic finger the way it distended up into the earth. He was scheduled to intersect the apex of the shaft again in thirty-six hours.

Only after crawling back into his rock cell, and only after the detritus of the excavation began to rebury the opening into the cavern did he dare to turn on the tiny compressor.

The sound was like the muted whir of a table saw, but it filled the tiny cell in the rock and sang through the earth.

Maybe he was too far away for *them* to hear it this time. Maybe *they* never came this close to the surface....

Then he heard the answering trumpet, which shook the limestone walls. Soon there was the scratching of giant claws against the rock, coming closer. They were using the tunnels he had made himself, when he first dug in to the cavern in his earth drill. They would be here in no time. With his teeth grinding from the tension, he ran the compressor until it filled the air tanks, and seconds later the nanotech machines covered the opening into the cavern with their detritus. Still he could hear the creatures that were coming up from the deep earth to find him.

They weren't albinos. The albinos were weak and stupid and contemptible. These things had never even shown themselves, but he heard them and he knew they were less human than the albinos.

They were getting closer. The loose pile of rock at the rear of his coffin was getting thicker, but slowly. The young man decided to increase the speed of the excavation. He wiped at the liquid smear at the front of the rock, collecting it into a smaller area, and the excavation continued in the tightest possible space. The young man slithered ahead at almost a foot a minute, dragging the air tanks along between his legs on the leather belt while the limestone walls squeezed him so close he couldn't take a deep breath.

He started laughing when he felt the digging below him. They had come to his cavern and found the loose earth of his little tunneling operation. Whatever they were—and his mind conjured wild visions—they were far too large to use his tunnels, no matter how loose the packed stone powder fill was that he left behind him. They had to dig up to him.

They were closer than last time. They *would* dig, and they just might reach him. He listened to the sound of the scraping claws.

He began to shiver, despite the hundred-degree heat. He estimated the progress of his pursuers and his own speed and calculated his odds of escape.

The odds weren't good.

He calculated the odds of suffocating himself before they reached him. Again, not good. His air wouldn't run out in time. His mind spun out of control as he thought of some other way of ending his life before they reached him; anything was better than letting them reach him. The nanotech robots were of no use. They would feed for only a short time on his flesh before their fermentation tanks were full of organic material. It wouldn't be enough to kill him. Was there a way to use the compressor to inject himself with high-pressure air and cause a reasonably quick death? No way he could think of with the tools he had on hand.

His only option was to make a run for it. He wriggled onto his stomach, slithered to the front and wiped together the nanotech goo into an even smaller area. The tunnel grew faster but the young man could barely move forward, the rock compressing his rib cage. His arms cried out in pain. He was forced to keep them distended ahead of him to elongate his torso and to keep from disturbing the tiny, glowing line of fluid. It contained swimming nanotech machines transporting excavated stone to the rear of the hot, bullet-shaped hollow.

The grinding from below grew more intense. Those creatures were scratching out their own tunnel as fast as they could, and closing in.

The young man knew he wouldn't make it. There was no way he could outrun them. The air became hotter when his tube passed into a granite layer, which crumbled less. The increased hardness of the rock made no difference to the nanotech machines, but the unforgiving texture of the granite was too much for the young man. He began to feel claustrophobic again, for the first time in weeks. The madness of his situation danced wickedly in his unstable mind. He chuckled at his own helplessness, feeling both horror and relief.

Those *things* would finally get him. His ordeal would soon end. He would be devoured, surely. Just as the albinos chomped up the blind cavefish.

That was funny. He laughed some more, then choked because he didn't have enough room for the deep breaths that laughing required.

When he stopped laughing, the scratching of stone below him had stopped. He was no longer being pursued.

Then it hit him. The granite strata was the answer. It was nothing to the self-sharpening teeth of the nanotech machines, but maybe it had foiled the creatures that were after him.

Hours later, his route of excavation closed in on the apex of the chamber. Here he was supposed to break through again and refill the air tanks. He had to do it, or he would suffocate. The next pit stop was a long way off.

Regardless of the danger, he was too intrigued to not take the opportunity to see what had chased him for as long as he could remember.

When the machines broke through the stone, he allowed them to create a hole in the rock too small for his thumb to fit through. That was enough to let in the air of the chamber, and it was enough for him to look through.

He saw only darkness.

He smelled something animal.

The disappointment was too much to bear. He *must* know what these things were.

"Hello down there!"

Talking to himself had kept his voice in good shape. It was answered with a distant screech. The creatures had given up on him and were already miles away. It didn't take them long to return to the cavern, snarling as they swarmed in from the tunnel.

They carried wadded-up balls of glowing matter. It was enough to reveal them for what they were.

What they were was unlike anything that the young man had seen before.

The things flung their glowing balls and spattered the cavern walls with the glowing entrails of cave salamanders. It illuminated the eight-hundred-foot shaft all the way to the top, where the young man looked out through his tiny peephole and laughed at them.

They screeched more. They dug their great talons

into the living rock and climbed up, up—but the limestone ran out. The granite was too hard for their claws to find purchase. They tumbled and slipped, breaking bony arms, cracking open their exoskeletal faceplates. One of them climbed to within a hundred feet of the young man, then plummeted, cracking its face open during the fall so that its skull split like a coconut, right along the ridge of its nose.

They screeched at the young man until the progress of his excavating machine forced him to move on. They were screeching until long after the tiny hole was covered with detritus.

The young man was chuckling. He was truly insane, and he knew it, but insanity felt good.

THE WORLD WAS in a nasty mood.

This was nothing new. The world was made up of nations controlled by people who had no business being in control.

Once, it had been survival of the fittest, and the most brutal caveman in the valley got to boss around all the other cave people. Then brains got bigger and people began working cooperatively to oust the brutes and give control to better leaders. Three million years later, the valleys were ruled by a new form of brute.

A politician was a human being who wanted power, and this by definition was exactly the wrong kind of person to be handed the reins of power. In some nations these brutes became dictators through their cunning, charisma and duplicity, always masked behind doctrine, always dependent on the whims of fate. Fate almost never allowed honest men to become dictators.

In other nations, they became prime ministers or presidents—through cunning, charisma and duplicity. They projected a false doctrine. They used public perception to distract the people from their evident lies. The people singled out one confident man or another to control their government because they had no real choices, and because they convinced themselves that the manufactured image of sincerity was genuine sincerity. The system was designed to bring charlatans to power. Fate almost never allowed honest men to be elected to high office.

Even the world's biggest democracy was not a democracy, but a democratic republic, where the culture of mass media and easy answers made a mockery of the democratic process. Yet it was still the best system of national government that could be found.

Which meant the other systems were flawed in the extreme.

When the leaders chosen under all these systems became agitated by forces beyond their understanding, they lashed out at whatever target was convenient. It felt good to do so.

The world became a despicable place.

**2**

His name was Remo and he had lately developed this thing about people who didn't get the recognition they deserved.

"I got maps of the Walk of Fame," said a street corner punk with crusty hair.

"I'm only looking for one star," Remo said.

"You'll never find it without a map," the punk insisted. "Just five bucks."

Remo considered it, then handed over a five. He was back a minute later.

"Hey, this map's no good," he told the punk. "It doesn't show the star for Alan Hale Jr."

"Sure does."

"Show me."

The punk rolled his eyes and snatched Remo's five-dollar map of Hollywood, flinging it open and stabbing one finger at the pages.

"Right there."

Remo looked at the spot the punk pointed. "Can't be."

"Can be."

"It's almost a side street. I don't believe it."

The punk sneered and thrust back the map. "I grew up in Hollywood, dude. I know every inch of the Walk of Fame. That's where they put Alan Hale Jr."

Remo scowled deeply. The punk couldn't decide if the man was about to start crying or whip out an AK-47 and begin a spree.

"Hey, you know how they decide who gets a star?" the punk asked. "It's all politics. True talent's got nothing to do with it. I guess Alan Hale Jr.'s people didn't work it good enough to get him a better spot."

Remo shook his head. "Maybe he wasn't a good actor, but he's still way better than most of the schmoes on this map."

The punk shrugged. "You ain't gettin' no argument from me. Look at all them people up the street. They been camped there for days, keeping a—what they call it?—a vigil. You know whose star that is?"

"Who?" Remo asked.

"That kiddy-diddler. Miguel Jackon."

Remo's eyes grew dark. "Are you telling me they give a primo star spot to that wacko and then they go and put Alan Hale Jr. next to a stinking alley? It's a crime. Somebody ought to do something about it."

The punk shrugged and looked away from the nerdy tourist. Something about the nerd's eyes made the punk uneasy. "Be my guest."

"I will."

The punk was surprised when his customer turned and marched up the street toward the crowd of Miguel Jackon supporters. Just what did that guy think he was going to do?

REMO WANDERED into the crowd, which had closed off the street around a mound of flowers, stuffed animals and handmade signs proclaiming undying love to Miguel Jackon: Miguel Is Innocent! and Free Miguel!

"What's going on?" he asked a woman with long braided hair and a face full of black mascara streaks.

"We're showing our support for Miguel," she said.

"Miguel who?"

"Miguel Jackon," she explained impatiently.

Remo did his best impression of an ignoramus. "What movies was he in?"

"He's not an actor—he's a singer, you jerk! How can you not know about Miguel Jackon?"

"Yeah, what are you, a retard?" demanded a dowdy, short man in a suit and tie that he'd been wearing for days.

"Hey, sorry, just a sightseer. But I thought only actors got stars on the Walk of Fame. How come they gave one to some old singer?"

The crowd grew uglier by the second. "He's not old!" insisted a pair of Latino women in matching Miguel Jackon satin jackets.

"He's the biggest star of them all!" the rumpled-suit man proclaimed. "Remember the Jackon Five, the band he was in with his brothers in the seventies? Remember *Thrillride?* He sold thirty million copies of that album."

Remo scratched his chin and looked at the grimy sky thoughtfully. "I don't remember any of that."

"He *must* be a retard!" insisted one of the Latino women.

"Wait." Remo snapped his fingers. "The child

molester! So this is sort of a memorial for all the kids he abused, huh?"

"Lies!" the short man spat.

"Those children lied to get Miguel's money!"

"Really?" Remo said. "I thought they had DNA evidence."

"More lies! They stole his semen and used it to frame him!" the mascara woman said.

"Truly?" Remo asked.

"He could never do that to a child," the mascara woman wailed.

"But what about the pictures? And the videos?"

"There were no pictures and no video," the Latino woman declared.

Remo grinned playfully. "You kidders. They're showing the video on the news right now." He pointed out the display of televisions behind the barred window of a nearby electronics shop.

"Oh, God, it's true," wailed someone.

"No, they're more lies! He couldn't have done it."

The supporters crowded down the street to the electronics shop and Remo slipped through them, stepped over the mound of flowers and teddy bears, and rummaged around for the sidewalk star of Miguel Jackon.

Seconds later, a great wrong had been righted.

THEY RAN THE VIDEO a hundred times that morning—a trash bin being lifted off the surface of an alley to reveal the Hollywood Walk of Fame Star of Miguel Jackon. Somehow it had been moved into a third-rate spot, where a big garbage bin was shared by a fetish shop and a Chinese food restaurant.

The camera slow-moed a cardboard container of discarded Chinese food plopping out of the trash bin and splattering right on the Jackon star. Sun-ripened pork lo mein covered Jackon's engraved name, and splattered far enough to deface the stars of the adjoining Gabors.

The sunny hostess chimed in, "Shortly after this exclusive footage was taken by *Good Day U.S.A.*, Miguel Jackon supporters discovered the star switch and caused a near riot."

The next clip showed an Asian in a filthy apron smiling toothlessly at the jeering crowd from behind a wall of police protection. "Law enforcement has refused to allow the removal of the disposal bin behind Happy Noodle No. 3," the voice-over said.

"Local ordinance says the garbage goes right where it is," a Hollywood police officer said in a sound bite. "Mr. Lung has the right to keep his garbage right there. We intend to protect that right at all costs."

The next clip showed rumpled-suit man proclaiming indignantly, "The Hollywood police are unfairly prejudiced against child molesters!"

"Meanwhile, you'll never believe whose star got moved into Miguel Jackon's old spot!" the blond announcer said, beaming. "His little buddy couldn't be more pleased!"

**3**

"What's wrong?" the skipper demanded. "Why aren't we moving?"

The first mate rolled his eyes. "We're going fifteen knots, Captain."

"The engines are going fifteen knots, Trine," Captain Moran said. "That doesn't mean the ship's going fifteen knots."

Yeah, right, the mate thought, checking the instrument cluster. It showed them moving across the Pacific Ocean at 14.95 knots. The captain was an old-timer who didn't trust electronics. He put his faith in the stars and the look of the ocean and crap like that.

"See?" the mate said.

The captain ignored the display and moved to the GPS position tracker. "Holy criminy. We haven't moved an inch in the last quarter of an hour."

The mate was about to protest, but the display showed him the captain was correct. They were staying in place.

"Didn't you feel the turbulence, Trine?" the captain demanded. "It woke me up."

"What turbulence?"

"The damn ship's working way too hard to maintain its course. We're going against some sort of a powerful current."

"Let me look," the mate said, and tapped out commands on the instrument screen.

"You don't need to look. There's not supposed to be any fifteen-knot current, not here," the captain declared.

"There must be," the mate insisted, but his global positioning system confirmed that there was no charted current.

The positioning sensor altered slightly, and the captain swore under his breath. "Now we're moving *backward*."

"That's impossible."

"Believe it, Trine. Dammit, something is up. Call Honolulu. I want to know what's going on."

Skipper Moran rang the alert, waking the entire crew. Trine thought that the old man was off his rocker. Something was wrong, yes, but it had to be an instrument problem, not a mysterious new ocean current.

He rang his Navy liaison at the Pearl Harbor naval base. The satellite phone crackled with interference as the mate asked for any reports of a localized southwesterly current in the vicinity, running at fifteen knots.

"Of course not. You guys smoking something funny out there?" the Navy operator asked with a chuckle.

"Not me, but I'm not speaking for the captain," the mate said defensively. "*Wahine* out."

The captain was changing course. "What did they say?" he demanded.

"They said there's no such current."

"Heavy weather?"

"Nothing," the mate said. "Captain, where are we going?"

"Anywhere away from here!" The captain had taken manual control of the *Wahine,* and he was adjusting the steering wheel-like helm minutely. "Feel that, Trine? She's still struggling. I'm trying to find the flow of the current."

"What?" Trine asked. He didn't feel anything.

"Did you ever steer a ship, Trine?" the captain asked, giving the wheel a slight adjustment, then stared into space. "There. That's got it."

First Mate Trine had no clue what the captain was talking about. He felt nothing.

"If we're going directly into the flow, we'll have the least amount of cross current to slow us down," the captain explained impatiently. "Now give me full speed. We have to fight our way out of this!"

Trine obeyed orders, bringing the shipping vessel *Wahine* up to full speed. The diesel engines rumbled belowdecks. Now, *that* Trine could feel.

Moran was tense. Was the captain actually afraid? Moran was past his prime, and he had certainly been left behind by the technological advancements of the modern merchant marine, but he still had a lifetime of experience aboard shipping vessels. Trine couldn't understand what the old man could possibly be afraid of.

The monitor on the position display changed.

"Well, now we're moving," Trine said.

The captain turned on him with haunted eyes. "Not very damn fast, we're not. The current's getting faster."

"How do you know?"

"Feel it, boy," Moran said. "The *Wahine*'s fighting hard."

SOON ENOUGH the mate could feel it, and everybody on board felt it. The *Wahine* struggled against a current that moved faster by the minute. The GPS showed that she had been pulled in reverse another thousand meters.

"We're losing it," the captain exclaimed.

"The GPS must be wrong," Mate Trine insisted.

"It's not wrong." Moran called the engine room. "What can you do to give us more speed?"

"Not much. We're red-lining as it is," the chief engineer said.

The captain was distracted by the display, showing they had lost another thousand meters in just a minute. "Mr. Viscott, I don't care what it does to the engines. You keep us moving. Override the safeties and give me speed."

"Captain—"

"I take full responsibility." Moran slammed down the phone.

First Mate Trine saw his opportunity for career advancement and he went for it. "Captain Moran, I cannot let you destroy the engines."

"Shut up and get me Honolulu, Trine."

Trine grabbed the on-board phone instead. "Chief

Engineer, this is First Mate Trine. I am relieving Captain Moran of his command of the *Wahine*. Disregard his previous orders. You will not disable the safety mechanisms on the engine."

"You idiot." Moran snatched the phone away from Trine. "Engineer, this is Moran. Obey my orders."

Trine marched into the rear of the bridge and found his side arm in its locker. He was back in seconds, just as the captain slammed down the phone again.

"Captain, I am placing you under arrest for deliberately attempting to destroy the engines of this ship."

"You're crazy, Trine. I said I would take responsibility, didn't I?"

"Those engines will cost three-quarters of a million dollars to overhaul. I'm saving the company a lot of money."

The captain sneered. "Bucking for your own ship, Trine?"

The first mate smirked. "Maybe."

"You're a moron." The captain's meaty paws wrenched the gun out of Trine's hands. "Next time, it'll work better if you turn off the safety." The captain flipped the safety off and leveled it at Trine's forehead. "You, I don't have time for. Put the cuffs on yourself and I won't have to shoot you."

Trine miserably obeyed orders. Well, he gave it a good try. Would it be enough to earn him a ship of his own?

Now the captain was calling Honolulu again. He was calling in a mayday and asking for air evacuation.

"No cutters—aren't you listening?" the captain

demanded. "We're caught in some sort of strong current. We're fighting it with everything we've got and we're still losing knots under the keel. You send a Coast Guard ship out here and they'll get sucked in just like us. We need an airlift ASAP."

THE COAST GUARD OPERATOR called in his commanding officer.

"Are you sure it isn't your instruments, Captain Moran?"

Coast Guard Captain Brotz jerked the telephone receiver away from his ear at Moran's thundering response, then handed it back to the operator and went over to the traffic control board.

"They are moving south-southeast at about six knots and accelerating," said the traffic controller.

"Could he have the ship in reverse and not even know it?" the Coast Guard CO asked.

The traffic controller shrugged. "Not unless he's got a screw loose. I'd say he's trying to pull one over on us."

"Why would he want to do that?" the CO asked.

"It's just a little more likely than not knowing he was in reverse. I didn't say it made sense."

None of it made sense. The information on Captain Moran's license showed he had thirty years' experience on the sea, in the U.S. Navy and then the merchant marine, without a blemish.

"I'm not taking a chance that Moran has a screw lose," Brotz decided aloud. He barked out orders for rescue choppers to get into the air. "Alert Captain Moran."

"I think I've lost him, sir. He doesn't respond. The *Wahine*'s blinked out."

*Blinked out* was their inexcusably blasé piece of jargon to say a ship had disappeared from all monitors suddenly and inexplicably. It implied the ship had gone below the waves. The room buzzed with sudden activity as the Coast Guard personnel launched into rescue-mission activities.

"We're on our way," radioed the captain of the long-range Coast Guard cutter *Reliant.*

"Thank God," said the operator. "*Reliant* is in the vicinity."

"Where?" Captain Brotz demanded.

"About ten miles south-southeast. Hold on, sir, and I'll give you better coordinates."

Brotz snatched the receiver that enabled him to join the operator's radio link. "*Reliant* commander?"

"This is Captain Burness."

"Gil, get out of there. Turn on a north-northwest heading and come on home as fast as you can."

"Norton, you crazy? We're on a rescue mission."

"We have rescue choppers en route. Let them handle it."

"Choppers out of Oahu? It will take them an hour just to reach the *Wahine*'s last position. It's a stroke of luck we're in the vicinity."

"Moran claimed there was an aberrant current overpowering his engines, Gil. I don't want you caught up in it, too."

"It's open water. No surge is going to surface enough to affect the *Reliant*," Captain Burness replied. "We could have a tsunami under our keel and hardly feel it."

"Not a surge—a current."

"There's no such thing, short of typhoon or an undersea volcano. Sun's shining, so I don't think it's the weather. Are there new volcanoes birthing around these parts?"

Captain Brotz hadn't even thought of that. He knew a volcanic eruption on the ocean floor could create tidal waves, but in the open sea could it create an ocean current capable of pulling in a powerful new freighter like the *Wahine?* Come to think of it, what else besides seismic activity *could* create such a phenomenon?

"Hold on, *Reliant,*" Brotz barked, then shouted at his meteorology data operator. "I want a report from the Navy seismology lab."

"On the line now, sir."

"What?" Brotz tromped to the desk and snatched another receiver. "Seismic? This is Brotz. You guys have activity anywhere in the vicinity?"

"Sir, we have activity everywhere in the vicinity."

"Well, what the hell is it? A volcano?"

"Maybe thirty volcanoes could create this kind of a seismic signature. We've never seen anything like it."

"You don't know. That's what you're telling me?"

"Correct. But we're working on it."

"Goddamn Navy!" Brotz slammed down one receiver and barked into the second one, "*Reliant,* you were on the money. Something geologic is happening and it's so big the seismic lab can't even ID it. Now get the hell out of there."

Brotz glanced at the traffic screen and the stricken face of the operator.

"*Reliant?* Talk to me."

*Reliant* was gone.

"Who's that?" Brotz demanded, jabbing at a new icon on the traffic screen.

"USS *Harding.* Navy spy ship on exercises. They intercepted the mayday from the *Wahine.*"

Brotz felt as if he were witnessing a chain reaction on a California expressway, standing there helplessly as one car after another slammed into the growing pile of wreckage. Were the *Wahine* and the *Reliant* really gone? Even on the unpredictable Pacific Ocean, catastrophe simply did not strike that fast. Ships took minutes or hours to sink....

He called for a connection to the Navy cruiser.

"Captain, your own Navy people report a major seismological disturbance throughout your vicinity. Two ships might be lost already. Don't risk the *Harding.*"

"You Coast Guard boys have sure lost your balls," replied the captain of the *Harding.* "Don't tell me you want to abandon the survivors? Those are your own people in there."

"Air rescue is on the way."

"Not fast enough. We're going in. Besides, this isn't a merchant ship and it's not a Coast Guard dingy. It's a Navy cruiser. We can handle a little strong water."

Captain Brotz felt ill, and the command center was eerily silent as he and his crew monitored the Navy radio chatter. *Harding* reported a strong current.

"Twenty-eight knots!" Brotz said under his breath.

*Harding* vanished. The icon on the traffic screen simply went away. No more radio communication came in from the ship, and the Navy radio chatter became frantic.

As the two Coast Guard rescue helicopters closed in on the last known location of the Navy cruiser, Navy command radioed Brotz and belligerently demanded surrender of command of the rescue choppers. Brotz declined. "You're welcome to listen in if you like."

Somewhere, Navy top brass was sputtering. Brotz didn't care.

"Sea is empty," reported the leader of the rescue team aboard the choppers.

"No wreckage? No oil?"

"Nothing. But the water is moving like you wouldn't believe. It's like a river down there."

"Pilot, what's your status?"

"Unaffected. We're fine up here, Base," the pilot reported. "Dropping a tracking buoy. Jesus!"

"What happened?" Brotz demanded.

"The tracking buoy, sir. It hit the water and started moving like a bat from hell. I'm pacing it at an airspeed of sixty-three knots."

"Coast Guard commander, this is Navy Command at Pearl Harbor. Your pilots are obviously incompetent. I want them under my command right now or it's your ass."

Brotz leaned into the monitor and examined the icon for the activated buoy, then he snatched the radio to the Navy. "Check it for yourself, Admiral, it should be on your screen. My pilot pinned it at sixty-three knots and climbing. Since the only bad decisions made here today were made by Navy command, I think I'll hold on to this one."

"Commander, there's a Navy vessel missing—"

"And a Coast Guard vessel and a merchant ship."

"But the *Harding* is a *Navy ship*," the admiral insisted. "Its priority outweighs a merchant ship or even a Coast Guard cutter."

Commander Brotz hung up on the admiral of the Navy.

"I've spotted the *Harding!*" radioed the helicopter copilot. "She's moving like you wouldn't believe, but she's afloat."

"We're getting interference," Brotz said. "Is there any visible cause?"

"Nothing, Base. The *Harding* is being pulled stern first. She's flopping all over the place. That nut thinks he can get free—he's rocking his thrust on the props."

Brotz barely made out the words behind the worsening static. On the monitor, the pair of icons for the helicopters flickered, as if the aircraft were dematerializing. "Pilots, pull out now."

"Negative, Base. There's no danger up here. We see something ahead."

"That's an order—turn around."

There was no response from the helicopters, ever, and their traffic blips blinked out.

ON THE OTHER SIDE of the world, a man was gasping for air.

"Mark, wake up." The young woman shook him

gently. The man's eyes went wide and he crawled away from her, against the metal bars of the headboard.

Sarah Slate never forgot the look. For a moment, Mark Howard didn't know who she was—or even what she was.

Then he saw her, remembered her and remembered himself. "Oh."

"What was it?"

He concentrated. "I don't even know." He looked at his hands. "I was something else. It was dark. The world was moving me and there was a light. It was going to—consume me."

"Eat you?"

"There were others, all of us being—channeled into the light. We were food."

"Food for what?"

The door rattled on its hinges with such noise and racket that Sarah turned, expecting an army to come pouring through it. It was a heavy old hospital door, and it remained closed.

"Open at once!" a voice squeaked from the outside.

Sarah rushed to the door and yanked it open, and was pushed aside by a figure no larger than a child. He was, however, unbelievably old, Asian and dressed in a brightly colored robe. Close behind him came a slapping of wild wings, and a purple bird as big as an eagle flew into the room.

"Say not the name," warned the old man, addressing Mark Howard as the bird settled on the blankets.

"What name?" he asked.

"That of the thing of which you dreamed."

"Were you eavesdropping?" Sarah demanded.

"Forgive me, young Slate. It was something that I believed must be done. I was on guard for just such a happenstance. I did not pierce the veil of your words until I heard the tumult of the Young Prince's awakening."

"What happenstance?" Mark asked.

"The tumult," the old man said. "The dreams come."

Sarah was peeved. "You just happened to wake up at two in the morning and just happened to hear us?"

"You did not awaken me. It was the others."

"What others?" Sarah demanded.

The old man shot out a finger so fast she couldn't see it move, and the finger pressed against her lips to shush her. He held it there as silence fell.

But there was no silence, after all. There were shouts, cries and screams.

"Oh, God," Sarah said. "It sounds like half the hospital. What's happening."

"Half of half, but that is a sufficient number of people in terror. The dream thing affects them, those with a particular bent and balance in their mind's landscape. It is the thing of which you dreamed, Prince Mark."

The man was listening to the cries from far away.

"Heed, Mark Howard," the old man said. "It may discover you and exert its will. Say not the name."

"I don't know its name."

"It may choose to tell you. Turn your thoughts away from it. Give it the least of your attentions."

"What is it?" Sarah asked. "Why would it afflict Mark?"

The parrot chuckled harshly. "An adept mind in dangerous company," it croaked, then looked surprised at itself.

"Quiet, bird," the old man scolded.

"Who is dangerous?" Sarah Slate asked, and she didn't offer the leeway for no answer.

"Remo."

"Remo's in Europe," Sarah pointed out.

"And me," the old man added. "I attract its attentions."

"And wrath," the bird added.

**4**

"I'm acting under the direct orders of my supervisor," Remo told the emperor of Sicily. "And I never disobey an order."

"It is a million dollars. Surely you can disobey one small order in exchange for a million dollars."

"Listen, Burpescusmi, I just shrugged off a career in the Extreme Naked Athletics for a million bucks."

"What?"

"On the other hand, I could have been the best Crocodile Outback Marathon runner that there ever was. Another easy million. Or ice-wall climbing. I could have done that blindfolded. Another million."

"I do not know what you are talking about," said the emperor of Sicily. "Please talk slower because of my English."

"Did I mention my TV career? Way more than a million bucks, bucko, and I would have got to bag more sleazy celebrity teenyboppers than you could shake your stick at. But I gave it all up."

"Why?"

"My father. He would have been irked. Now, you

want to know who's really irked? Me. Why? Miguel Jackon."

"Ten million dollars," the emperor said. Even crazy men had their price, right?

"Not bad. If you had it. Which you don't. Did you hear about Miguel Jackon? The whole business with the star in Hollywood. That was me. I moved it. But it's not what I wanted to do. You know what I wanted to do?" The American began snapping imaginary bones in his hands. They weren't especially powerful-looking hands, but the wrists were thick as the drive shaft on a piece of construction equipment.

"I can get you ten million U.S. dollars by daybreak."

"If I cared, which I don't. I'm already rich, see?"

"No government agents are rich. Except in my government."

The American's smile was made all the more chilling by the malevolent brown eyes. "What you call a government I call organized crime."

"Yes, we are organized, yes, and now official, too. We have the legitimacy of statehood."

"You think because some slimeball mafioso declares himself king he really is king?"

"Yes, that is true," declared Don Bertilescessi. "Sicily has always been under the oppressive rule of the mainland Italians. Too long have they dictated their will to the Sicilian people. Until now there has been no man with the strength of will to take a stand against the dictators of Rome."

"Doesn't make you legitimate."

"We have been recognized by other heads of state! This makes us legitimate!"

"Just because a bunch of other international criminals say you're not a criminal doesn't mean you're not a criminal. You know how many innocent people have been killed during your reign of power? One for every rice grain in my breakfast bowl."

"We are fighting for our freedom!"

"You're a thug. A bully. You're a coward."

The emperor of Sicily grew red in the face. "No man alive today has ever called Don Bertilescessi a coward. All are dead!"

"I know. Take, for example, that village mayor from up in the hills."

"Exactly!"

"He said that it was cowardly of Bertilescessi to hold the families of the Italian government as hostages."

"Yes!" Bertilescessi hissed.

"So you sent the other thugs who work for you to kill the mayor. And his family."

"He got what he deserved!"

"Hello? Stupid man? You proved how cowardly you really are."

"I am not a coward!"

"You're chickenshit. The wonderful wizard wouldn't know what to do with you."

The emperor of Sicily attempted to kick, or swing a roundhouse, or surreptitiously extract the dagger from his sock garters. He wasn't capable of moving anything below the neck. The smart-ass from America had paralyzed him with a nerve pinch of some kind.

"You call me a coward when you have incapacitated me! A real man would fight fair."

Remo nodded. "You have a point."

REMO and Don Bertilescessi, the self-installed emperor of Sicily, came to a gentlemen's agreement.

The don's upper ranks were invited to his penthouse suite to see that the agreement was fairly executed.

"Come in, everybody. I'm Remo and you're not."

There was confusion and distrust, and there were many drawn weapons. One of the don's top men asked a question that Remo didn't understand, but he assumed it was your standard "What's going on?" The don muttered quickly in response.

"Here's the deal," Remo announced when eight armed and unpleasant Sicilian mafiosi were milling around in the penthouse suite that was the don's private bedroom. "The don and I have come to an agreement. We're going to have a fight, fair and square, man to man."

There was a flurry of raised firearms.

"Do not shoot!" the don ordered. Remo was now holding his wrist, and the don knew what sort of pain could happen when Remo squeezed the wrist.

The second slimeball in command issued some rapid-fire demands, but the don interrupted him.

"Speak only English."

"Thanks, Don," Remo said. "Now, everybody knows that the don here is a big sack of cowardly shit, just like the rest of you—"

"Don't shoot!" the don squealed.

"He says he's not. We're going to have a fight to determine who's correct. The don gets his choice of weapons. I fight without weapons. If I win, the don goes on Sicilian television and tells the viewing audience that he is a coward and a worthless hunk of dog droppings. Got it? You guys—I'm trusting you now—will make sure that he follows through.'Kay?"

The high-ranking hoods, who also served as the upper ranks of the Sicilian government all week, came to the conclusion that this American was a lunatic. But until the don was free of the lunatic, they played along.

"Okay, Don, choose your weapon." Remo adjusted the don's spine, and Bertilescessi regained the use of his arms and legs. He smiled self-assuredly, got to his feet and strolled across the room to his men.

Now Remo was on one side, and the don's army was on the other.

"Kill him," the emperor of Sicily ordered.

The second in command was waiting, with his finger on the trigger, for this very command, and he fired even as the words were spoken. The high-powered Glock handgun cracked like thunder.

Something happened very fast. The second in command staggered and stared down at the big bloody hole where his manhood used to be, then he slumped against the wall and slid down it, hissing like a leaky tire.

"Ha! What a buffoon!" Remo was now standing behind the don, spoiling any other shots.

"He was my brother!" the don gasped.

"Your brother was a total idiot."

"He was a great man!"

"Is that why he shot his own privates? Anybody else going to try spoiling the fight?"

The don didn't know what was happening, but he ordered his men to stand down. "We will fight, as I have sworn I will fight."

"Call the local news," Remo added.

"Let us wait to see the outcome." The don selected a stubby Uzi submachine gun as his weapon of choice. He checked the magazine and, without so much as a handshake, began firing at his opponent.

Somehow he missed and missed and missed while Remo shuffled and slithered around the penthouse. When the submachine gun chugged to a halt, the penthouse was in tatters.

Remo fingered a smoking hole in a seventeenth-century Sicilian tapestry. "Your weapon must be defective, Don."

The don snatched a revolver from one of his men and triggered it repeatedly at Remo, who leaned a little this way and a little that way until the revolver clicked.

"We did agree on one weapon," Remo pointed out, but Bertilescessi snatched up a short-barreled combat shotgun and blasted a hole in the wall where Remo was standing. Remo was standing somewhere else now. More holes blossomed in the walls. The don threw the shotgun at Remo, who ignored it, drifting like flash of shadow up close to the don and using one of the most recognizable hand-to-hand combat moves in the business—the Stooges' two-finger eyepoke.

"Ouch. Did that hurt?" Remo asked the gasping don, who slithered to the floor, moaning in pain.

A human beer barrel brought his pistol down on Remo's skull, only to have it slapped out of his hand at the instant before impact. The sting turned to raging pain, and the human beer barrel saw his hand was a limp skin sack full of broken pieces. The gun was imbedded in the forehead of another man, who didn't know he was dead yet and gargled as he collapsed.

"I expected you guys to stand by the word of your don," Remo said. "Where's your integrity?"

Another man answered by firing his own submachine gun. He traced a line in the wallpaper. Remo was still standing there, with smoking holes in the wall behind him but none actually in him.

Remo appeared to take one long step that carried him across the room, as if his legs were elastic, and he adjusted the aim of the submachine gun. A few rounds peppered the chest of the gunner's neighbor, and then Remo pinched the barrel and the last round blew up the Uzi in the face of the assailant.

"I guess I shouldn't have expected anything better," Remo said.

The bodyguard whose Uzi was appropriated by the don looked for another weapon. He found the blood-soaked Glock lying on the carpet, and he tried to use it.

"Obviously, that gun is malfunctioning," Remo told the guard, who found his manhood splattered on the floor just like the don's brother. The man died just as readily. "Anybody else want to give it a try?" Remo showed the gun to the three survivors.

One of them fired his own piece right at the heart of Remo Williams, but his aim was off slightly. The bullet hit the Glock in Remo's hand and ricocheted back into the gunner's own chest.

"I think it's cursed," Remo said, tossing the Glock.

The other two men were without weapons, but when the gun landed on the carpet in front of them, they wouldn't touch it.

"Didn't I tell you to call the TV news?" Remo said. They stared at him. "Well?"

One of them went for the Glock, and the other man tried to stop him. Somehow, the Glock went off in the tussle, with a little help from Remo. The don was just blinking his eyesight back as his last two men flopped dead from the same bullet.

THE RECENTLY self-proclaimed emperor of the Independent Kingdom of Sicily resigned as the world watched.

"I am a worthless piece of human trash," he informed them over his video feed. He spoke in English for some reason. He was broadcasting from the luxury, high-security apartment from which the government had operated. "I am a coward and a bully. I'm not a man. I'm just a slime-wall."

A hand came into the shot and dragged the emperor out of the camera's view. There was whispering off-screen as the camera's automatic lens adjusted to bring the background into focus. It was a slaughterhouse. The government of the don had clearly been eviscerated.

"Excuse me," the don said as he was thrust back in front of the camera. "Slime*ball.* I am a slime*ball,* not a wall. I will now release the 120 political prisoners...."

He was yanked out of the shot and shoved back in.

"The 120 innocent hostages will now be released. I, and the cowards who grovel at my feet like filthy dogs, should be arrested and charged with mass murder. Also, we are morons."

The emperor looked off-camera and raised his eyebrows. "Anything else?" the world heard him ask.

Remo yanked the power cord to the camera and its lights went out. "That ought to do it." He nodded at the wide-screen TV on the wall. "Look, you're on CNN Europe already."

Remo was thrilled at the instant success of the don's nifty video hard-link to the local news station. The don had used it for the past few days to make proclamations to his new subjects. Now the don proclaimed to the world that he was an imbecile and a coward. He was worse than finished—he was emasculated.

"Kill me," he pleaded.

"Sure thing," said Remo Williams.

**5**

Sir James Wylings had been born a leech. He had lived a leech. Being a leech on society was what Wylings knew. He was good at it.

But that didn't mean he couldn't remake himself into something better. He was convinced that all his famous, noble forebears had earned their royal status. So had Sir James Wylings, as far as the world was concerned. But Wylings himself knew the shameful truth. His knighthood had come about through the manipulation of events and, frankly, a little mass murder. You couldn't arrange to save a starving camp full of refugees without allowing a good number of them to actually starve first. Wylings tried not to think about that part of the scheme. After all, it was only inland Africans who did the starving. His great-grandfather had a term for such people: "ignorant savages." It was such a quaint old-England turn of phrase.

Sir James imagined the old duke saying, "They're just ignorant savages, my boy. Any token of civilization you can give them makes them worlds better off than they were before. Aren't those ignorant

savages better off because of the blessings you provided?" The old man wouldn't have allowed anybody to answer that before concluding, "Of course
they are! You touched their lives with the magic fairy
dust of English culture! If they weren't ignorant savages, they'd understand that it was well worth the
lives of a few ignorant savages."

That mind-set was totally lacking in the modern
world of the twenty-first century. It really wasn't so
long ago, the time of the British Empire, when England ruled the world.

Bloody England today was nothing more than
America's manservant, and every time the Americans got mud on their face, England was right there
getting spattered, too.

Not that Wylings wanted the U.K. to be popular.
What was the value in that? He wanted the U.K. to
be powerful. He wanted his great-grandfather's
British Empire back. A leech such as himself could
find a real niche in a nation intent on good old-fash-
ioned colonialism.

He'd been drawing up plans for years, but they all
looked like crazy schemes in the end. He had been
wielding his influence conservatively, creating the
perfect image. He held roles in the British government and was perceived as competent and loyal. The
competence took some back-room game-playing to
create, but he was genuinely loyal to the British
crown—although to a crown that did not necessarily still exist....

But maybe, one day, his version of England would
be reborn. Maybe, just maybe, he would cause it to

happen himself. Maybe all the craziness in the world this week would give him a leg up—if he only worked it just right.

**6**

Being in Palermo when the crowds came into the streets was a big ego boost for a guy who was already feeling pretty good about himself.

Any other man would have been relieved to escape with his life. Remo Williams had gone into the don's penthouse without concern. He had faced truly dangerous enemies in the past, but the don's thug club wasn't one of them. Actually, it was kind of a fun outing.

Now it was even more fun. There was laughing and cheering and kissing going on. Every house was awake and celebrating. The Sicilians knew how to throw a party, and the ouster of the don was the best reason of all. The man had slaughtered an amazing number of civilians. Lord knew how many more people would have died if the don had held on to control for another month, or even another week. Hell, just one more day. All the thanks, Remo thought happily, goes to me.

"FIRST YOU GO to the United Kingdom. Then you can go to Sicily and France."

This was the directive given by Harold W. Smith, Remo's boss.

Remo stood in the dingy office and carefully made his decision. "Not this time, Smitty. I'm calling for a change in priority. I go to Sicily first."

The old man Smith considered it and nodded. "Understood. We'll change your flights to get you to the island soonest."

"Really?" Remo almost couldn't believe it was that easy. "Then Basque."

Smith considered this. Remo felt the need to defend his decision. "See, there are people dying in Sicily and there are people dying in the Basque region. In England, nobody's dying yet and you don't even know if there's a real danger."

The younger man at the second desk nodded as if he agreed with Remo.

"I see. You called it. You get it," Smith said. He added, "I fully intend to honor our new agreement, Remo. Arguing at this point would accomplish nothing for either of us."

The old man was suspiciously agreeable, but Remo took him at his word. Smith's word was good. Remo went to Palermo first.

He was glad he did. A twelve-hour stop in England would have given the bloodthirsty don time to butcher another hundred "traitorous" men, women and children.

Instead, they were dancing in the streets, shooting off fireworks, whooping and honking their car horns at three in the morning. Nobody paid attention to the American in the T-shirt, and none of them knew he was the one who had freed them from the bloodthirsty don. It didn't matter. Remo Williams felt like the man of the hour.

He didn't need a parade or accolades, but he did need to know he was doing some good. He had worked long and hard to get the right to make at least some of his own decisions, and this was his first taste of it.

The taxi crawled to the airport, but Remo told the cabbie to stop apologizing—the streets were full of music, dancing and impromptu anti-Mafia demonstrations. It was gratifying just to be there in the middle of it. It was okay that he wasn't out dancing in the ring of Sicilian lovelies with the long, flying black hair. He wasn't a party kind of guy.

REMO WILLIAMS WAS a totally different kind of guy.

Right now, there was only one human being on the planet who was anything like Remo Williams. That man was an elderly Korean who had remained back in New York, interrogating a parrot.

Remo and the old Korean were the only two living Masters of Sinanju. Sinanju was the name of their art, and Sinanju was the name of a tiny Korean fishing village. For five millennia, the muddy little village had spawned the greatest assassins the world had ever known.

The men of Sinanju became assassins out of necessity. The bay on which they lived offered poor fishing. Assassin work became a way for the men to support the village.

For hundreds of years the village was supported

by several assassins at any given time, under the leadership of one Master. Then came a time of change, when the greatest of all Sinanju masters discovered a new body of knowledge. The art of Sinanju was the original, and the greatest, martial art. The art made the Master so effective that from that point on, only one assassin was required to provide income for the entire village.

The Masters used their bodies, minds and breath more fully than other men could. This gave them great abilities. They moved with the swiftness of flickering shadows. They fought with the strength of great beasts. They killed with extraordinary ease.

Other martial arts came in time, but they were murky reflections of the shining light that was Sinanju.

When this new knowledge was bestowed upon the great Master named Wang, he slew the other assassins of Sinanju, who were warring among themselves. Wang then started the tradition of one Master and one student. A Master would train a boy of the village as his successor. The old Master might retire when his protégé became a full-fledged Master in his own right, or the old master might surrender his title as Reigning Master to his successor and retain his active status until his successor took on a trainee of his own.

Rarely, if the retired Master lived long enough in his retirement and his protégé trained a successor of his own, there could in fact be three Masters living at one time, but the lineage remained distinct. There was no confusion over the transition of authority down the line.

The tradition had been violated in the naming of Remo Williams as the Reigning Master of Sinanju. He was a white man, where for five thousand years all other Masters were Sinanju Koreans.

Not that Remo had any say in the matter. He was drafted. There he was, happy as a clam, living his mundane life as a New Jersey beat cop. He spent his time arresting lowlifes, drinking beer with the boys and smoking his way to lung cancer. What more could you ask for? Then his life turned upside down. He was framed for murder. He was tried and convicted with unprecedented speed. He was sentenced to death in the New Jersey electric chair. He was fried and he died.

But the death didn't take. Next thing he knew, he was being trained for government work.

The government work happened to be for the same people who arranged for his convenient death sentence, which made Remo disinclined to work for them, but it was either work for CURE or they'd kill him again. They'd do it right this time.

So Remo Williams went to work for CURE, a secret branch of the federal government that had a mandate to use any means, legal and illegal, to protect the stability of the U.S. He was trained to be CURE's enforcement arm. He was trained to be an assassin.

One of Remo's trainers was the old man from Korea. He was named Chiun, and he had been lured to the United States by a generous offer and by an old Sinanju prophecy.

Could Remo Williams be the white man of the

prophecy, the one who would become a great Sinanju master?

Unlikely. Remo was a buffoon who ate cow flesh, drank distilled spirits and inhaled the fumes of burning tobacco. He was an adult where all previous masters began training as children. Still, Chiun began to train Remo.

And Remo learned. He absorbed Sinanju as if he was born to be Master. He and Chiun became inseparable, and Remo one day attained the rank of Master of Sinanju.

Years later, he succeeded Chiun himself as Reigning Master of Sinanju.

A white guy from Jersey—who'd have thunk it?

One benefit was that he had seen more of the world than other guys from Jersey, even the enlisted men. Remo had even been to the Basque region of France before.

By afternoon, he was in an infamous Pyrenees mountain town named Duero. Once it had been a safe haven and a tourists' mecca, where the slightly adventuresome travel and art aficionados would come to experience the best of Basque's artistic talents. Duero was an artists' colony devoted to nonviolent separatist activities, with poetry cafés, small shops selling handmade crafts and tiny studios selling the most sensitive inspirational paintings.

The unofficial mayor of Duero was the man known as the Poet of Peace, Martin Copa. He held court at a small, smoky café, where he and the other poets would read their heartfelt pleas for freedom for his people. They called him the Martin Luther King of the Basque separatist movement. Like King, his gently confrontational style made him popular—and made it difficult for the government to rationalize any measures against him. His avowal of nonviolence made him politically untouchable in Spain or France.

Up until a week ago, his critics had called him weak, or effeminate, or worse. They didn't call him that anymore.

The Poet of Peace was now known as the Basque Burner.

Martin Copa had transformed overnight, and it seemed as if half the town had transformed with him. One day they were reading free-form lyrics to the finger-snapping crowd, the next they were calling for armed violence. After a day-long demonstration in the streets of Duero, the mob was agitated and bloodthirsty—most of all Martin Copa.

He personally set fire to the mosque in Toulouse as his mob nailed the doors shut. TV cameras recorded every second of it.

A cleric and a band of Muslim men charged Copa's mob. They begged for the doors to be opened. They offered themselves up to the mob in exchange for the lives of those inside the burning building. The mob kicked and pummeled the fathers while their wives and daughters burned up inside the mosque.

That was on Monday.

The manhunt was unprecedented in its scale, and yet Copa could not be found in the vast Pyrenees Mountains. On Tuesday, his mob struck a second time, setting fire to a government building and another mosque in a town on the River Garonne. The police guard on the mosque could only hold off the suicidal poets and painters for so long.

Wednesday saw France in a state of martial law in all regions west of Paris and Lyon. The Basque Burner remained at large, but thank God he had not struck again.

On Thursday night, the manhunt abated as the government called for negotiations with Copa and faced criticism for roughing up innocent Basques. Martial law remained in effect.

Duero's tourist business had died down considerably. In fact, on Thursday, there was just one traveler—an American journalist, with an American attitude.

"I'm sure some of you people are legitimate freedom fighters, whatever that is," Remo told the man behind the counter at the café. "But some of you are just murderers with a rationale."

"And what are you to judge who is right and wrong, American?" asked a local who was hunched over a wooden table with a metal cup.

"I wouldn't know right if it came and spit in my face," Remo admitted. "But when something's really and truly wrong, that I know. Terrorists who set fires and burn kids at church? That's definitely wrong."

"Some people do not see it that way," the drinker said. "Some people think it is wrong for us to be forced to endure the tyranny of France and Spain."

"Maybe that is wrong. I don't know. But burning up the mayor of that little snotty hamlet on the river, just because he's a part of the same country you have a problem with? Definitely wrong. Absolutely one hundred percent wrong—only stupid people think it's not wrong."

"If the message is heard, then it is right," the drinker insisted.

"No, sorry, definitely wrong."

"What of the foreigners. We do not want them here. We do not like foreigners."

"That I don't even understand. They weren't in your town and why do you care if they're in your country when you want out of the country? But, okay, I'll give you the benefit of the doubt. Foreigners are bad. Fine. Even so, killing families of foreigners at the mosque is definitely wrong. If you don't think it is wrong, you're a dope. An imbecile."

The drunk muttered into his metal cup, and a silent figure at the bar spoke up. "You wouldn't say that to Martin Copa if he were here."

"Sure, I would. Who is Martin Copa?"

"He is the leader of the freedom fighters. He is the one called Basque Burner."

"You mean the loser who torched those innocent people? I'd tell him to his face that he's a loser and the stupidest piece of trash in these here hills."

The tavern owner stepped in nervously. "American, you go home now. You drink too much." He snatched Remo's beer mug, only to find it was still full.

"You really want to meet Copa?" asked the quiet man at the bar.

"Yeah, sure, but I heard he's a puss-boy who hides

in the mountains. Only comes out to burn up little girls and old ladies."

"Maybe I could put you in touch with him," the man taunted.

Remo shrugged, attempting to look as if he was trying to look tough. "I'm game."

THAT WAS HOW he ended up strolling alone on a dirt road in the foothills of the Pyrenees at dusk. If he were anyone else, he would have been walking to his death.

When the sun set behind the mountains, dark closed in quickly and Remo was in the cool stillness of night. The forests around him were still, and before long, he was miles away from anywhere.

Any other man would have been afraid for his life and rightly so. Remo wasn't. What concerned him was his acting ability. Had he been convincing? Would he really make contact with the Basque Burner, Martin Copa? If his blind date stood him up, he might end up wandering the hills for days looking for Copa. France, even this part of France, wasn't Remo's favorite place.

"Thank goodness," Remo said when someone shot at him.

It was a single round from a big rifle, and it was a shot intended to provoke, not kill. Remo didn't even flinch.

"That's just what I expected from Martin Copa and his band of pansy-asses," Remo said, projecting his voice so that it carried into the hills. "If you don't have the balls to show your face when you incinerate women and children, there's no way you'd expose yourself to an unarmed American."

More rifle shots echoed among the hills, and they pocked the crust of the earth around him. Only one was on target. Remo felt the approaching pressure waves of the bullet and dodged it by rotating his body just enough so that the round missed. Then he announced to the Pyrenees foothills that Martin Copa was a female cat.

"Does that mean the same thing here as in America?" Remo called.

He heard someone uphill reloading urgently, then begin firing again. Remo slipped aside of a few on-target rounds.

"Yawn. You've proved your point, Martin. You're a coward. Everybody sees that now."

Vehicles and men began coming down the hill and Remo's spirits improved as gunmen closed in around him.

"Man, if there's one thing I'm good at, it's pushing buttons. Which one of you is Copa?"

There was a flurry of conversation. Remo didn't catch much of it.

"Who are you, American? Why did you come out here all alone?"

"I'm traveling with my crippled grandmother, and I knew if I brought her with me then you all would be to afraid to show your faces."

"What did you say?" the English-speaking man demanded threateningly.

"Hey, back off," Remo said. "Pee-yew. You sure you people aren't French? 'Cause you *smell* French."

The English speaker swore and moved in close, delivering his rifle muzzle into Remo's stomach. He was wearing only a beige T-shirt, and the rifle muzzle should have bruised his guts, maybe even done some internal damage.

"Oops. You slipped." Remo was now holding the rifle by the muzzle in two fingers, as if it were a ripe fish. "Jeez, even your gun has BO."

The English speaker snatched it back and rammed it at Remo's gut again, only this time he threw all his weight into it. Somehow, the English speaker's feet were flying out from under him. He landed flat on his face in the dirt.

"Oops. I can see you're an amateur with firearms," Remo said, offering the man a hand, which spurred laughter from the others.

The English speaker jumped to his feet in a red rage, raised his rifle and fired as his companions shouted for him to stop.

Too late. The rifle boomed—but it blew back into him, removing the flesh from his chest and throat down to the bone. The wounded man crawled around the dirt making horrible noises out of the hole where his esophagus had been, then died with a rattling breath.

"Now that's funny!" Remo said. "Who am I?" He pretended to be crawling around on all fours, wheezing noisily. "Aw, come one, guys, you gotta admit, it's funny. Stupid man go boom?"

The others were amazed, not amused. One of them inspected the exploded gun and quickly found the crimped end of the barrel. They looked at Remo suspiciously, then herded him up the road.

"Guess that wasn't Marty Copa," he commented. Nobody answered him.

They reached a dark farmhouse after a two-mile walk. Even in the dim forested foothills, Remo easily made out the scorch marks around the windows. Remo read volumes in it. Martin Copa found an ideal base of operations and convinced the previous owners that living here was no longer a good idea.

They found an authority figure in the basement at the end of a rough-hewn wooden table.

"I hope you're really Martin Copa," Remo said, "'cause I'm fed up with all these French ticklers he sends out to do his dirty work."

Remo was ignored. The man at the table conversed anxiously with Remo's captors, and stood up to briefly inspect the mutilated corpse, which had been carried with them.

"Wait, let me tell it," Remo said. "It went like this—you're gonna love it." He growled and acted out the foot-stomping rage of the rifleman and the pantomimed triggering the gun, then stretched the skin of his face back and did the crawling around and wheezing act again.

"These guys didn't laugh, either," Remo said. "Boy, you all need to lighten up."

The leader took his seat again and stared at Remo from the blackness, agitated but trying hard to remain threateningly still. Remo stared back. What the leader didn't know was that Remo Williams could pierce the blackness and see his consternation.

"Who are you?" the leader demanded at last.

"No, who are you? I'm done talking to peons. I

want that chickenshit Copa to show his face for once. Or is he too—?"

"I am Copa."

"You're lying. Know how I know? Because I'm a grown man and everybody knows—and I mean *everybody* knows—that Martin Copa wouldn't face a grown man even if he did have fifteen armed bodyguards. Hell, he wouldn't face a grammar-school bully with only fifteen men to protect him."

The ranks of gunmen understood enough English to get Remo's drift. They muttered angrily.

"I am Martin Copa. Who are you and why do you wish me to kill you?"

"If you're Martin Copa you won't kill me. You'll have one of your stinky petes do it for you."

"Are you a fool?"

"You don't know how often I get that." Remo smiled. "You sure you're Martin Copa? *The* Martin Copa? The guy who murders innocent children?"

"I am Martin Copa and I slay the fascists who exert their will over the Basque people!"

"Those kiddies in the day-care wing at the Arab church were really being tyrannical, huh? If you're Copa the Coward, then where's the rest of your rank ranks?"

"Are you truly with a newspaper in New York?" Copa asked.

"No," Remo sighed, finally tiring of this humorless bunch. The least they could do was provide a little amusement before being decimated. The Sicilian don, for instance, had been good for a song and dance.

Well, now he had Copa and he could wrap up the job. "This has to be a good cross section of your Basque Bastards or whatever the hell you fools call yourselves. I guess this will have to do."

"Do what?" Copa demanded, also coming to the end of his patience. "What are you here to do, American? Surely you have some purpose."

"I'll show you my purpose," Remo said, and he began moving.

Gliding steps carried him across the room to nudge one of his gun-toting escorts. The man's head flew back, into a bolt in the wooden support girder for the house above. The bolt was so long it emerged between the gunman's eyes.

The others were too stunned to react. Remo used the silence to push two more heads together. The crack was tremendous and the result was a fusion of brain and bone that didn't separate as the bodies collapsed together on the long wooden table.

Then came the shouting and the firing and the mayhem—and the whistling. Remo was giving them his rendition of "As Time Goes By" as he slaughtered them.

They should have been able to locate him from the whistling after a gunshot shattered the lightbulb. Remo slithered among them, leading some of the tracking gunners to shoot their companions. Remo's senses warned him when any bullets were homing in on him and he sidestepped them.

Bullets might sometimes travel faster than the sound of their shot, but they always tended to compact the atmosphere ahead of them and around them.

These pressure waves were so subtle as to be undetectable to the vast majority of human beings. Remo didn't fall into the category of "vast majority." His superior senses felt those waves, although if asked he couldn't have described accurately what he was feeling. His agile instincts caused him to analyze and react to the pressure waves. His magnificent capabilities of movement were more than up to the task of dodging bullets.

But, just for variety, he slithered under the table and jabbed his stiffened hand into assorted kneecaps, not so much cracking the bones as liquefying the entire joint. Bone and cartilage, tendon and muscle ligaments were pulped, and bodies fell face first on the tabletop and then rolled to the floor screaming in pain. Remo got to his feet again to take care of the lucky few who had sensed somehow that being near the table was a dangerous thing.

Remo ran his one extralong fingernail around the neck of a gunner, who lost his head, literally. A few more died when Remo's fingers inserted themselves into their heads via the temple and whisked their brain matter into a kind of puree. The fallen screaming ones were silenced with quick kicks.

The battle was over a minute after it began.

Martin Copa, the Basque Burner, was the one left alive. He was trying to see into the blackness and figure out why the noise had stopped.

"That was something, huh?" Remo said.

Martin Copa triggered his handgun.

"You know what's so funny, Marty? Half your guys shot each other."

Martin Copa tried to find Remo by the sound of his voice and blasted into the blackness until the magazine was empty.

"Missed," Remo said, inches from the man's shoulder. Copa spun and brought the handgun butt down hard, but never hit anything. The gun was lifted from his fingers, and when it was replaced in his hand he could feel the extended barrel was curling like a pig's tale.

"Who are you?" Copa demanded.

"I read some of your poetry on the wall at the café in Duero. You were an awful poet."

"It translates into English not well," he retorted, for want of something better to say.

"As bad as it was, you should have stuck with it. You're a way better poet than child-murdering thug." The voice seemed to be coming from all points in the blackness. Copa was twisting and turning to find it. "Listen for a second. What do you hear?"

"I hear nothing," Copa said, voice shaking.

"Exactly. It's the sound of your future," Remo said. "You're going to join your friends now."

"No! Wait!"

Remo didn't wait.

**7**

England's power had faded. It was no longer the great British Empire, although it still pretended it was. It was hardly even a United Kingdom anymore, just a few dank North Sea islands under centralized control and a smattering of minuscule colonial remnants.

Sir James Wylings was a man out of time. He was an English gentleman in the strict eighteenth-century sense. Not for him the shattered empire of today, the age of homosexuality, the century of British obeisance to the European Union it had once lorded over and the time of rampant disdain for royalty and all it represented.

He was a throwback immersed in a world of throwbacks. His life was a carefully limited series of private clubs, foxhunts and social engagements with the dismally small clique of old, titled money that still survived in the twenty-first century. Sir James Wylings and his peers spoke of the modern world in abstract terms, and always with disdain. In this company, the discussion of current events was deemed to be in poor taste.

But etiquetté be dashed when a greater need arose, and today the need was vital. There was one thing England would not tolerate and that was the further diminishing of what was left of its empire. Take, for example, the islands off of South America. When the Falklands attempted to steal themselves away from the Crown, the Crown went and took them back. Taught those miserable bastards a thing or two.

Still, they were just the bleeding Falklands. Who gave a rat's bloody ass about the bleeding Falklands?

Now the crisis was real. This time it wasn't some insignificant island that nobody had ever heard of.

This time it was Scotland.

Not since the days of Wallace had there been a serious threat of Scottish independence. Sure, there was always a small underground knot of freedom fighters at work, but they were at best halfhearted terrorists. The Scottish people never paid them much attention, and the British government paid them even less.

Until now.

Overnight, a grass-roots independence movement had sprung up in Scotland, and it was just one of hundreds of independence movements all around the world that had gone from obscurity to vitality. It was as if there was something in the air, spurring on the egoists. The Sicilians declared their independence from Rome, while the Basque separatists were running amok. Moscow was having a time just keeping straight who was trying to secede from Russia and take which plots of land with them. It was all rather amusing—until it hit home.

Rowdy protests erupted in London and Glasgow. Protesters demanded London grant immediate independence to Scotland. They demanded reparations for years of "occupation" and the surrender of all British holdings inside 1766 Scottish territorial claims.

The last part was what galled men like Wylings.

"There was a time when ownership meant something," he opined while sipping a Scotch at the club. His audience included Dolan and Sykes, both excellent chaps, both members of Parliament.

There were murmurs of agreement.

"Every time we turn our backs we're getting more of our property taken away," Wylings complained. "I've bloody well had enough of whining ingrates claiming ownership over sovereign British territory."

"Yes, certainly."

"Quite right."

"Well, of course it used to belong to someone else. You go back far enough and *everything* belonged to somebody else, right? But it doesn't belong to somebody else now, because it belongs to the Crown, because we had the gumption to go and take it."

"Yes."

"Naturally."

"Only in the twenty-first century could that count for nothing," Wylings concluded.

"Hmm."

"Yes."

"Unless we make it count for something."

Dolan nodded as if he understood perfectly. "What do you have in mind, Wylings?"

"Listen," Wylings said with uncharacteristic fervor, "we need to show these Scots gits who's boss. If we let them push us around, there'll be radicals from every scrap of land we have left trying to give the Queen the boot. We need to make an example of the Scots."

Dolan and Sykes looked expectant.

"Let's neuter the bastards. They want to be more Scottish, well, we'll just take away whatever Scottishness they've got left. Once they start getting the opposite of what they're fighting for—well, they'll back down in a big hurry."

As Dolan and Sykes listened to Wylings's plan, they were all smiles.

"You've got a real head for the political game, Wylings," Dolan said. "I predict you'll sit in Parliament some day."

Wylings had a drained look on his face, but it was just an act. "God forbid! Besides, why should I bother when I have a couple of excellent chaps like you willing to listen to my suggestions?"

LATER, WYLINGS SIPPED his Scotch alone. His excellent chaps had scampered off to do his bidding like the good little lapdogs they were. Wylings had cultivated his friendships with Dolan and Sykes when they were just lads, knowing even then that they were bound for positions of power by virtue of their intelligence and breeding.

Over the years Wylings had played with them to amuse himself in different ways, and occasionally obliged them to throw some government contracts to the family concerns. It kept Wylings wealthy without requiring him to actually get involved in the business of business; he wouldn't allow his noble hands to become sullied with corporate ink.

When he was in his thirties, his friends in government helped him engineer a little public awareness. An American shipment of food supplies was lost while en route to Africa to aid starving victims of intertribal war. Wylings had one of his companies reroute a shipment of foodstuffs from its intended destination in Rio de Janeiro to Africa. Included in the shipment were seed corn and tents, and the small, displaced Nairobi tribe loudly proclaimed that Wylings had single-handedly ended their famine and saved their people from extinction.

For this well-publicized act of selflessness, Wylings received his knighthood at an exceptionally young age. No one ever bothered to really investigate the loss of the original American food shipment. Likewise, there were no questions asked about the shipment of food, tents and seed corn that Wylings's scrap-steel-hauling division just happened to have on hand at the fortuitous moment.

Wylings always played his cards well. He knew how to make the system work. Without any real effort on his own part, he had become one of the most respected and influential back-room players in the British government.

All at once, the jitters came and bit him. His brow broke out with a sudden sweat, and Wylings lowered the crystal glass to the surface of the bar, where it rattled noisily for a moment. Wylings mopped his brow with a linen handkerchief, monogrammed in gold thread. His eyes darted around, but there was no one around. No barman on duty at this time of the night. Members served themselves after 2:00 a.m. Nobody else in residence.

Wylings breathed a sigh of relief. Sometimes, when he wasn't careful, the little rodent of nervousness darted out of its hole and crawled into the open before he could give it a good swift kick. Wylings prayed that no one would ever see his jitters.

Two hundred years ago, his great-great-grandsire was exactly the same kind of man, but the nature of those times meant that he could make great contributions to society and to the good of England. Now, such a man was only an outcast and a throwback.

IT ALL CAME to a head far earlier than Wylings had even dreamed of. In fact, he had to cut short his next afternoon of tennis when he got the news of the brewing altercation in London.

"This is the scene on Downing Street where angry Scotsmen are gathering by the hundreds to protest the new law that was rammed through Parliament this afternoon. The law prohibits the wearing of kilts or tartan colors anywhere within the United Kingdom and is effective immediately. This was the scene in Parliament today."

The television in the locker room showed a Scottish member of Parliament attempting to speak. He was red-faced with anger, shouting to be heard, and still the heckling drowned him out. All Wylings heard was something about the new law being "patently illegal."

"Put on some trousers, you bleeding fairy!" responded someone in the crowd.

By evening the protests in London came to a head. After issuing a warning and giving all kilt wearers within London city limits a three-hour grace period to change their attire in accord with the new laws, they began making arrests.

Wylings watched with Dolan, Sykes and a close-knit group of like-minded patriots at the club.

The BBC anchor followed the protest coverage from locale to locale. At one point, he announced, "We're getting reports of violent resistance being offered by the kilt-wearing criminals...."

That nearly brought the house down. Wylings and his mates had their heartiest laugh in many a day.

"Whoever heard of a violent Scotsman!"

"Outside of thrashing the beer girl at the football match, you mean!"

They sobered up when the BBC mobile camera began broadcasting evidence of the Scots fighting back.

**8**

Sir Frederick Cottingsharm had the disease. It was like some sort of global plague that came and infected a person and made the person extremely moody. The events of the past few hours made it clear that Scotland was seeing a major outbreak—brought to a head with the help of British prodding.

Fred Cottingsharm was snarling when he saw Sir James Wylings standing on his doorstep. They were old acquaintances. They played golf. But the disease made Fred Cottingsharm into a Brit-hating isolationist Scot, just like all the maniacs raising hell in London.

"Fred, thank goodness I reached you before you left," Wylings said.

"What do you want, British?"

"We're not enemies, Fred," Wylings said, then lowered his voice. "I'm on your side."

"What do you mean, British?"

Wylings leaned in close and said in a quiet voice, "I've got Scottish blood, Fred. And a Scottish heart."

"You? You're the perfect little royal, you are."

"All the better to help the Scottish cause. Fred, I've been working with SCOTS for thirty years."

Cottingsharm sneered. "SCOTS is a fairy tale."

"SCOTS is real. We've been working behind the scenes to gather evidence against the Crown. Fred, I have certain documentation with me that you need to see, right now."

Cottingsharm was wary, but he swung the door open and allowed Wylings into his expensive London flat. The front parlor was stacked with old chests and new suitcases. Like many angry Scots, Cottingsharm was fleeing the land of the enemy.

"All right. Tell me about it," Cottingsharm dared.

"Scottish Control of Territorial Scotland is a tiny organization, and we keep our mouths shut. That's why so many people believe it doesn't even exist. We're just seven souls, but each and every one of us has taken on government roles that give us access to various legal archives. We're putting together an indictment of British theft of Scottish territory. The records we've found show an orchestrated, centuries-old conspiracy by the Brits to take Scotland away from the Scots plot by plot."

"Tell me something I don't know."

"And wipe out Scottish culture."

Cottingsharm stared at him.

"Erase it. Like it never was. That's what the Crown's been up to—for centuries! And you're one of the victims."

"What do you mean, Wylings?"

"I speak of Cottingsharm Cottage."

"The cottage? You've lost me."

Wylings nodded seriously, but inside he was exuberant. Cottingsharm was eager to believe in anything that would stoke his irrational anti-British sentiment. "The cottage was stolen from the original Frederick Cottingsharm," he whispered. "I have proof." He patted his blazer.

"Cottingsharm Cottage was sold to the Gracels in 1596, and we got a fair price for an old stone hut," Cottingsharm said. "Lord Gracel tore it down and built Loch Tweed Castle."

"Wrong, Frederick. Even your family history lies to you. It was the first Frederick Cottingsharm, your ancestor, who actually built Loch Tweed. By rights, the castle belongs to you. It is Cottingsharm Castle!"

Cottingsharm looked confused but the idea invigorated him. He was ready to swallow the worm, the hook, all of it. "How could that be?"

"It was extortion. The Gracels did it, working with the Crown. They took Frederick Cottingsharm's daughter and secreted her in London. They promised your ancestor to return the girl, but only if he would give Gracel the newly finished castle—and he had to agree to forsake all claims, even past claims, to the castle. *It's all right here.*"

Triumphantly, Wylings flipped the envelope onto a parlor table. Cottingsharm opened it nervously and pulled out a photocopy of a centuries-old document.

"Look at the signatures. Does that not resemble the penmanship of your ancestor?"

"Yes," Cottingsharm gasped. "It is nearly identical."

"The other signature is Hartford Gracel."

"I see. This is an agreement to a ransom, just as you said!"

"Exactly," Wylings said. "Irrefutable proof."

"Absolutely irrefutable," agreed Cottingsharm. He began to pore over the faded text of the document, which Wylings had created on his iMac that afternoon using MicroFlop RelicCreator version 2.2. The software translated any text into the English vernacular of any given era between 1066 and the present day. It printed using dynamic fonts that simulated the inconsistencies of human handwriting. It had even come with a free six-month membership to MicroFlop Internet Portal, which gave Wylings instant online access to TV listings, movie show times and his up-to-the-minute horoscope.

"English bastards!" Cottingsharm fumed. "They stole my castle!"

Cottingsharm had swallowed the story completely. This was too easy.

"But you can get it back," Wylings said with determination. "The Scots are standing up against their oppressors. They're flexing their muscle at last. Cottingsharm, this is your moment to reclaim your heritage, your real estate and your family honor."

Cottingsharm's eyes were glowing with determination and no deliberation—a good thing, too, since Wylings couldn't explain any of a hundred major holes in his bit of fanciful history.

"Frederick, will you go reclaim your castle?"

"I will," he proclaimed. "With my determination as my talisman and this ancient document as my sword, I shall do battle against the English and take back my family home!"

Wylings smiled grimly. "I'll help you load up the van."

**9**

The Mad Scots had only been in existence for twenty-four hours, but already they were the most feared street gang in London, period. The local Yakuza branch was going to learn that the hard way.

"You know why we're the toughest bastards you ever saw, Chink?" Stewart McGarrity hauled the Yakuza leader off the grimy alley cobblestones, and dangled him by the collar of his jacket.

"I am Japanese, not Chinese," the young Yakuza captain said weakly.

McGarrity's fist slammed into his jaw.

"A Chink is a Jap is a Charlie. You got piss-yellow skin. Why do I care what p'ticular kind of yellow? Now, I asked you a question. Do you know why we're the baddest bastards in London?"

"No. Why?"

"Because we got a cause. We got something to fight for. All you piss-colored Chinks ain't got nothing to motivate yer, see?"

"Hey, fairy boy!"

The call came from the far end of the alley. All eyes turned. The beaten Yakuza man smiled with bloody teeth when he saw the assembled reinforcements.

"More Chinks!" McGarrity exclaimed.

His five companions chuckled.

More than twice as many Japanese street toughs advanced to meet them.

"You calling me a fairy boy?" McGarrity taunted. "Look at yourselves, Chinks! All that shiny hair and shiny leather jackets and piss-colored skin. I can't even tell the boy Chinks from the girl Chinks!"

The Japanese point man sneered. "A man in a dress has no room to talk," he said. "Do you think to earn respect wearing a skirt in public?"

McGarrity tittered. "It ain't a skirt, Chink. It's a kilt. And you gotta be a real tough bastard to go into the streets wearing one, don'tcha think?"

This made sense to the Japanese and for the first time it occurred to them that the Mad Scots might not be bluffing. Could a bunch of high-country pretty boys really be that tough?

The Mad Scots had all the confidence in the world. They grinned at the outnumbering Japanese as if they couldn't wait to get at them.

"You know what we do for fun back home, Chink?" McGarrity demanded. "We throw fucking boulders. I thrown boulders a lot bigger than any one of you!"

The truth was, Stewart McGarrity hadn't been much involved in local sports. In fact, most of the Mad Scots that Stewart knew had come from the Fine Graphic Arts College in the Hills, which taught painting, sculpture and eclectic graphic arts. The

College in the Hills had produced some of the most critically acclaimed—and commercially unpopular—artists of the last thirty years. Stewart was majoring in experimental geometric charcoal sketching.

But he had seen boulders tossed all his life, and right now he felt strong enough to toss two or three of them. So he snatched up the Yakuza captain and tossed him overhead. The man was too beaten to fight him off, and found himself sailing into his own men and snapping his spine noisily. He felt the paralysis but his vision kept working for several seconds—long enough to see the Mad Scots go mad on his street toughs.

Stew McGarrity arced through the air, kilt drifting up obscenely, his still shiny formal Oxford shoes landing heavily on the fallen bodies. McGarrity's meaty fist slammed into more surprised faces, and his fearless mates were right beside him. They clobbered the Yakuza faces wherever they saw them. A knife slithered out at McGarrity, but he worked around it and got a little sliced up for his trouble, but it was just a scratch. Nothing to worry about.

One of his boys got it a little worse. Arthur Butler withdrew the switchblade that had impaled his lip and reached almost to the back of his throat. He sucked in the blood and grunted, "Dat stings, yuh piece of piss." He propelled his assailant's face into the alley wall.

McGarrity looked this way, then looked that way. His heavy brow wrinkled between his deep-set eyes.

"You could 'ave saved me another one of them mouses. This bunch was 'ardly worth getting outta bed for. Come on, let's go see if we can find a real fight."

They hit the streets. McGarrity's band of toughs was just one of the cells of Mad Scots wandering London that night. The Mad Scots weren't so much an organized street gang as an angry mob, but they did have the gang colors: every man jack of them was in a kilt displaying his family tartan. Those without a known pedigree simply adopted whatever tartan was most convenient. The clan didn't matter, really. It only mattered that they were Scots and that they were mad as hell.

The kilts served another useful purpose. On the streets of London, where tempers were running high, the kilts were an invitation to pick a fight. McGarrity knew it was just a matter of time before he and his lads crossed paths with more English pig-dogs who would be itching to take them on.

"Stew!" A young ruffian in a kilt and a bloodied faced loped up the street. "Come on, there's a big blow about to go with the London leather boys. We're rounding up all the Mad Scots to give those faggots a what-for."

It was music to McGarrity's ears. He'd had enough of the Asian pansies that passed for gangs in this part of the city. "That sounds about right to me," he grumbled.

They jogged after their friend, other young Scotsmen—and not a few women—accumulated around them, until they had an army of one hundred tartans.

"I'm hoping we're going to get some good London ass to whup, boys, but I got a feeling this is gonna be another mouse hunt," McGarrity complained.

Butler grunted. "Yeah, unless dey they got the fuggink American Marines backin' up dere asses, dis many Scots lads'll make mush of 'em, whatever many dey got."

McGarrity laughed. "Butler, yer a friggin' sight to see!"

The Scottish gangbangers guffawed at Butler's expense. He took it good-naturedly and examined his reflection in a storefront window, which showed his pierced lower lip was now swollen four times its normal size. It was purple and blotted, and the wound continued dribbling blood down his chin to soak into the front of his woolen shirt.

"I loog like a freegin' zombie," he announced.

The Piccadilly streets were deserted until they came upon the band of London tough guys who were lying in wait for them. The unlikely assortment included street trash, sneering punks, leather boys and British street gangs, followed up by nervous-looking British bobbies. The cops weren't about to step in yet—they were outnumbered ten to one at this stage. Reinforcements in riot gear were arriving in panel trucks.

Stew McGarrity put on a big grin. "This could be a worthwhile romp, after all, lads."

The two sides came together and the battle was on.

**10**

"You can't go to Piccadilly. There's a bleeding riot going on there!"

"Just drive."

"What?" The cabbie turned on his passenger, not believing what he was hearing. "People are getting killed!"

Another man got in the cab. The newcomer was as small as a child and as old as any human being the cabbie had ever seen. His beard consisted of a few threads of pale whiskers on his chin, and there were tufts of hair over each ear. The old man was Asian, wearing a bright robe.

The American gave him a look. The Asian clearly didn't understand how taxicabs worked in the Western world. You don't just go getting into other people's taxis.

"Hey, Little Father," the American said, and the cabbie realized they knew each other. "Didn't expect to see you here."

"The Emperor has requested I hasten to your side. I boarded the first available aircraft for London."

"Huh," the American responded, not sounding

happy about the news. "Let's go, mac," he said to the cabbie.

"Look, fella, I am not gonna take you into a war zone. People are dying."

The elderly Oriental man was sitting still as a statue, his hands in his sleeves, obviously as deaf as a post. The younger man sighed.

"Look, I have a job to do. My patience is gone. Now, drive this cab to Piccadilly or I will."

The cabbie was infuriated. "Mate, think of the poor old bloke at least. Those bangers will beat him up just for looking like an old Jap gigolo."

The cabbie briefly glimpsed the American reaching over the seat—fast—and then he was propelled through the door, out of the cab and onto the curb. He scrambled to his feet just in time to see half of his driver's seat back topple out of the open door. It had been sliced down the middle. The old man's hand was being withdrawn from the open space.

It couldn't be what it looked like. Because it looked as if the old man's fingernails had just done a machete number on the car seat—steel springs and all.

"I think a thank-you would be in order," the American said as he walked around the car and sat in what was left of the driver's seat. "I did just save your life."

"My cab!" the cabbie started to say.

"You really want to get back in with the Jap gigolo sitting right behind you?"

"No…"

"Maybe you want to try to forcibly remove the Jap gigolo…"

"Stop saying that!" the tiny Asian squeaked.

The cabbie couldn't answer and the cab was gone. He picked up the half of the seat back and held it close, like a frightened child with his most comforting stuffed animal.

"You just can't do that—that's all there is to it. Killing people indiscriminately attracts attention. There are some ethical reasons, too."

"You heard what he said of me," Chiun replied icily.

"But he wasn't even saying that *he* thought you looked like a—" Remo stopped when Chiun glared at him menacingly in the rearview mirror. "Whatever he said, it was what he thought the gangbangers were going to think you looked like. So he was really doing you a favor."

"And I was doing the world a favor by removing another English bigot from the population of procreators. It was you who committed a crime against humanity by preventing me from it."

"I give up. Anyway, you'll get plenty more chances to bloody your fingernail pretty soon." Remo turned on the radio.

"They're having a go at it twenty years from now," exclaimed the disk jockey over a fading Toyah Wilcox track. "Bodies are piling up in London. There are reports that more than a thousand Scots have converged in Piccadilly to do battle with riot police. Scotland Yard spokesmen earlier said they're pleased that the gangs are coming together of their own accord as it will make it easier to take them under police control. But the latest reports say the riot squads are being driven back and British army commandos are going in to do the job. Proof positive that the twenty-first century is completely blinking mad! We recommend you stay right here with us, in good old 1985!"

A synthesizer began repeating a soulless two-chord progression.

"I believe the announcer is delusional," Chiun observed.

"Sounds like the Mad Scots aren't lying down easy."

"I do not believe it. The Scottish could never threaten Britain's stability."

"We'll see in a minute," Remo said. He balanced on the seat with half a back and considered Smitty's dire warnings. The growing agitation all over the world had resulted in city-wide riots. The problem was that the agitation was general. Sure, a bunch of Scottish thugs were causing all the trouble now, but there had been reports of Londoners turning aggressive. And not just the lowlifes. Regular, middle-class English citizens were starting to join the fight against the Scottish invaders. If those numbers grew, the battle could consume the city and shut down the British government for days—or indefinitely. Even Remo was having a hard time buying into it.

Chiun interrupted his thoughts. "We are instructed to bypass the peccadillo in Piccadilly."

"You've been spending too much time with that bird," Remo said. "Did you just say something dirty?"

"No. Emperor Smith requests us to not engage the street thugs in London. Instead, we are to go directly to the Scottish castle."

"Why?" Remo demanded.

"The Emperor will explain it all when we are on the helicopter."

"What helicopter?"

Chiun's breath control was perfect. He didn't need to sigh, but he did sigh, the sound of a man who has endured unfathomable irritation for an eternity. "The helicopter that will take us to the castle in Scotland."

"Where are we supposed to catch the helicopter?" Remo asked. "Wouldn't the airport have been a likely place?"

Chiun explained as if he were teaching a child to keep his hand away from the open flame. "The Emperor did not see much chance that I would intercept you at the airport. Therefore he bade me to travel to the Piccadilly battle zone and locate you there. The helicopter is standing by."

"Got it," Remo said. "So Smitty's not expecting us to phone in right away. We've got some extra breathing room."

"I do not require extra breathing room. I breathe perfectly."

"I'm pretty good at it, too. Here we are."

The streets were deserted and they soon began showing the telltale signs of battle. Destruction. Bodies. Remo stopped the cab when they reached the outskirts of the violence.

Troublemakers in bloodstained kilts had a scraggly band of riot police trapped against a brick wall.

The cops' riot gear was now in the hands of the Mad Scots, who were using the clear acrylic shields to bash the London police in the head and face. There were only a couple of survivors left; bodies were everywhere.

"Watch this!" barked a happy killer as he brought the shield down on the face of a riot cop who was begging for his life. The cop's face flattened against the shield. The bloody, crushed expression was vivid for a moment, then the face slid off and the man collapsed in a pile. "Lookit that! Haw!"

"Let me try." Another Mad Scot raised his shield over his head, but his would-be victim wasn't cooperating. He protected his head with both arms.

"Put your face up, bobby."

The riot cop was mewling wordlessly.

"I said, show me your fucking face!" The Scot kicked the cop in the back. The cop went rigid, grabbing for his back, and the Mad Scot brought the shield down on his momentarily exposed face.

The cop whined and his assailant barked happily, and then everything went into a wild reversal. The shield changed direction and flattened against the face of the Scot who was holding it.

But this time the face *really* flattened, like a soft clay face under a rolling pin.

"Hey, wank, he was one of us," complained another Mad Scot.

"But I'm not one of you," Remo explained.

"He's a Yank, not a wank! Get ready for sleepy time, piece of American shit."

"I'm ready, but first I just have to ask. What's this all about?"

"What do you care?"

"Yes, what do you care?" Chiun stood on the sidelines looking peeved.

Remo opened his mouth, closed it. "Even if one of them did give me an answer, it wouldn't mean anything, really."

"You have gained great wisdom," Chiun said, and he stepped forward, striking out in both directions. His hands seemed to reach three times their length, and his fingernails plunged into living flesh and bone like dipping into a bowl of tepid water. He rotated his wrists with a flick and was back standing where he had been.

Two Mad Scots lost perfectly circular sections of bone, heart muscle and meat, as if the cavity had been formed with the sharp end of a sawed-off beer can. Blood flooded out and their bodies collapsed into it.

Remo moved into the attackers with deft, efficient movements. Some he touched lightly on the chest and neck, and they dropped hard. Others he pushed and shoved with finesse, sending the Mad Scots flying into garbage cans, walls and each other. They hit with such tremendous force they were crushed or broken beyond repair. In seconds there was nothing left living in this small corner of London except for a few cowering riot police.

The Masters of Sinanju strolled along the street, intercepting pockets of fighting that amounted to nothing more than one-sided cop beatings. Remo's ire was rising with every murdered policeman he counted.

"You know what?" he announced. "I changed my mind again. I do care."

He was talking to a Mad Scot whose tartan was sodden with blood. Blood oozed from his sash. Blood trickled from his skirt. It dripped from his farm boots to the ground, which was a long way down. Remo had one hand flattened against the gangbanger's massive stomach with such force it kept him firmly pinned against the wall of a clothing store.

"Can't breathe," the fat Scot gasped.

"Neither can that guy. Or that guy. Or those guys in the gutter. Answer the question."

Chiun waited in repose.

"Don't know what yer talking—"

"Don't be stupid. It's a simple question and I want a simple answer. Why?"

"Why what?" the fat man gagged.

"Hands off, Yankee fucker," ordered one of the fat Scot's friends.

Remo wondered if the Mad Scots accepted only chronically obese members.

"Fine," Remo snapped, and took his hands off the four-hundred-pounder, but not before giving him a little extra bit of a shove—which smashed his abdomen with force akin to being rolled over by a big truck. The four-hundred-pounder made a grotesque noise, then his body fell heavily and permanently.

"You fu—"

Remo snatched the leader of the Fat Pack by the

face and held it tight—so tight the others heard the cracking of skull plates. The leader swung his crowbar and his handgun at Remo's arm, but Remo shook him by the head with enough force to render him semiconscious. He hung, suspended by his face.

"Are any of you *not* as stupid as you are fat?" Remo demanded.

"Fuck—"

Another foulmouthed fatty was on the verge of triggering his 12-gauge at Remo from ten paces away. Remo crossed the distance, flipped the gun, nudged the man's trigger finger and returned to the fat leader before the leader fell six inches. The shotgun blast disemboweled the gunner.

"I want an answer and I don't want to hear the word 'fuck' again. Got it? Now answer." He aimed one deadly finger at the closest Fat Scot.

"What's the question?" the gangbanger stuttered.

"Why. The question is why."

"Why what?"

The stuttering Scot was backhanded with such ferocity he never saw it coming and he never felt it hit. The others saw it. They saw the crushed head detach messily and arch into the night.

The rest of them ran but they didn't run far. Something pummeled into them and sent them sprawling onto the bloody streets. It was the body of their huge leader.

"You. Answer," Remo ordered the fallen leader.

Dimly aware of what was going on around him, the leader of the Fat Pack said, "We've been wronged. The British enslave us."

"Not good enough." Remo pulled him to his feet by his head and twisted it 180 degrees. "See those cops? They're dead. You murdered them. I used to be a cop. I don't like it when people murder cops. I especially don't like it when they murder cops without even having a good reason. Now I want to know why."

The leader had lost his ability to speak—or breathe or think—when his spine was twisted out of its socket. He was dumped and Remo went to the others, who were now lying paralyzed among heaps of the dead police.

"Well? Got an answer? You give me a good answer and I'll let you live. How 'bout you? No?" Remo snapped his palm into a skull and broke it. "Next! You?"

"Uh—uh—uh—"

"If I had a dime for every time I heard that answer from a politician and/or murderer," Remo replied acidly, and then he snapped out the killer's lights.

"By reason of insanity!" the next man shouted.

"That I believe," Remo answered.

"So you won't kill us?"

"Not kill you? Crazy or not, you're a piece-of-shit cop-killer. Bye."

He grabbed the man off the ground and dropped him on his last surviving buddy. Dropped him hard. Dropped him with such force that the bodies could never be separated.

A BAND OF LESS CORPULENT Scotsmen homed in on the battle, looking worried. They didn't understand how the slim white man in the T-shirt was annihilating their brethren. They also didn't understand the little old man in the silly dress, but he was harmless, at least.

"Get that fu—"

"I too have heard enough of your unimaginative foul-mouthery," Chiun explained as he used the Scotsman's momentum to steer him into the wreckage of a nearby car. The Scotsman was moving so fast that the wreckage tore him apart. Chiun grabbed the next pair by the wrists and pulled. Their arms didn't just dislocate—they detached. Chiun stepped among the growing numbers of attackers as the gunfire started. He spun and drifted around the spray of bullets, dancing gracefully out of it. Bullets peppered the other Scotsmen, but the old Korean was untouched. Chiun came up to the gunners and killed them by tapping on their chest. It was a pattern that fluctuated the pulse until the heart began beating wildly and uncontrollably. The victims rolled on the streets as their hearts beat themselves to death.

Others died from quick slashes across the throat or brain-stopping insertions of his spikelike fingers.

Remo glowered malevolently at Chiun's side as the last of the horde fell over. He was eyeing another band of hesitant Scots down the street. One of them began firing an automatic weapon. Remo didn't flinch, but he grabbed an iron cover from a sewer inlet and deflected the bullets upward. The automatic weapon ran dry. The band became more worried—and more agitated.

As they began storming angrily across the street,

a torrent of deformed automatic rifle bullets rained down on them, knocking one man unconscious and gouging a few others before they fled.

Chiun and Remo moved down the middle of the street, observing the last surviving remnants of the riot police withdrawing from the battleground, leaving scores of dead behind them. The gunfire from the crowds turned on the hovering news choppers, and then a growing chorus of voices began closing in from the side streets.

The Londoners were fighting back. Angry mobs of civilians, young and old, poured into Piccadilly from all directions, brandishing tire irons, handguns, chains and at least one pitchfork. The Mad Scots were overjoyed. The two sides clashed and the blood began to fly.

"It's a circus," Remo said morosely.

"Let us leave them to their entertainment. The Emperor expects us to move on to more important things."

"I'd rather stay and deal with these thugs."

"In your dreams, bloody American swine!" The Scotsman who attacked was a true classic—he had the tartan sash and the kilt and his weapons came from the antique golf bag on his back. He chose a five-iron for this particular Master of Sinanju, but the five-iron left his hands and went around his neck. It was a fine old set of clubs, and the hand-forged steel shaft should have been unbendable. Sure enough, when he tried to unbend it from his neck, it wouldn't budge.

They left the golfer gasping for his last breath.

REMO FOUND the folded Post-it note in the last place he looked—in the back pocket of his chinos. There were sixty or seventy numbers on the note—it seemed that many, anyway. How could anybody be expected to poke out that many numbers without messing up even one of them?

"Pork Emporium."

Problem number two: if he did get the wrong number, how was he supposed to know it? Smitty had reinstituted the system that screened out wrong numbers. Remo was supposed to talk to whatever computer-simulated character picked up the line. Eventually the computer would verify his identity and patch him through to CURE.

"Need to order some pig parts," Remo said. "Feet. Pickled. What'll a gross run me?"

"Plain or extraspicy?"

"Plain, of course. Nobody in their right mind would want to cover up the natural taste of pig's feet."

"Okay, but plain's extra. We delivering?"

"Wait, there's more to the order," Remo said. "Pork rinds. I need six pallets. Extrafried."

"Son, ah never heard of *extra*fried pork rinds."

"Really? You ain't et till you et extrafried pork rinds," Remo said.

"What?" Harold W. Smith asked. "Remo, what on earth are you talking about?"

"Don't give me that," Remo answered. "It's your screening system, not mine. Incidentally, I still don't believe they're fake. I can even hear their breathing.

Anyway, this thing in England is bigger than you thought."

"That's what I was afraid of. The latest news coverage shows the city falling into mob rule, and there are reports of a growing organized resistance by London civilians. What's your estimate, Remo?"

It was odd—not so much the question as the tone of voice. Smith was asking Remo for his honest opinion, as if the answer would be actually credible. Remo responded by making a genuinely straightforward answer.

"This end of London is in the crapper, all right. But there's one thing wrong with what you heard. You said 'organized,' right? Trust me, there's nothing organized about any of this. The maniacs in kilts are nothing more than maniacs in kilts. They don't know why they're running amok—they're just enjoying it while it lasts. The civilians? My guess— wait." Remo dropped the phone and stepped up from the sidewalk to the top of the eight-foot red phone box, where he observed a few warring bands fly violently and heedlessly into one another. He stepped down.

"Yeah, the Londoners are just as nutty. If it weren't for the kilts you couldn't begin to tell the two sides apart. Oops. Hold on a sec."

DR. SMITH HELD the telephone to his ear and watched the windows of muted news feeds coming through to the large LCD monitor mounted under the glass desktop. It was unreal, the raw footage of so many scenes of violence—as if someone had edited together the shots of conflict from an entire season of a police reality show. How could it all be happening at the same time, right now?

Then, making it feel more unreal, Smith was provided with a soundtrack to accompany the video. The phone relayed curses and exclamations in brogues and Cockney and even an "I say." There were also the sounds of crunching bones, smashing bodies, breaking glass.

"Wouldn't you know?" Remo said. "We were at ground zero for a second, but then everybody decided to give peace a chance."

Smith could picture it. Remo in the telephone box, Chiun calmly standing nearby and the ground littered with fresh corpses.

Mark Howard nodded to Smith from across the room. He had been waiting for the call from Remo. He had traced it and dispatched the waiting helicopter to the exact location.

"Chiun's probably told you that the trouble's becoming serious in the Highlands," Smith reported. "My fears about the Scottish target are confirmed. We're getting you on-site ASAP. I asked Chiun to join you, in case the situation becomes extremely serious."

"Not sure how much worse it can get," Remo said.

"It can get *much* worse," Smith replied.

THE U.S. NAVY HELICOPTER loomed out of the London sky and settled its skids on the garden at the center of a roundabout.

A quartet of Navy SEALs popped out and swept the street with their submachine guns. They were experienced SEALs. They'd been everywhere. They'd done all that. Except this.

"Hi," said the slim, dark man in a beige T-shirt, chinos and expensive-looking leather shoes. He was following a silent figure who was as small as a young boy, but as old as Stonehenge.

Around them was a charnel house. The SEAL team commander had never thought he would actually see the gutters running with blood but that was certainly the case here.

"What happened?"

"There was a fight," said the younger man. "Maybe you noticed the folks of London town having it out."

"Yeah, but not like this. Who won?"

"Nobody won. They wiped each other out completely."

"You mean no one got away? Not one person?"

"Don't think so. Anybody escape, Little Father?"

"I let no one escape," squeaked the old Asian man indignantly. "You insult me." The tiny senior citizen stepped from the street into the Sea Hawk, five feet off the ground. He made it look effortless.

"Is he saying he killed all these people?" the commander asked.

"Humor him," said the younger one. "He's very, very old and—" The younger man finished by twirling one finger in the vicinity of his ear.

"You should live to be as old and half as wise," retorted the old Asian, who was now out of sight inside the rumbling helicopter. The old man couldn't possibly have heard what the young man said.

The SEAL commander couldn't make any of this fit together. None of what his eyes saw meshed with any explanation he could muster. And the implication that the old man had wiped out this crowd of rioters—impossible! This pair wasn't even armed.

And yet they were VIPs who rated a personal and immediate U.S. government transport, even when all British-based equipment and personnel were supposed to be helping the U.K. in their time of crisis.

"They ain't shot," murmured one of his SEALs.

The commander didn't know what his man was talking about, then he gave a last glance at the field of the dead and understood. There were some gunshot wounds, but nearly all the dead had been killed—quite obviously—by some form of horrific manual damage. A head torn off. A chest cavity smashed in. Lots of cut throats and foreheads with unnatural-looking holes in them.

Was the old man telling the truth? Had he truly, honestly wiped out all those rioters barehanded?

The SEAL team leader got into the helicopter and called for the pilot to take off, then sat and examined his two VIPs as he would have watched a pair of poisonous snakes. This lasted until the old man said something to his companion in a language the SEALs didn't know.

Remo sighed. "He says take a picture, it will last longer."

The SEAL team leader was startled. After all, Chiun had his back to the SEALs, so how could he know he was being stared at? The SEALs began looking at everything except Remo and Chiun.

"That is not what I said," Chiun added, speaking in Korean. "You failed to relay my promise of decapitation."

"They got the message and you're not supposed to decapitate SEALs, remember?" Remo also spoke Korean, the only language besides English in which he was fluent.

"I am certainly permitted to act in self-defense," Chiun sniffed.

"Since when is being looked at an attack?"

"It is an affront."

"An affront is not the same as an attack." Remo thought it over and added, "Is it?"

"Yes."

"Next time, deliver your own threats."

**11**

There was more to Loch Tweed Castle than met the eye. The magnificent castle, home to British royalty for centuries, had become a dual-purpose palace in 2003.

Nobody was paying much attention to the castle. Nobody ever paid much attention to it. It was big but had deteriorated. There were more impressive castles in this part of Scotland. It was on private land, its historical importance was minor and its original furnishing had been lost in a bad fire in 1961, so there was nothing to study. There was almost no good reason for anyone to want to come to Loch Tweed Castle—and that was just how it was supposed to be.

The Tweed-Smythe branch of the old family had the place now. They liked the extra income from the British government, and it was quite easy to look past the Armageddon devices in the basement.

HECTOR TWEED-SMYTHE was smoking a pipe when he came to the front doors. His houseman was right about the large number of unexpected callers. Not a friendly-looking lot, either.

Tweed-Smythe spotted a familiar face in the crowd and waved the man over. For some reason, his old chum was on horseback.

"Good lord, Cottingsharm, this is a party you've got! Are you hunting, then?" Tweed-Smythe tried to sound friendly.

"We're hunting backstabbers, Tweed-Smythe," declared the belligerent on horseback.

"Well, before you're off, care to come in for a spot?"

"You're trespassing," said the man on the horse.

Tweed-Smythe stumbled over his words. "You've gone a little daft, old man. This is Loch Tweed Castle. Been in my family as long as I know of. A man can't trespass on his own land."

"This home was stolen from my family by yours."

"Oh, come on!" Tweed-Smythe was too perplexed to remain unruffled. "This was Cottingsharm land once, I believe. Is that what you're talking about?"

Cottingsharm smiled disdainfully. "You're putting on a lousy act, Tweed-Smythe. 'Twas a Cottingsharm built this castle—"

Tweed-Smythe dropped his pipe hand. "What?"

"Only to have it stolen from him by the blackmail of your first Lord Gracel."

Tweed-Smythe protested. "What are you saying? Gracel built this castle himself. He gave your family a good price for the plot, as I recall. Where did this fairy tale come from?"

"Not a fairy tale, but God's own truth," Cottingsharm insisted. "Here!" He thrust a few stapled pages at Tweed-Smythe, who was just now recalling a bit of news about angry Scots that he'd overheard on the tube last night in the kitchen. Hadn't thought much of it other than to joke to himself that maybe the Scots were starting a war of independence.

"These are made on a copy machine," Tweed-Smythe protested. "I think they're from Kinkos."

"They're evidence of theft!"

"I'm seventy-one and I never heard tell of a claim by the Cottingsharm to the castle."

"Your family erased the evidence. Now I have come to reclaim what rightfully belongs to me and my family. Every man here is my blood kin, and you owe every last one of them payback for the wealth that the Cottingsharm line should have shared these last centuries."

Tweed-Smythe was aghast. Damned if it wasn't the pansy-arsed Cottingsharm clan, every adult male in the village. The county was rife with stories, both recent and ancient, about their, er, gentle nature. The Cottingsharm folk were notoriously passive and famously cuckolded by the wives from other villages. How in blazes had Frederick convinced this bunch of sheep-lovers to take up arms?

Maybe they were ill. The look in their eyes, and in Frederick Cottingsharm's eyes, was shiny and sickening. Tweed-Smythe became very afraid.

"Maybe you ought to see what the courts have to say about this, Cott." Tweed-Smythe handed the pages back to his acquaintance. He remembered his pipe and he put it back in his teeth.

"The courts?" Cottingsharm snarled. "The English courts? They no longer have jurisdiction!"

The pipe came right back out. "I beg your pardon?" Tweed-Smythe asked.

Cottingsharm answered by pulling out his sword.

Tweed-Smythe chuckled nervously. "Really, Cott! Come inside and we'll talk this out."

"Here's a better idea." Cottingsharm thrust the sword into the old man's heart. Tweed-Smythe died thinking that Freddy Cottingsharm wasn't quite a pansy-arse after all.

Cottingsharm raised his bloody sword. "Now let's take what is ours."

With that, he led his army of friends, relatives and neighbors into the old castle, killing every living thing. Old Mrs. Tweed-Smythe died in the Red Parlor from multiple sword and scythe cuts. The maids were cornered in a linen closet and hacked with farm tools. Four purebred Himalayan cats, and their on-call groomer, were cut down viciously.

Cottingsharm's old sword didn't have nearly enough blood on it. "That's all?"

"That's not all," said the man behind the wall in the dining hall as he slid it open to disgorge a half-dozen SAS commandos. "Drop your weapons."

"In here!" Cottingsharm called excitedly to the others. "Here's the fight!"

More recruits to the Cottingsharm cause entered the dining room in a hurry.

"Wait—stop! Get back!" The SAS commander was waving his submachine gun at them. This was nothing more than a bunch of civilians with old swords and new pitchforks.

Cottingsharm's eyes were gleaming. So were the

eyes of the others. It was an insane glow, and it didn't let reality stand in its way.

Cottingsharm didn't worry about why a team of SAS commandos was staged behind a secret wall in Loch Tweed Castle. He didn't care about their superior firepower. All he cared about was the need to pop the balloon of anger inflating in his head.

He led the charge, swinging his family sword and shouting like a true Highlander on the attack.

"Ah, bloody hell!" said the SAS team leader. "I guess we have to fire."

They fired their submachine guns in controlled bursts that took down Cottingsharm in an instant, along with three of his comrades in arms. The rest should have run screaming in the other direction, but they just kept coming. The SAS room-brooms blazed again.

The funny thing was, no matter how many fell, more kept coming in. Who'd have thought there were this many sheep farmers in the whole district? Then the commando's mind did a quick assessment of the numbers and of the team's remaining ammo.

"Christ, they're gonna get to us," he exclaimed. "Pull back."

They started the armored wall moving, raising howls of disappointment from the locals, and a few of them threw themselves bodily into the opening to slow it down. The motor strained and the wall shuddered. The SAS guns went dry peppering the bodies before kicking them out of the path of the door.

Shotgun blasts filled the dining room, coming from within the ranks of the locals. The blasts chopped holes in the Scottish ranks, but tore up a pair of commandos, as well. The Scots didn't care about their own losses and they charged en masse. The wall crunched the bones of those who got in front of it. The bodies went limp—but the wall jerked and finally stopped trying to close. Civilians scrambled through the gap.

The commandos scuttled away, but Cottingsharms were coming as fast as they could shimmy through the door to pursue the SAS.

The standoff occurred when the hundred-yard stainless-steel corridor descended into an expanded working area. The floor was steel plate and the underground chamber was filled with machines operating inside stainless-steel enclosures, some ten feet on a side. The air tasted metallic and the lights above were directed at the ceiling, which diffused it into a harsh, high-key illumination. The sounds from the steel enclosures were...unusual.

It was all unusual, and the Cottingsharms couldn't seem to care less. They weren't angry at steel boxes. They were angry with people. People who could fight back and make them even angrier, they hoped.

The shooting started and never seemed to stop, and all the while the steel boxes churned and hummed.

**12**

Remo looked over his shoulder and asked the SEAL team leader where they were going.

"You don't know, sir?"

"It slipped my mind. There were a lot of distractions during that phone call."

"Oh. Loch Tweed Castle, sir."

Remo nodded. "Oh, yeah." He asked Chiun, in Korean, "Do they have a Loch Tweed monster?"

"Please think three times before you speak," Chiun answered. "This will save me much wasted response."

"Tweed would be hard to swim in, I think," Remo added. "Maybe he only wears it to go to the pub."

Chiun tried to ignore him.

"The Loch Tweed monster, I mean. What I can't understand is why I've never heard of this place. Nessie would be a nothing compared to this guy. A plesiosaur in a tweed jacket is more interesting than some old naked plesiosaur."

Chiun glared at Remo. "What are you talking about?"

"Just passing the time."

"What is the thing you mentioned that might or might not be naked?"

"A plesiosaur? I think it's a kind of dinosaur that some people think survived in Loch Ness."

"Why do you bring up the subject of this creature?"

Chiun was on edge, and he hadn't been a minute ago. What had Remo said? "Just talking to hear myself speak. Why so interested?"

"You give credence to insane science with regards to things that survive from ancient times," Chiun said. It was an accusation. "You must trust the past for itself, Remo."

"Chiun, I don't know what you're talking about. I was just wondering if we would see a dinosaur in a tweed jacket in the lake. You could say I was being less than serious."

"I never know," Chiun said in a whisper, although they were speaking in Korean and the helicopter noise meant the others couldn't hear, regardless. "You joke seriously and pepper your most heartfelt thoughts with foolishness. How am I to understand when you are sincere?"

"Sorry. Chiun—"

"Sorry will not save your life."

"What do you mean? What kind of danger am I in?"

Chiun glared at the bulkhead, frowning.

"You're mad because I didn't ask for money at the negotiating."

Chiun waved it away.

"Then why?"

The ancient Korean turned to him quickly. "Because you disdain that which is ancient!"

"You?"

"I am not ancient! But someday I shall be and then I shall be consigned to science!"

"Little Father," Remo said gently, "I don't know what you're talking about. Honestly. What does that even mean, consign you to science?"

Chiun pursed his raisinlike lips. "Remo, I see the domination of the machine growing. I see men everywhere blindly surrendering to it. There was wisdom in the past, and not all explanations can be translated into the language of technology."

Remo nodded slightly. "Now I understand."

"You do?" Chiun asked haughtily.

"I do. This is about Sa Mangsang."

Chiun nodded but sighed. "Your words are right, Remo, but you do not understand. *This* is about the thing you named." He waved around the interior of the helicopter, but somehow he was including all of the British Isles and all the world. "This is all caused by that entity. It is he who stirs the boiling gruel pots of humanity's sanity."

"I know, Chiun."

"You don't believe."

"It's kind of hard to believe that a sleepy South Seas squid has the Scots in a snit."

"Joke if you must! And yet it is so."

"I don't see how."

"It does not matter how. There is no plainer way to tell you than that—or to tell Emperor Smith. The knowing how is of no moment."

"If it will help us learn what's happening so we can do something about it," Remo said.

"I have said what can be done—nothing. My words are not enough."

"But not because they are your words—because Smitty can't sit there and do nothing."

"So he sends us out on busywork."

"It's something," Remo said. "And Smitty doesn't believe there's a connection anyway."

"He believes nothing, and you are little better. You only know or do not know. You only trust what some logistician or intellectual claims is truth. When you don't have that truth, you force your problem into one of the boxes of science and chop off the unneeded details until it fits some explanation. But know this, Remo Williams—science explains nothing accurately."

"Where would Smitty be without his computers, Little Father?"

"My fear is where you will be because of them. The Dream Thing stirs, and soon even Mad Harold's idiot electronics shall decide that the blame for all this lies in that entity. He will send you there."

"So?"

"There is nothing worse that could be done."

Remo pondered this in silence. The helicopter was beginning its descent when he said, "Little Father, what would you ask of me?"

"To believe in that which is unproved."

"To have faith."

"Faith, yes," Chiun agreed. Then he added hurriedly, "This is not about the carpenter from Galilee who now appears in blood-and-guts films."

"Of course not. I know what it's about."

"We shall see," Chiun said, only partially satisfied.

The satellite phone on the wall buzzed, and Chiun composed himself more perfectly. The SEAL team leader handed the receiver to Remo.

"General Rozinante for you, sir."

"Thanks."

The SEAL commander gave a hand signal to his team, and they quickly donned headgear and switched on a music feed. It was the oldies station out of London that considered itself to be ensconced in the culturally superior 1980s, and at this moment was playing a Spandau Ballet song to prove it.

"General Rosey-somebody?" Remo asked.

"Are they isolated?" Smith demanded, his sour voice tinged with a heaviness that made Remo worried.

"Yeah. They can't hear us. But they couldn't have anyway—you know we're in a helicopter?"

"I know. This is bad, Remo. Very bad."

Very bad. Smith was as emotionless as they came, but he was clearly concerned.

"How bad?"

"Worse than I had thought. Worse than my worst-case scenarios."

Remo looked over the bulky phone at Chiun.

Smith was almost rambling. Smith never rambled. He pulled himself together in a hurry. "Here's what we've got. Military research, under the castle at Loch Tweed. It's a joint U.S.-British research effort. Whoever is responsible made damn sure it was a secret, even from the President."

"Why?"

"The Folcroft Four sniffed it out," Mark Howard said, coming on the line. "The security didn't fit the cover story. It's supposed to be nothing more than a U.S.-U.K. terrorist-response strategy-planning facility."

"So if it's not that, what is it?"

Together, Mark Howard and Harold Smith told them what it was. It took a minute for Remo to catch on.

"I got it." He felt like biting the phone in half.

"The place has been hit aggressively. Contact is lost. The nature of the cover makes it low on the list for a military response."

"Are there not conflicts occurring throughout Scotland?" Chiun wondered aloud. Remo relayed the question.

"The castle is inside Scotland and owned by an English family," Mark admitted. "This could be just one more of those small-time conflicts."

"Anybody believe that?" Remo snapped. "Smitty? Junior?"

"I'm hopeful—" Smith started.

"What does your gut tell you, Smitty?" Remo demanded.

"Without more facts—"

"Forget it."

Remo hung up feeling angrier than he had felt in weeks.

**13**

"It's a war zone," said the SEAL after talking to the pilots. "You sure you want to debark here?"

"Yes, thanks." Remo shook his head at the proffered backpack. "No thanks to that."

"You have to jump. You're not getting a touchdown. We don't know what's going on around here." The SEAL was adamant. "You jump and we'll take your friend to the base."

"We'll jump together," Remo said. "No parachutes for either of us."

The SEAL leader and the pilots argued for a full five minutes as they scanned the terrain for a jump-off point. They closed in on a hilltop in what looked like a peaceful countryside sheep pasture.

"Here's the deal," the SEAL team leader said. "We're 3.3 miles from the place you want to be and he'll take you down to the hilltop. Skids no closer than five feet to the ground. That's the pilot talking, not me. You'll be totally exposed."

"That'll do just fine."

"If this helicopter doesn't get blasted out of the air while we're dropping you off," the SEAL added, "you'll probably get shot dead when we leave."

"We'll manage. He's scrappy." Remo nodded at Chiun, who showed his disdain. "Or was it Grumpy?"

"Your funeral," the SEAL said with a shrug.

There was no one within sight when they stepped out of the helicopter onto the treetop. The SEAL saluted them grimly. Remo gave him the Vulcan V-sign. As the Sea Hawk was vanishing on the horizon, they were in a world as peaceful as a travel brochure. There wasn't a soul in sight as they glided swiftly over the fields to Loch Tweed Castle.

The castle grounds were well-kept, but the castle's glory was faded. The loch was narrow and looked cold, the color of gunmetal. The red blood spills were hard to miss.

There were just a few corpses outside. Remo and Chiun could hear the clamor of battle waging in-side—deep inside.

There were more bodies inside. In the large din-ing hall was an armored, motorized false wall that was still trying to close, even with a few bodies in the way. The motor must have been a good one, be-cause it had managed to soften up the corpses con-siderably.

"Another hour and it'll fulfill its function," Remo observed, then shouldered the armored wall gently. The movement drove it off its tracks and the motor screeched in protest before locking up. They fol-lowed the long subterranean corridor and found the battle aftermath.

The Cottingsharm villagers had finished with their deadly foe, whoever they were, and were now taking out their aggressions on a stainless-steel cube. There were several such cubes, ranging from the size of a British roadster to a Ford SUV. They were thick walled. The Cottingsharm attackers were only making pockmarks in the surface.

"Who are you?" shouted one of them, charging at the new arrivals with a blunted pickax. "You British? You Tweeds?"

"Neither," Remo said. "What are you, a florist or something?"

"What?"

"Your occupation. Your calling."

"I'm a Scot. Sheep farmer."

"You ever paint or write poems?"

The man blushed and toed the stainless-steel floor. "I do make up some pretty rhymes."

"I'm a singer," volunteered the brute who was using a sledgehammer on the steel cube. "Listen to this." He sang in falsetto about suicidal young lovers as he raised the hammer and brought it down.

"I asked you to stop," Remo said, now holding the hammer. The singer looked at his empty hands and his voice died with a perplexed sound. "See, Chiun, just a bunch of those 'sensitive' types you were talking about."

"I never doubted this. What is the point?" Chiun asked.

"The point is, we don't need to go wiping them out just because they've got Sa Mangsang in their heads."

"Shush!" Chiun barked. "Have I asked you to refrain from speaking the name?"

"He's who we should be going after. Not these guys. They're victims."

Before either of them could answer, they heard the distant song of metal striking metal.

"I shall dispose of this," Chiun said, and he streaked into a tight back corridor at the end of the steel room, speeding into the earth faster than most humans would drive. He emerged into another smaller laboratory a quarter mile from the first. There was one man there with a hammer, pounding at a metal cube that was brushed aluminum rather than steel. The softer metal yielded to the attack.

"Beautiful!" the attacker said as Chiun stopped several paces short of him. The man was watching his arms become engulfed in sparkling, viscous fluid—like mounds of gemstone fragments swimming in clear glue. "The Cottingsharm family treasure," he explained joyfully. "I never knew it even existed."

"It never did, or I would have known of it." Chiun's announcement didn't seem to reach the old Scot. The man began to sing a different tune.

"It hurts! It's eating me."

"It is hungry," Chiun said with a shrug. "Do not ask me to explain it."

"Make it stop!" The man took a step toward the old Asian, his body now alive with shimmering rainbow colors that became scarlet as the tiny machines ate through the dermal layer and exposed the Scot's lifeblood. The man collapsed.

Chiun glided away, avoiding the splattering fragments of bloody fluid. He didn't understand what this substance was, but he knew enough to stay away from it. Even the skills of a Sinanju Master were insufficient to do hand-to-hand combat with enemies the size of mites. The ancient Master snatched up the fallen hammer and scraped it rapidly on the skin of the aluminum cube. The friction became tremendous, and soon enough the steel was orange-hot and smoking.

The Cottingsharm villager was silent, his skinless corpse slumped lifeless in a spreading puddle of blood that glowed scarlet in the surgical lights. A moving mass of rainbow colors trickled and pushed through the puddle, distending the blood spill toward the old Korean. It was reaching for Chiun. It knew he was there.

Chiun waited until it was inches from his sandals before he placed the orange hammer head into the thick fluid. The heat boiled the liquid in the center, and waves of opaque whiteness grew larger as the tiny machines were cooked.

Tiny droplets of substance separated themselves from the main mass ahead of the killing heat and moved away in all directions, making their escape.

Chiun exercised patience. The mass of sparkling stuff turned into frosted crystal floating on boiled black blood, but only when the transformation was complete did he remove the hammer. The heat in its head was still enough to soften the steel. The leather handle was smoking, and Chiun's fingers danced over it like the rising and falling legs of a millipede—never resting long enough on the hot surface to burn his own skin.

He placed the hot hammer head into the small patches of liquid, sizzling them.

"I tire of ill-tempered machines," he announced. The final splatter of fluid had now become a starlight cluster of droplets, all fleeing in opposite directions. "I despise killing machines whose only use can be dishonorable. You are no better than a flagon of poison."

Chiun didn't know if the things could hear him or understand him. Common sense said they shouldn't exist at all.

"And exist you shall not," he concluded as he heated up the hammerhead again on the rim of the aluminum cube. The droplets traveled at snail speeds. One of them was heading toward a crack in the rock.

"I think not," Chiun announced, and placed the hot steel gently atop the droplet, boiling it instantly. He touched the other droplets one after another, careful not to splash them. Soon all were cooked.

Chiun examined the rock, searching for microscopic escaping droplets. It was a ridiculous exercise, and yet he understood the need for it. His eyes were magnificently sharp, but would they spot an individual germ-sized machine making a run for freedom? Even Chiun had his limits. Still, it looked to him as if the tiny machines were in the process of breaking off into smaller and smaller batches—halving themselves. If that was the case, then Chiun had stopped them while they were still grouped in colonies of thousands of individuals.

"Fah!" he said in disgust, coming off the floor into a dignified stance.

He left the small laboratory.

Then he came back.

He stared at the aluminum box, now scorched black, where he had heated his hammer.

He closed his eyes and stood with his hands in his sleeves. His wrinkled face became loose with relaxation, yet he stood like a mountain. His power was immense and subtle. The buzz of the lightbulbs was like the engines of large jets until he put the noise aside in his thoughts. The sounds from far behind him were like the racket of a house being hammered apart until he dismissed them. Then there were the smaller sounds, the infinitesimal bits of information that came at him from the movement of the air.

Finally, he put that aside, too—and this all in a matter of a few heartbeats. Here in the earth, where the bombardment of information was reduced, he could feel what he might never have felt....

The thing that pricked his skin was so tiny it was like something from a dream, and yet Chiun stiffened and opened his eyes at once. He controlled his revulsion, willing away the prickling of crawling flesh that had come to him. This sensation was unlike anything he had known before—and he had communed with devils.

This was so small as to be alien. All the more repulsive was that it was made by man.

He stood before the blackened aluminum box and peered into the open hatch, from whence Cottingsharm had extracted the mass of tiny machines. One or more of them remained within. One of them was looking at him; Chiun *felt* it.

He stroked the threads of his beard, then began to work again with the hammer. He rubbed the head around the openings, superheating them, making the exit impassable, then feverishly heated the entire exterior of the aluminum. The hammerhead became hot but the aluminum remained gray. The superheated air hissing through the cracks indicated when the entire interior had reached oven temperatures.

Chiun dropped the hammer and watched the aluminum box for a moment; he could never know for certain that he had succeeded in killing it.

Not kill. It was not alive. It was a machine. He wasn't killing it, but simply dismantling it. Why was the greatest assassin of the modern age doing the work of a junkyard dog?

That's what Remo was for.

**14**

"What took you, Little Father?" Remo asked impatiently. "Sounded like shop class down there."

Remo's store of bizarre and meaningless comments was endless, and Chiun dismissively waved a hand. "One of the cells was breached. I destroyed the contents."

"How?"

"It matters not."

"It matters a lot. How'd you kill them?"

Chiun pursed his lips. Remo was an excellent pupil in some ways. Decorum was not one of them. He had never learned to understand when it was best for all involved to leave some things unspoken. Chiun felt justified by what he had done, but Remo would give him no peace. Still, it would be best to admit it now.

"I used a hammer," Chiun said hastily.

"What?" Remo asked. "A *tool?*"

"Yes. A tool. When one fights unnatural foes, one must adopt unnatural methods. What other way was I to incinerate the tiny devices?" Chiun haughtily explained his method of destroying the mechanisms in the flowing substance. "Tell me what better way to dispose of these abominations?"

Remo shrugged sloppily. "Hey, if it works, why not? I'm sure I couldn't have come up with anything better."

They passed in silence among the cubes, which made slithering sounds that were muted by the thick stainless-steel walls. The Cottingsharm army was lined up along one wall. Some were breathing; some were not.

The quiet was strange and foul. Chiun's skin felt like it was tingling. He was too alert, too aware. He kept thinking he felt the prickling of those tiny little eyes on him.

"This place makes my flesh crawl," Remo declared.

"I hope you are joking. I have long ago instructed you in the mastery of crawling flesh," Chiun said.

"It's this place. It's this stuff. These things. I don't even know how to talk about them. I just know they're wrong. And did you notice the brand name?" Remo jabbed a finger at the etching in the stainless steel: Property Of The United States Of America. "Makes me feel ill."

"I assume this is another feeble joke." Chiun observed Remo halt at an emergency containment booth. Behind the glass was a bodysuit of shiny material and an airtight helmet like those donned by the space shuttlers.

The sign read In Case Of Emergency, Break Glass. The neatly piled hose inside was of a different makeup than the water hoses Chiun was used to seeing.

"Look. A spark igniter. That's a welding torch. The hose has welder's gas. Probably high-temperature stuff to patch up a box in an emergency breech. Still, not enough gas to blow this place up."

Chiun regarded his pupil reproachfully. "My method of creating heat with a hammer would be faster than that tiny flame. Let the Emperor care for disposal of the nanomachinoids."

"Trust Smitty to do the right thing? I don't think so. But you knew that, didn't you? You want me to shoulder all the responsibility."

"You are Reigning Master and contract negotiator. Not I," Chiun sniffed.

"Whatever. You can blame it all on me. Maybe we could feed a garden hose from the gas main in the house."

More ridiculous words pouring from the mouth of Remo, the Obviously White Master of Sinanju.

Chiun started to respond, but instead he suddenly ran. He ran in fire.

REMO HEARD the clicks of a hundred tiny valves, flush-mounted in the stainless steel all around them and opening all at once. The sound of a hissing snake strike filled the vast chamber——it was the release of gas at an immensely high pressure. Remo was already running. Chiun was at his side. The vast chamber seemed longer than when they came through the first time.

Floor slots opened to suck the old air out and

make room for the flammable mixture. More tiny flickers in a dozen places produced sparks. In under a second the room was filled with hydrogen and billowing with flame.

Remo and Chiun were out of the chamber, but the gas clouds were in pursuit, reaching out for them and the hallway had its own incendiary system that was now sparking to life. Flames embraced the Masters of Sinanju.

Only their speed saved them from the flames. They literally outran the conflagration and emerged into the space behind the hidden panel in Loch Tweed Castle. They slipped out of the dining hall and through the finely decorated old chambers, then emerged onto the front steps.

"Hallo? Who're you?" demanded an SAS colonel, leader of the counterassault.

"Fire inspector?" Remo could feel the pressure waves thundering through the house behind him, and he stepped off the old flagstone porch just as the front door exploded open behind him. The double doors flipped through the air like a thrown magazine, and the SAS commandos craned their necks to watch them land in a decorative pond and crush the last existing mating pair of Tweed-Beige swans.

The SAS colonel couldn't believe he was alive. He'd been physically removed from the front of the building. He swore he saw the bloody doors flying at him for a fraction of a second....

"Where'd he go?" the commando demanded. "Where's the old man, too?"

The SAS agents were tearing their eyes away

from the horror in the brick pond. None of them had witnessed the escape of the two men on the porch, but they were gone.

"Didn't any of you see anything?"

"Oh, God!" One of the commandos had discarded his weapon and was half running to the pond, where a crippled, gasping swan came staggering from the water and collapsed. The colonel had always suspected Butch Butler was a closet sentimentalist. "Butler, retrieve your weapon!"

"Brighton" Butch cuddled the swan and sobbed as it went limp in his arms.

"Damn it all to hell!" the colonel exploded as more of his elite squadron broke down in tears. "Buck up, you pansies! Come on!"

Heckler & Koch submachine guns rattled on the flagstone steps as the weeping commandos huddled around the dead bird. The noncriers were trying to keep from chuckling.

"What is so goddamn funny?" he demanded, then the flames caught his attention again. Loch Tweed Castle was a bonfire. "Has anybody called the fire department?"

## 15

Okyek Meh Thih was a strange man from an ancient time, and he didn't know many of the Elder stories—stranger stories, from a far more ancient time.

He didn't know their meaning, didn't understand the words, but he knew they were important. But were they so important that he should turn his back on his People when they needed him most? This was truly the most terrible crisis the People had ever faced in his lifetime, and as far back as the legends told since the People first came together in the jungle.

"These are the most vital of all the legends I would tell you," said his teacher, his grandfather, Chak Meh Neh, to the inquisitive boy that Okyek Meh Thih had been. That was almost three hundred months ago.

"But how can they have importance when they are not about the true gods?" Okyek Meh Thih had asked the old man. "We pray to Curupira to lead our hunts and we ask Little Black Shepherd to help us find those who become lost in the forest. Saci causes us little troubles, but at least our prayers to him have a purpose—to beg him to take his mischief elsewhere. These are the spirits who deserve our attentions."

"And who taught you of all these holy beings?" the old man demanded of the boy.

"You taught me this, so I know it is true," the boy replied.

"Then you will hearken to what I say now. This is the greatest truth you will ever learn from me."

The boy who was Okyek Meh Thih agreed that he would put his trust in the old man's words. "But, Grandfather, help me to understand. This story you told does not fit with all the other knowledge that you have given me."

The old man nodded in agreement. "I felt the same way when I heard these special stories. I asked the same questions. I will give you the same answer, which is this—the ways of the gods are variegated. They act differently to different Peoples. For this reason, some Peoples shun Curupira, where we honor him. Likewise, some gods seldom meddle in the affairs of men and some gods are concerned with mankind not at all. Thus, there is little to tell of these gods."

The boy considered this. "Such a god is Chuh Mboi Aku?"

"Yes. He cares only for the human beings who know the way to speak to him, or so I have heard. There has not been a People to my knowledge who can speak to Chuh Mboi Aku—not in ten thousand months. His importance lies not in what he has done, for he has done nothing but sleep the eons away. His importance lies not in what he might do, for he ignores all prayers and all blasphemes directed to him. His importance lies only in what he *will* do, someday."

With that, the old man took his protégé to the cave in the mountain where the old inscription was. There was a central illustration and some decorative symbols. Okyek Meh Thih could make nothing of it. "Is this Chuh Mboi Aku?"

"No. It is the ruin of the world that will come when Chuh Mboi Aku awakens. He shall take the water of the seas and send the water from the hot heart of the world, and soon thereafter, the world will end. It is a story that doesn't fit into the other stories of the gods and men, and as difficult as it is for you to grasp, so it would leave our People in confusion. Confusion would only distance them from all the gods. It is a mercy for them to not know. We, who keep the wisdom of our People alive, are alone burdened with it."

Okyek Meh Thih was dissatisfied with this. He wasn't a secretive boy, and the old man had never required secrecy of him before. What value was there in hiding any truth from his People?

"Who inscribed this? It is old."

"It is older than our People. It is from the time of the empires, when our forefathers were counted among the ten thousand tribes that were now and then part of the great kingdoms, which came and dissolved. There is a story of the man who painted this, that he came from an unknown land, by an unknown means, speaking an unknown tongue. But this man strove to spread his warnings of the end of the world."

"And yet," the boy Okyek Meh Thih asked cautiously, "he was regarded as more than just a madman?"

"Not until long after he was dead. His carving remained, ignored, until the visions of the People, in generation after generation, spoke of the same fate of the world."

Okyek Meh Thih couldn't help but think that the inscription was of something different altogether. "This picture, what is it again?"

"The water from the hot heart of the earth." The old man would sit there and answer his questions for hours, if necessary. His grandfather possessed inexhaustible patience.

Okyek Meh Thih traced his finger over the small bumps drawn on the wall at the base of the fountain of water. "Are these the rocks from which the water springs?"

"Those are the trees of the jungle."

The boy saw the picture anew. "Then the water from the hot heart of the earth will tower over the jungle like a mountain?"

"And the rain will fall, scalding all living things," the old man added.

Okyek Meh Thih bowed his head. "Forgive my insolence, but I have disbelief in my heart that I cannot put aside."

The old man said nothing.

"This insults your honor. How may I amend the crime?"

The old man waited to speak, although the boy could see the answer forming. "You are wise to have your doubts. The truth be known, I never fully believed in this until I had the dream of the thing, Chuh Mboi Aku. Only then did I believe. You may dream of it. You may not. There are those in the village who may dream of this thing, and you will recognize the influence of Chuh Mboi Aku when these unfortunates come to you for a cure for their sleeplessness. Chuh Mboi Aku is real—this I believe. Chuh Mboi Aku will end the world as this picture shows—this I have never fully believed."

It was a revelation that this venerable old man was capable of doubting any aspect of the traditional faith of his People.

"You will be like me, I hope, Grandson," the old man continued. "You will live in doubt until your dying day. This I pray. For the only evidence to allay such doubts..." The old man nodded at the wall.

The boy trembled at the thought. "Then what is the benefit of anyone, even Caretakers of the People, having this knowledge?"

His grandfather made a wry smile. "I know not, save this one thing. There is a task that falls upon you, should the thing that makes dreams make too many. When his dreams begin to cause true disruption to the People, then it is for you the task of coming here to this cave, to speak the pleas for enlightenment to Chuh Mboi Aku."

Okyek Meh Thih was now more confused than he had been. "Leave my people in their time of need? It is not the way of the Caretaker—you taught me this. To speak to a god who has never listened? Why?"

The old man spoke sternly, and he was a man who never angered. "Because it is your most important command and your only binding duty."

The boy was amazed.

"We will likely not speak of this again but for one time, when you take the oath to be Caretaker for the People and follow all the duties of the Caretaker, and I will demand of you this vow—to carry out your duties of obeisance to Chuh Mboi Aku without fail. Boy, tell me now if you will not be able to make me that promise during this rite."

The boy was taken aback, and his mind was in turmoil, but the old man was willing to wait for the answer. The old man waited for a long, long time.

"I will swear to this duty, and I will commit to it again when I take the mantle of the Caretaker." The old man only nodded. "I perceive, Grandfather, that you understand this little more than I," the boy suggested.

"Grandson, you are wise beyond your years and insightful beyond all Caretakers who came before you."

"Do we know even who mandated this duty to the Caretakers of the People?"

The old man nodded. "This we do know. This is the one thing I have not told you. It was Quoo Uhl who declared this duty."

"Ah." Quoo Uhl was the one who founded the People, gathering together the wanderers of the forest many generations before. Now the boy remembered that Quoo Uhl's story began with him coming down from the mountain into the forest. "If you had told me this before, it would have been easier to make my decision." Before the old man could comment, the boy added, "But this way you have been provided with a truer measure of my faith."

The old man smiled.

Okyek Meh Thih became closer to the old man that day, and he kept the secret of the inscription of the god who ignored mankind, the one called Chuh Mboi Aku. They had left the cavern then, and the boy's memories of the place were pleasant, for here he had grown high in the eyes of the man he most esteemed.

But that man was long gone, and Okyek Meh Thih was older and sitting alone in the cavern of the dismal elder god Chuh Mboi Aku. He was speaking his plea of enlightenment, in the presence of the ridiculous painting. Why was he keeping company with a power that ignored him when he should be down in the jungle being Caretaker to his People?

Without even his bird for company.

He missed the bird.

He wondered where his bird had gone.

# 16

The young woman caressed the bandaged leg of the purple bird and examined the creature. It scrutinized her in return.

Sarah Slate was in her early twenties and looked younger, but she possessed wisdom beyond her years. It was as if the eclectic knowledge of her globe-trotting forebears had collected inside her.

She knew the science behind the creature. It was *Anodorhynchus hyacinthinus,* the hyacinth macaw, family Psittacidae, subfamily Psittacinae. Macaws were the biggest parrots, and they were native to South America. They could live sixty years or more, and ate nuts and fruit. They could be tamed and kept as pets.

This one wasn't exactly tamed, wasn't exactly a pet. There was much to this animal that was inscrutable. It knew a few dozen dirty limericks in English. It also possessed an intelligence that was far beyond that of any normal bird.

But the intelligence came and went, as if a human personality was wrestling for control of the bird's mind. Sometimes it came through strong and clear, but usually it was just a drift of static beneath the surface.

Chiun, Master of Sinanju Emeritus and the caretaker of the great bird, had entrusted its care to Sarah, whom he honored and regarded above most others. She was also the only other human that the bird seemed to accept—probably because she had nursed it back to health when its leg was wounded by an angry resident of Folcroft Sanitarium.

The creature had arrived at the sanitarium exhausted and confused, and in search of Chiun. They were old acquaintances. Chiun and the bird had met in the Caribbean months before. Chiun was suspicious of the creature, which made Sarah feel foolish. When she had witnessed its intellect she had been willing to believe whatever words came out of its big beak.

Soon, Chiun did understand the message the parrot was bringing him—but it was too late. The damage was done. The thing Chiun called Sa Mangsang had been stirred from its slumber. Chiun blamed himself—and Remo—for carelessly allowing the awakening to occur. Sarah doubted it. She had heard of the meeting between the man and the bird at a tourist resort on a Caribbean island. The bird hadn't been unusually communicative then. Why should Chiun have paid attention to the creature?

Chiun spent hours questioning the bird, hoping to get something more from the creature, but the bird had nothing more to say. It was simply the bearer of bad tidings, or so Chiun concluded. Sarah wasn't convinced.

"Chiun doesn't see you like I see you, bird," Sarah told it. She spoke to it constantly, and it always seemed to be listening. "I can see you struggling. You wouldn't work at it if there wasn't more for you to say."

"Exactly, Sarah," the bird said.

She smiled and rested her chin on her hands, her elbows on her knees. The bird shuffled its feet on its eye-level perch, favoring the good leg, and cocked its head.

"When you say things like that I think you're really listening."

"I'm always listening."

"But how do I know when it's *you* speaking, or the bird?"

"Trail mix!" the macaw demanded.

"I thought so." She smiled and stroked its head, but her disappointment was bitter. The bird seemed so lucid sometimes. It couldn't be a trick.

Or could it?

The bird was obviously a superior mimic. Its repertoire of dirty limericks was world-class. Was it possible it had been trained to speak a bunch of conversational phrases? Could someone have even coached the bird to respond to certain emotional phrases and voice tones? Had someone crafted the bird's behavior to give it the illusion of intelligence?

The longer Sarah spent with the bird, the less believable its intelligence became.

But she had witnessed some amazing exchanges that couldn't be passed off as good training. There had to be more to it than that.

There was a flapping of huge wings, and the bird weighed down on her shoulder as she retrieved trail mix from the hospital cupboards. She had a small kitchen setup, with a hot plate and a minifridge. She felt more at home here, with Mark, than she did in the big mansion in Providence, Rhode Island, the ancestral home of the Slates.

"Dee-ya dee-ya dee-ya," it murmured as she opened the trail mix. It was the mumbling it made when it was about to get a treat, or sometimes when she stroked it. It was like a purr. She held a palm full of mix and allowed the bird to pick out pieces with its great beak.

It bent its head and hooked a raisin, and the tip of the beak drilled into her flesh and froze.

It was looking right at her, and it mumbled, "Hear us now, Sarah. The more you feed it, the bigger it gets."

It ate the raisin.

## 17

"You mean, you were about to sabotage the entire fa-cility?" Harold W. Smith asked peevishly.

"Yes."

"That's unconscionable. Incidentally, it's far be-yond the scope of the new contract's areas of au-thority sharing."

"Why?" Remo demanded.

"It's a matter of national security," Smith said.

"Uh-uh. You can't claim national security. Every-thing we do is national security."

"I meant national defense, specifically," Smith insisted.

Remo bit his tongue and it didn't help. "Smitty, there's a few big words I get, like 'genocide.' What I saw in the basement at the Tweed's castle was for genocide. Not defense."

"Remo, perhaps you don't understand—"

"Not homeland security or nation rebuilding or shocks and awes. It was WMD taken way over the top."

Smith sighed heavily. "All this is moot since you were not the ones who initiated the self-destruct. I assure you, the order did not originate with CURE."

"We do not doubt your sincerity, Emperor," Chiun sang. He was seated on his reed mat on the floor of the London Ritz-Carlton. "Doubtless Remo tripped over some sort of electrical cabling. Perhaps he leaned accidentally against the automated-destruction lever."

"I don't lean."

"You lean often and carelessly."

"You're making that up."

"You are likely unaware this is happening."

"The question remains," Smith interrupted, "who initiated the attack, if not Remo?"

"You tell us. Weren't you watching the blips and bleeps in real time?" Remo asked.

"We were doing our best. Believe it or not, everything the U.S. government does is not known to us. The system at Tweed was nearly one hundred percent physically isolated—they had almost no data channels into or out of the system. It's one way of heightening security."

"Nearly one hundred percent isn't one hundred percent," Remo said. "You did get in?"

"We were able to worm our way inside. It was barely enough to get more than a system ping." Smith added, "Remo, is there any chance that one of your prisoners regained consciousness?"

"C'mon, Smitty. You serious?"

"Yes."

Remo looked at Chiun. Chiun looked at the infinite horizon of their Ritz suite.

"No. They were very unconscious. None of them would have woken up soon, and even if they had we would have heard them—we were in the same laboratory they were."

"Any chance there were other people in the facility that you did not notice?"

"What are you, nuts?"

"I feel compelled to ask. Please be forthright about this, Remo. The consequences—"

"You mean, be straight? I'm being straight. To the best of my ability I swear there was nobody else in the room. No closets. Even the toilet was out in the open. It was me, Chiun and the microbots."

"Yes," Chiun agreed.

"Hey, Smitty, are you thinking that the little mechanical guys blew themselves up? Why couldn't it be just an automatic self-destruct in the computer system?"

"There wasn't one," Smith stated flatly. "The agency in charge of the research ordered the self-destruct application purged from the operating system. You have to understand, Remo, the Department of Defense has got some serious catching up to do after their technology losses to the Fastbinder arms sales."

Remo scowled at the ritzy print on the hotel bedcover. Jacob Fastbinder had done great damage to the U.S. military research effort, stealing and selling billions of dollars' worth of innovative technology.

"That's a crock, Smitty. We didn't lose anything. We just have to share what we have with everybody else."

"That's the same as being behind when you're the only world superpower."

"Can the crap. We're still not talking about conventional unconventional warfare. We're talking about continent killers. Did you figure out who's behind the development? I bet it's not your standard-issue secret government agency."

Smitty was quiet, then said, "You're correct. It's a small, secretly funded offshoot of the Anglo-American diplomatic effort."

Remo snorted as he became more agitated.

"It's almost completely unknown by the British or the U.S.," Smith continued.

"And you? How long has it been on your radar?"

"Since I ordered you to Scotland," Smith said. "Even then my intelligence was sketchy."

"Look, this is the point, Smitty. If I'd known what was in Scotland, I wouldn't have made a stink about going to Sicily first."

"I know."

Remo fumed quietly, then blurted, "Dammit!" He kicked the telephone stand. It was polished oak one moment, toothpicks the next. "Just me throwing a fit," Remo barked before Smith could start asking about the racket. "What else?"

Smith had nothing else. Remo hung up the phone, and glowered at the morning sunlight on the Thames. The view from the Ritz was spectacular. Normally the CURE budget mandated less costly hotels, but this was one of the few hotels that would open its doors after dark during the "Scottish troubles."

The haze in front of Remo's eyes made everything look dismal. "Dammit, Little Father, look what I did. The first time I went and flexed my new muscle, and

I screwed it up. See, I should have gone to bloody old England first of all, got rid of the minibots, then gone to Sicily. Just like Smitty wanted me to do."

"This would have accomplished what?" Chiun asked, his voice rising like a song.

"Those crazy Scottish guys at the castle were going to open up those cans and dump whatever was in them on the world."

"But they did not."

"It was too damn close. If I would have listened to Smitty, it wouldn't have been so close."

"What of the Sicilian criminal?"

"He'd have kept. Besides, the Sicilians are fighting for control again. I saw it on the airport TV in France. They're all up in arms again, so what good did getting rid of the don do?"

"He would have kept murdering the people, which you went to stop. You did stop it. It is satisfying to see you follow through with your intentions."

"That doesn't take the situation in Scotland into account. Chiun, what if I am too late next time?"

"You will never know," Chiun answered flatly. "You ask me to assure you that you will never second-guess yourself into witnessing failure? Remo, you will achieve all your least-desired goals if you allow the nuggets of doubt to ferment. *That* is the path of ruin."

"What, thinking things through?"

"Thoughtless thought. Pointless consideration."

"What makes thinking about something thoughtless?" Remo demanded.

"When it is not constructive?"

Remo tried to make sense of it. "Whatever."

"Pay heed, hireling!" Chiun barked. "I will tell you of Master Cho-gye."

Remo gave the Thames the evil eye and combed his memory for Master Cho-gye. "Worked for the Japanese a lot? Suspected of letting one of the Sinanju hand gestures slip?"

"Yes. Cho-gye denies this failing in the scrolls, but he protests his innocence too adroitly, and the spoken history has more to say of Cho-gye than his written record. I suspect he is guilty of revealing this secret. What is more, that was not his only failing. Master Cho-gye was—" Chiun cocked his head "—too careful."

"Too careful. Thanks for the advice. Good story."

"He was compelled to caution to a ruinous degree. A keeper of strict records and a writer of unambiguous words. Cho-gye was a Master who was bound by the ideals of the perception of perfection. It was he who once wrote of the need to document all the Sinanju method in the scrolls."

"Come on—not really. A how-to manual?"

"Exactly. A ridiculous notion."

"Sure. You could put some of the stuff into writing, I suppose. But only a fraction of it would really be learnable from a book. Cho-gye must have known that if he was a true Master, right?"

"Yes, and yet his desire for order compelled him—it is believed—to actually perpetrate this fallacy. If this is so, and if these pages were once stolen from him—"

"Bam—seventeen centuries later you have Bruce Lee."

"And worse still, Mannix movies."

"You mean *Matrix?*"

"The silly films with the Keanu actor."

"That narrows it down to about a hundred flicks. But yeah, I think you mean *Matrix.*"

"His were not the first or last secrets stolen from us. The point to be learned is that Cho-gye's need for order compelled him to take foolish steps."

Remo's mood darkened again. "I see."

"You do not."

"I got it, okay? Remo has to go prove just how bright as a button he is and the world almost gets a loose WMD as a result."

"You see nothing. You think I have delivered the morale of the account so quickly? It takes more words than that to dispatch my message into your obscenely large Caucasoid brain pan. *Listen.*"

Remo listened.

"Cho-gye was a skilled Master, and yet he might have been a better clerk, for he codified his employment terms to such a degree that emperors became reluctant to bargain with him. Codify means he wrote out his contracts to an unwarranted length. He would negotiate for weeks or months. For Cho-gye there was no such thing as a simple payment for a simple task completed."

"Look who's talking."

"You fail to listen! Did I not say 'simple task'? The contract we have with Mad Emperor Harold is for years of service. Cho-gye would hammer out such intricate written agreements prior to accepting a simple job of one assassination. His need for order became a thing that compelled him strongly—as important in his eyes as the urgency of providing for the starving babies of Sinanju. Now, when Lord Agumi made war on Lord Hawa, Cho-gye journeyed to Japan to offer his services to the highest bidder. It is said that his preconditions for accepting employment required a night and a day of courtly oratory."

"I can imagine," Remo said.

"Of course you cannot. Cho-gye spoke on and on, putting even the Lord himself to sleep until only the court scribe was awake to transcribe the salient points of the oratory—and he only for fear of death should he succumb to slumber. Still, both Agumi's and Hawa's courts managed to endure this oratory and both sought to employ Cho-gye. Thus the negotiations began. The discussion with Agumi came first, and the negotiations went for ten days. Agumi became so overwhelmed with the details that he begged off of further bargaining. Not because the price was too high, but because the negotiations themselves were so onerous. Onerous means unpleasant."

"I know what onerous—"

"But of course you do. Cho-gye went next to Hawa, who thought previously that he had lost his chance to employ a Sinanju Master. He was on the verge of calling for surrender to Agumi rather than face certain defeat. Now, he thought, with Cho-gye it is I who shall be victorious. And, as with Agumi, Cho-gye commenced negotiations for the assassination."

"One assassination?" Remo asked.

"Agumi wished to employ Cho-gye to assassinate his foe, Hawa, and Hawa wished to rid himself of Agumi. Certainly unlike the years of service that I negotiated carefully with Emperor Smith. And which you altered shabbily."

"My negotiations weren't shabby."

"I digress. It was indeed quite shabby. Cho-gye's discussions dragged on for weeks. Know this— Hawa had long ago succumbed to Cho-gye's wiles and agreed to a fair but exorbitant fee for the service. You must understand that the fee was not the issue, but only Cho-gye's obsession with covering all contingencies. This endless discussion drove Hawa mad."

"I know *exactly* how he—"

"Catastrophe ensued. When Hawa could endure the torture no longer, he called Agumi to meet. Agumi was in fear of Hawa coming to an agreement with the Sinanju Master. He was in greater fear of Hawa dismissing Cho-gye unsigned, for surely Cho-gye would then approach Agumi again for more talk. Therefore, in a matter of minutes, the warlords agreed to put a halt to their conflict rather than endure Cho-gye."

Chiun nodded to signal that the morale of the story was delivered.

Remo knitted his brows. "Peace broke out?"

"Exactly. Cho-gye was dismissed."

"Without a fee?" Remo asked. "I don't believe it."

"You think I lie? You, who have never known me to speak a dishonest word?"

"I didn't literally mean I don't believe it," Remo

said. "I just mean, it's an amazing thing that Cho-gye allowed it to happen and more amazing still that he wrote about it in the scrolls. Wasn't he humiliated?"

"Of course. To lose a commission is a transgression by a Master upon all of Sinanju. The winter was very cold that year. There would have been great sorrow in the hearts of the people, for they are always aware that their old acquaintance starvation might come again at any moment to visit them, and once again they would be forced to execute the ritual of sending their babies home to the sea."

"Uh-huh," Remo said. "If I remember my Masters like I know I do, Cho-gye's first assignment was also something worth putting in the scrolls. Didn't he bring home a fortune of a thousand coins of gold from the king of an Indonesian island?"

Chiun didn't confirm or deny.

"Well, am I right?" Remo asked. "Don't answer. I know I'm right. So, this business with the Japanese peaceniks couldn't have left the village destitute, unless Cho-gye had frittered away all the coins. Did he?"

"No."

"Maybe he liked the whores in Hamhung. Is that where all the gold coins went?"

"Of course not! The coins were not frittered."

"Not to mention all the other fees he had earned since then, and that doesn't take into account the piles of gold from the Masters before him."

"Perhaps the threat of starvation was less immediate than what you perceived I was implying," Chiun declared icily. "Did you take away anything of meaning from this valuable lesson or was it all wasted breath?"

Remo considered that. He didn't answer the question, but asked, "What happened next?"

"For a man who insisted on such forethought on paper, Cho-gye acted rashly when he was informed that the war had been canceled. Thinking he could not return to Sinanju empty-handed, he hurried north, overland, until he found another conflict, where his services were purchased. It was only on his way home that he overheard rumors among the soldiers that Hawa and Agumi had become friends over their shared misfortune of having endured the negotiations of the Master of Sinanju. It was then, and only then, that Cho-gye understood that he had caused himself to lose a substantial gold payment."

"Uh-oh. Did he go on a rumor-killing spree like Yeou Gang the Younger?"

"This never even occurred to him. He returned home in shame, but his shame changed him. He left his obsession behind him. No longer did he insist upon extended negotiating sessions. He accepted employment on honor, not paper documents. Even his writings in the history became efficient to the extreme."

"I guess he learned his lesson," Remo said.

"But have you learned Cho-gye's lesson?" Chiun probed.

Remo concentrated on that for a moment.

"Sorry, Little Father. I'm trying to figure it out."

Chiun shook his head slightly.

"I know it doesn't have anything to do with writing stuff down. I don't even use sticky notes." Remo sounded genuinely distressed.

"It is simple, Remo," Chiun said, but said it more gently. "There are tasks that appear constructive, but in truth they are obstacles. Sometimes, this truth only becomes plain when the obstacle has not just stumbled us, but has stopped us. Or rather, you."

## 18

The bird. Okyek Meh Thih awoke from his trance with a start. Why had he not thought of it before?

The old man looked around, disoriented, until he recalled that he was inside the cave still, high in the mountain, and the plea for enlightenment still droned from his lips. He had been in a meditative state when the memory of the bird returned to him.

The bird had been a gift from his grandfather on the very day they left the cave. In fact, it was in obtaining that gift that the grandfather suffered his fall.

"This is for me to do," the old man said, dismissing his grandson's offer to climb the tree.

"I will go," the young Okyek Meh Thih said, laughing at his grandfather's joke. But it wasn't a joke.

"Only I know what to find in the tree. I have seen it in my dream."

"Grandfather, direct me to it. I fear for you should you climb the tree."

"Gather our People as I commence to climb."

The boy was astounded.

"Do as I ask, Grandson."

The boy flew away on feet that seemed to have wings. He didn't know what the old man intended to do, but he hoped the presence of the others would help talk sense into the old man. Chak Meh Neh was too old to be climbing great trees that reached high into the canopy of the rain forest.

The People heeded the calls of the boy and within an hour they were gathered around the base of the tree. By then, their Caretaker was high above them.

"You will care for our People," the old man called down.

The People were amazed—the man was performing the rite of the Caretaker from high up in a tree. Why?

"I will care for our People," the boy replied, voice proud and carrying up to his grandfather and even higher into the tops of the high trees.

"You will ease their suffering of spirit, of body, of mind," the old man called.

The boy repeated the famous words, and then came the final line of the oath, which now had new meaning to the boy.

"You will carry out your duties as you have sworn to carry them out."

The old man was high up in the tree now, and the boy spoke his words with great emphasis. He wanted the old man to feel his sincerity.

"I name you Caretaker of the People," the old man said, and he continued climbing until he could not be seen. They heard him call once. "I have found my gift to you. It shall be in my pouch."

The attack came about then. The cries of the angry

creatures were raucous, but the old man never made another sound. The people were weeping and the new Caretaker started up the branches in a rush, in defiance of the old man's order. But it was too late. The attackers caused the old man to lose his perch, and down he came, careening off a hundred branches before striking the jungle floor.

The new Caretaker saw that the old man was broken. Weeping, he ascended. He found his grandfather's pouch dangling from a branch. The attackers fled, not knowing what had become of their precious nest, but knowing it was now gone.

The newly appointed Caretaker descended slowly, taking great care of the pouch and its fragile contents, which he tied close to his warm stomach.

When he came to the ground again, the old man was still, and the sad procession returned to the village, where the new Caretaker performed his first official rite.

Now, three hundred months later, he felt his bitterness fade away. His memory had reawakened his resolve to keep the duties his grandfather assigned him. The man was wise and compassionate, and he would not have given this charge to Okyek Meh Thih unless there was a grave reason. So the Caretaker continued to speak his Plea of Enlightenment to the god who would not hear him.

## 19

The gift inside the pouch was a clutch of two eggs, which Okyek Meh Thih tended constantly.

One of them was spoiled but one of them hatched finally, and for weeks he cared for the chick, mashed up larvae and nuts for it to eat, held its quivering body next to him for warmth. The People were delighted with the present. Surely, they said, they had not lost their wise old Caretaker at all.

Okyek Meh Thih smiled at this, but he wasn't ready to believe that his grandfather was alive and well inside the chick.

It had robust health and became strong, and the People called him Chak with much affection, and so his name was Chak. He became full grown in twenty months, bigger and more vibrant than any of his brothers who flew among the treetops.

Chak would go to the swarms of purple giants who winged among the upper canopy. Sometimes he would join them for days at a time, but always he returned to the Caretaker, and then he would be on the Caretaker's shoulder hour after hour. Okyek Meh

Thih wore shoulder pads of layered hide to protect his flesh from Chak's giant claws.

He was reminded of the inscription every so often, as he cared for his People and attended to their problems, physical and emotional. Sometimes they would come to him with sleeplessness from bad dreams. As his grandfather, long deceased, had explained to him, this came when Chuh Mboi Aku's own powerful sleeping mind sent wisps of itself into the minds of those who were sensitive to him.

Okyek Meh Thih had a tool that his grandfather never had. It was a book on psychotherapy. An anthropologist had gifted him with it decades ago. The anthropologist had been a friend, and had perceived the intelligence in Okyek Meh Thih. "You would be a professor if you were to come to America with me."

"I'm quite happy here and my People need me. Would I and my People be happier if I were to go to America?" Okyek Meh Thih asked the anthropologist.

"No, of course not."

That settled that. Okyek Meh Thih loved his book and he used his smattering of reading skills to absorb it, until he knew the entire book and his reading skills were much improved.

The book had almost been lost once. It was two years after the anthropologist had visited.

"We saw the film on public television and our hearts went out to you," said the missionary. She was a stern woman with her hair pulled back and knotted so tightly that her mouth was taut and her tongue snaked out like a lizard's. The mouth was good for nothing. She couldn't catch flies with it for all her tongue flicking, and she couldn't speak any sort of common sense.

"Please explain again what you are here to do for my People," Okyek Meh Thih asked. "I do not mean to offend, but I cannot understand."

The missionary took his hand. "We're here to help you with your plight."

Okyek Meh Thih thought he knew the English word *plight,* but he didn't understand the missionary's meaning. "We have no plight."

"We're here to raise you up from your misery and filth and to give you the gift of civilization."

Okyek Meh Thih was rarely so confused. "We have no filth and no misery. Perhaps you have found the wrong People. I understand there are sometimes many Peoples featured on public television."

"This filth! This misery!" She was becoming exasperated as she pointed to a cooking pot and a sleeping hut. Then she shot an accusing finger at a young woman who was bringing a gourd of water. "This immorality."

"Ah!" Okyek Meh Thih said. Now he remembered the warnings of the anthropologist. The missionaries would come with visions of what was moral and what was not. Altering the Peoples to meet their own definition of morality was what they strove for. Somehow, a great deal of their efforts revolved around the hiding of the breasts of the women. The People, the missionary pointed out with much indignation, wore no clothes at all.

Indeed, the missionary and her husband and her four young adult helpers went to great lengths to impress upon the Peoples that the human body was a sin. Seeing it was a sin. Allowing it to be seen was a sin.

When the chief missionary became exasperated by the People's inability to understand her edicts, Okyek Meh Thih stepped in and offered her a compromise as a gesture of politeness. The People would agree to don clothing for one day if the missionaries would go naked for one day. In this way, both Peoples would share their experience and develop greater respect for one another.

The lady missionary didn't see this as a reasonable compromise. In fact, she became enraged and violent. She disrupted Okyek Meh Thih's village temple and she found his book on psychotherapy. "Filth!" she named it, and threw it into a cooking pot.

Okyek Meh Thih retrieved it, cleaned it in pure water, and set it out to dry in the sun.

Then the woman missionary turned her rage on the bird, Chak. "Who put English filth into the mouth of this evil beast?"

Okyek Meh Thih answered that the beast wasn't evil, and he asked her to refrain from saying so, for she insulted the People in a way she could not understand. As for his bawdy poetry, it had come from the anthropologist.

"The creature learns our words with much skill, so my good friend taught the poetry to the bird. My good friend assured me the poetry of the bird would be of much assistance to the People when the missionaries came."

The woman sputtered. The bird chose that moment to perch above her and recite one of his favorite poems.

> For fifty-odd years the old maid
> bitter and angry she stayed
> she'd be way less grumpy
> if she'd just try some humpy
> 'cause what's more fun than getting laid?

The woman went into paroxysms of fury. "Did you *hear* it?"

"Pushed your button!" the bird squawked excitedly.

The woman found herself the center of attention, and she turned more red than any human being the Caretaker had ever seen. She responded in the only way she knew how.

"That bird is possessed of evil! It is God's will that it be removed from His earth." She snatched a burning stick from a cook fire and attacked the bird.

The great purple macaw laughed and his head followed the pretty flames swinging back and forth under its branch. The People were mortified. Chak was more than just a favorite pet of their Caretaker and a friend of all the People—he was, maybe, the embodiment of a revered forefather.

The People, all of them together, escorted the missionary and her companions away and invited them never to return.

THE ANTHROPOLOGIST'S BOOK was swollen from getting wet, but still legible after it dried, and from it

Okyek Meh Thih found a method for dealing with the People who came to him dreaming of the old god called Chuh Mboi Aku. The book told him that most dreams among all human beings were about one subject only.

"It is a phallus," he would tell them. "You dream of the fertility that blesses you and your family."

"But in my dreams, the thing came out of the jungle was tall as a mountain," the dreamer might tell him. "It rained down hot on the jungle for miles in all directions, farther than the People have ever ventured."

"You dream of the magnificent semen of your bloodline, so powerful it has touched even other Peoples," Okyek Meh Thih told them. "Did you not share your semen with the women of the People of the River Down the River when we met for our Feast of Peoples? I think your great semen has blessed those Peoples just as it has blessed ours."

This tale worked well with men, as well as with women, and it transformed their night terrors into delight. His grandfather would have been proud of him.

Rarely they came with the other tales of Chuh Mboi Aku—the dreams in which they laid their eyes on Chuh Mboi Aku himself, who was possessed of multiple tentacles that writhed and snatched up prey. "Those are phalluses," Okyek Meh Thih told his People. "You are dreaming of the many wonderful penises of your blessed bloodline and the splendor of those penises, for you and your brothers and father and sons and nephews all hunt well for the People and protect the People and spread your wonderful semen magnificently among the Peoples!"

It was gratifying how splendidly these explanations worked for him. The book was truly invaluable. Clearly, the wisdom of some from beyond the jungle was great—although clearly some, like the missionary, were great fools.

And the lie of the phalluses was a harmless one, for who would have thought the dreams would ever come true? For a hundred generations the dark secret of Chuh Mboi Aku was kept by his forefathers, and never had it come true.

Now the dreams were suddenly coming all too frequently. There were many of the People who were having the dreams every night so that they couldn't sleep. They had the dreams every time they collapsed into just a moment of slumber. They awoke in terror.

"No more can we accept these interpretations of towering manhood," they proclaimed. "What else could they be?"

That was when the father had come with his daughter, who was in madness from her dreams and her torment of sleeplessness. That was when the Caretaker decided to go search for answers in the mountain, in the cave. It seemed unlikely that he would find enlightenment there, but his grandfather said that he must meditate on the painting...

So he turned away from his village, feeling like he was betraying them all, and walked away from the People in their hour of greatest need.

**20**

The office had seen better days. Decorated in the era of sock-hops and greasers, its upkeep had been limited to only what was absolutely necessary to keep it functional.

Dr. Smith wore a sour expression, which was perfectly at home on his unnaturally gray face.

"Smitty?" asked Remo's voice from the speakerphone.

Harold W. Smith was elderly, but today he looked ready for the grave. "I'm here, Remo."

"Somebody dying?" Remo asked.

"The oceans," Chiun answered from the same phone.

"I am not convinced of that yet, Master Chiun," Smith said.

"Choose to disbelieve, if that comforts you—it matters not, Emperor."

"The ocean is low?" Remo asked.

"Not noticeably," Smith said.

"As of yet," Chiun added.

"The ocean levels have indeed dropped," Smith said, then clammed up when there was a knock on the door and a young man entered, walking almost at a normal pace and barely limping.

"Hey, Junior," Remo said.

"Remo, good to hear from you."

Remo sounded more worried by the second. "It is?"

Mark Howard's desk was positioned awkwardly in the room. He and Smith had been sharing office space for months, ever since Mark Howard's leg was seriously injured. His own office was so tiny his wheelchair couldn't fit inside. He was out of the wheelchair now, but neither Smith nor Howard showed an inclination to change the arrangement.

Harold Smith was director, and Mark Howard assistant director, of Folcroft Sanitarium, in Rye, New York, a private hospital and mental health facility.

The two of them also made up the entire management staff of the smallest agency in the United States government. The agency was called CURE, and Folcroft had always served as its base of operations and cover.

CURE operated differently than other agencies, taking no orders and operating without oversight. Only the current President of the United States of America knew of the existence of the agency, and even the Commander in Chief was not empowered to give orders to CURE. He could only suggest missions. The one command the President could issue to CURE was to shut it down.

It had existed for decades, but even the surviving former Presidents no longer remembered that they had once been party to the wide-scale violation of the Constitution of the United States that was CURE.

Exposing CURE would have destroyed the agency. Its methods of operation were so blatantly illegal, it would never have been allowed to continue. Smith and Howard, as the intelligence gatherers for the organization, violated right-to-privacy laws every day. They stole information from U.S. and international intelligence organizations with impunity.

The CURE enforcement arm did the true rule-breaking. Remo, and Chiun were assassins on the payroll of the United States of America.

Putting this kind of power into the hands of any one man would have seemed like an act of national suicide. How could any man wield such unrestrained, unsupervised power without being corrupted by it?

Harold W. Smith had done this. For years, he alone had managed CURE's intelligence gathering and directed Remo and Chiun in the field. Smith never abused his power.

His assistant was Mark Howard, a young CIA agent installed on the whim of the President. Smith had never asked for an assistant, had never wanted an assistant. If he were to search for an assistant it would have been a massive data-crunching operation to find a suitable trainee—one without a hint of corruptibility.

Smith had come to realize that no search he could have conducted would have yielded him a better candidate than Mark Howard. The young man had proved himself in unexpected ways. He was a patriot, he was ethical and yet he was young enough to see the twenty-first-century world through a clearer lens than Smith could.

In a few years—perhaps twenty—Mark Howard would be ready to run CURE on his own.

Today, Mark Howard was lucky he could stand on his own two feet.

"Junior," Remo said, "you sound like you look—like hell."

Mark Howard slumped into the squeaky, ancient chair behind his old desk. "Not sleeping," he explained, and just saying it seemed to be an effort.

"No one sleeps within those walls, or elsewhere," Chiun intoned in his melodious voice. "All around the world, those whose minds are sensitive to certain vibrations are agitated in their dreams. This place brings many such minds into close habitation. The young Prince Regent is even more attuned to this disturbance than the inmates of Folcroft."

"Please don't call them inmates," Dr. Smith said. "They're patients."

"Pardon me, Emperor."

"Please don't call me Emperor," Smith replied automatically.

One of the rules of the assassins of Sinanju was that they worked only for kings, emperors, popes and regents—never for those of a lesser rank. Harold W. Smith was probably on par with the President himself in terms of real power, but without the title. Chiun had long ago taken to addressing him as Emperor, which befitted his station better. Also, it sounded better in the Sinanju histories. Smith no longer tried so hard to dissuade Chiun from using the term.

"So, what are the dreams like?" Remo asked.

"Do not answer," Chiun snapped. "You would be wise to refrain from foolish questions. Have I not told you of the dangers we face, unique to us, in this time?"

"I don't see how it can hurt to know what the dreams are all about."

"It can hurt grievously if it stirs His thoughts toward us."

"Master Chiun, I have not accepted your theory of these events," Smith said.

"Have any of my predictions failed to transpire?" Chiun posed. "I predicted a tumult in the ocean. It has happened, has it not?"

"It has," Smith agreed.

"It has?" Remo asked. "Hey, I've been up to my eyeballs in work for the last forty-eight hours."

Mark Howard tapped out commands at his desk. "They're calling it a storm of interference, or the vortex. The number of lost ships and aircraft is eighty-three at the moment. Missing, believed dead, are more than five hundred. The first report was from a freighter bringing produce out of the Marquesas Islands to Oahu. Within hours there were eighteen ships and aircraft lost. Coast Guard, navy cruisers. We sent in a B-1 bomber and two extremely high-altitude drone aircraft. They go in, we lose them, and they don't come out."

"What's that mean—storm of interference?" Remo asked.

"All communications black out in here, no matter what the transmission method," Mark explained. "Radio, infrared, microwaves, even laser-based line-of-sight, nothing gets very far inside the storm. It's even interfering with our spy satellites in the metasphere, 350 miles up."

"Why so many ships?" Remo asked. "Why didn't people get out?"

"They tried." Mark shrugged.

"There was a current. A flow of water converging on the eye of the storm," Smith explained.

"From all directions," Mark added. "Flowing into a central point."

"Like a bathtub drain," Remo said. "He will drink the seas dry, Little Father?"

Chiun said nothing.

"And then destroy the world," Remo added thoughtfully.

"I think we're jumping the gun," Smith said. "There's no way that can happen."

"The seas do shrink, Emperor," Chiun pointed out.

"How much shrink are we talking?" Remo asked.

"The Pacific has fallen 1.8 millimeters in the last day and a half, and the pace seems to be picking up."

"That doesn't sound like much," Remo said. "On the other hand, that's a hell of a lot of water, isn't it?"

"The displacement is almost incalculable," Smith said. "Regardless, the water must go somewhere. The most extreme estimations of empty space that could exist below the Pacific will be reached in less than a day. The drainage can't go on much longer."

"It will," Chiun replied.

"There's simply no place for the water to go, Master Chiun."

Chiun didn't reply.

"The limits must be reached within twenty-four hours, at which point the oceans will stabilize," Smith declared. "Then we will see what, if anything, CURE should do."

"Remo must not be drawn into the twilight realm of the Dream Thing, Emperor," Chiun intoned. "Nor I. We own an obligation to that one. He would take control of the Masters of Sinanju if he can."

THERE WERE NO MORE major problems requiring Remo's attention—only a thousand minor ones, in every nation. Smith asked Remo and Chiun to come back to New York until they could come up with a better course of action.

After the call was done, Smith was unsettled, still trying to make sense of it all.

Chiun frustrated Smith. The old Master could be inscrutable, and his adherence to his knowledge was admirable, but right now Smith needed that knowledge.

Smith didn't know if he should accept that these bizarre events were related, as Chiun believed, or simply appeared to be. The bird, the global disturbances, Chiun's recent vision in New Zealand—each was a unique, improbable planet circling the binary stars of two cataclysmic events: the massive disturbances of the oceans and the seething discontent in every nation.

If they were related, then what Chiun knew could be invaluable—and yet Chiun refused to dispel the fanciful notions of the legend to find the truth at the core. Smith felt like a scientist trying to understand the nature of a comet, but his only eyewitness was a medieval peasant who was convinced he had seen Satan streaking through the heavens.

He summoned the two Masters back from Europe because there was little more they could do beside extinguish minor fires—and because he hoped to be able to have a meaningful exchange of ideas with Master Chiun.

"Chiun's Moovian legends have no basis in reality, and still I find myself buying into them because I can't accept doing nothing," Smith said aloud.

Mark asked, "Do you believe the water level will stop going down within twenty-four hours?"

Smith frowned at the desktop, his hands idly bringing up a window on the screen below the glass desktop. The screen contained various estimates of the possible volume of contiguous sub-Pacific caverns. "Every rational scientific estimation says it should have stopped already," Smith stated. "Unless you give credence to Dr. Belknap."

Mark Howard's wristwatch vibrated, reminding him to get to his feet. Sitting for more than fifteen minutes still made his leg ache. He circled the desk and looked at Dr. Smith's display window.

It was a deceptively simple table. The top box contained the bulleted names of scientists, universities or think tanks that had developed estimates of the possible course of the ocean drain. Next to each name was their estimate in total time. The box on the bottom showed the names of the more improbable theorists. The hollow-earth believers, for example, who claimed the earth was actually an air-filled sphere. Neither Smith nor Mark Howard gave them much credence, but their theory allowed for the seas to indeed drain indefinitely.

In the middle of the window was a single name inside its own box. Dr. Stephen Belknap, a seismologist from Oregon State University. Nobody had ever heard of him until yesterday, when he went public with Tectonic Hollow theory. He postulated that, as the tectonic plates drifted during the past few hundred million years, ripping apart Earth's single super continent to form the continents man knows today, it formed an air-filled chamber under Earth's crust.

"Even the experts that are working with the benefit of data about the most recently discovered cavern systems haven't been able to accommodate the volume of water the oceans appear to have lost," Smith said. "Belknap's looking more credible by the minute."

Mark wouldn't have agreed yesterday.

His leg didn't hurt but he was weary, body and soul. The bad dreams hadn't allowed him to sleep soundly in days. He needed just a few minutes.

He rested his head in his hands.

**21**

Mark Howard sank through the oceans slowly at first, watching the water grow darker until it was black. Then he moved faster. The fish that existed here provided their own glowing lights, and they made trails going past Mark.

He was aware he was in one of the Pacific Ocean's deep trenches. Somehow, he knew he was twenty-one thousand feet below the surface when he finally touched bottom—and slipped into the earth.

The blackness was the same, but it felt different. It was the mealy coarseness of soil, and Mark felt miles and miles of it pass. He sensed what his destination would be: the talk of the evening news, the infamous Tectonic Hollow.

Mark, who had not been afraid at first, was afraid now. He pictured himself standing inside a rock chamber hundreds of miles across, nothing but emptiness, emptiness, emptiness until it finally reached the rock hardness of the wall. The fear was claustrophobia and agoraphobia combined, but Mark was too terrified to appreciate how unique it was.

He tried to stop. He reached out to the earth,

clawed at the dirt, but he was only a shadow, a help-less phantom without substance.

He shouted at himself to wake up and for an instant he felt the dream fade—then he was dragged back into it by a thick tentacle that constricted his bad leg and pulled him down.

Mark Howard tried to kick it off, and the pain in his leg was severe—as if the old wound were freshly inflicted. He couldn't see whatever it was—and whatever it was, it wasn't as horrifying as where it was taking him.

Mark lunged at his leg and dug his fingers into the tentacle. It loosened, then squeezed harder.

Then Mark arrived at his destination.

It wasn't what he expected.

It was worse.

SMITH NOTICED his assistant was dozing at his desk, head in his arms. Smith went back to his screen. The young man deserved any sleep he could steal.

Mark gasped.

"Mark?"

Mark was trying to dig into the onyx desktop with his fingers, then he curled up in his chair, a low groaning sound coming from deep inside him. Smith went to the young man and touched his shoulder.

Mark got to his feet, pushed against Smith and fell against the wall, hard. It shook the office. The look on Howard's face was slow in coming—horror. His eyes were wide and his mouth dropped open, and Mark Howard made a long sound like a foghorn calling to the drowning passengers of a sinking ship.

SARAH SLATE burst into the hospital room and found herself halted. Smith had her by the arms. She would have never thought the gray old man was so powerful.

Mark was shirtless on the platform, surrounded by doctors in the triage center that served as Folcroft's emergency room when necessary. An IV was in his arm and a mask was on his face. A nurse pushed a needle into his arm and injected something.

"What happened?" she demanded.

"We're not sure." Dr. Smith added in a quiet voice, "He fell asleep at his desk and experienced something traumatic."

"But he's unconscious."

Smith looked at her helplessly.

"He may have hit his head when he fell against the wall," reported one of the doctors. "We'll check him out. Probably just a mild concussion. Don't worry."

"But what about his leg?" Sarah demanded.

"His leg wasn't affected," the doctor said, and stopped when he noticed the stream of red soaking Mark's pant leg. Everyone saw it then, and there was a second of surprised silence. It was at that moment that the blood began spattering noisily on the floor tiles.

SARAH WAS FINALLY KICKED out and sent back to her suite to stew while the doctors performed tests on Mark Howard. She expected Smith to call with news, so when he knocked on her door personally her mind leaped to horrible conclusions.

"He's in no danger," Dr. Smith said. "He's sleeping."

"Don't screw with me. Is he comatose?"

"I don't believe so," Smith said. "There was no trauma to the head. I never thought there was, actually. This is similar to his past episodes...." Smith became uncomfortable.

"They are this bad?" Sarah asked.

"Almost never."

"What about his leg?"

"He tore open a section of the scar himself. The damage was minor. Five stitches."

Sarah shook her head lightly. "I don't know if I should be relieved or not."

Smith was startled when the hyacinth macaw crossed the room in a flurry of purple wings and touched down on her lap, then comforted her by rubbing its head against her collarbone. She stroked it.

Smith wasn't at ease with this girl. Woman, he reminded himself, even if she did look too young to vote.

Sarah Slate had come to Folcroft unexpectedly, to tend to Mark when his first grievous leg wound was inflicted while trying to save her life. They now shared a suite in Folcroft's private wing.

She was in her young twenties, a wealthy heiress from Providence, Rhode Island. Sarah was well-educated, quite intelligent and extraordinarily intuitive—and she knew about CURE. But how much did she know about Mark Howard?

Each time the bird rubbed its head on her chest, it lifted the dangling gold charm and dropped it against her skin. The charm was the symbol of the House of Sinanju and a gift from the Master Emeritus.

"Dr. Smith, what does this mean?" she asked.

"How can I know without knowing—what he experienced?"

"You said almost never. When these experiences affect him to this level, it means something is reaching for Mark specifically, right?" she demanded.

"Maybe that this place is being targeted," Smith replied. "Mark's is the most receptive mind to receive the communiqué."

"Attack, you mean?"

"We can't assume that."

She glared at him. "Sure we can."

## 22

Henry Lagrasse was alive. That was his first clue that something was very, very wrong.

He should be in Davy Jones's locker. Him, the rest of the crew, the whole damn ship.

The ship! Was he still aboard the *Reliant?* That mystery prodded him into opening his eyes again, however painful it was. The light was as diffuse as late twilight, but he still blinked for a minute. His head pounded. When he was knocked out, he had landed on his left arm and now it was numb.

Yes, he was on the deck of the *Reliant,* which was sickeningly motionless. It must have washed ashore.

Impossible. They had been caught in a whirlpool, the cone maybe ten kilometers in diameter. The *Reliant* was rushing into the vortex faster than she had ever moved in her entire existence. The current was drawing them in, and they were powerless to stop it.

Then he remembered the island—yes, sitting right in the eye of the vortex. The vortex shot the *Reliant* into the stony shore of the island. The Coast Guard cutter bottomed out, her hull flattening, and her enormous inertia kept her moving. The hull screeched and threw up plumes of sparks, and somehow Lagrasse kept to his feet while his Coast Guard brothers and sisters spun off the deck like toys.

Then came the other ship, a burning pleasure yacht that had arrived on this strange shore but minutes before. The *Reliant* plowed into it and twisted to one side—and Lagrasse remembered seeing the deck come at him. Then nothing.

The ship must have ground to a halt finally. But what was this place?

He got to his feet and rode out the waves of nausea. The stillness of the cutter was sickening. The *Reliant* was never supposed to be perfectly still. She should always be in motion, moving with the water.

He stumbled to a nearby corpse. Katrina. First mate. Lagrasse tried to position her head in a more natural position, but it kept rolling to the side.

He crept into the superstructure. The bridge was a mess, full of broken equipment and broken people. The entrances belowdecks were all blocked. The hull was pancaked underneath the deck. Anybody belowdecks was flattened.

But was there anybody belowdecks? They had all been on deck when the crash came, right? The commanders had said they might—just might—have a helicopter rescue en route. Considering the circumstances, everyone had stayed abovedecks in the vain hope of making a quick exit.

So where were the others?

Lagrasse's eyes focused better now. He crawled over the rail, dangled and dropped. He landed on someone.

One of his shipmates, but he would never know who. He turned away from the mess and circled the *Reliant*.

His mind didn't like what his eyes were seeing and attempted to shut it out, but Lagrasse shook his head clear.

What he had seen during the crash was all true, all still there. The crushed *Reliant* was on an island of black, hard stone, and the hard current rushed at the shore—then flowed under the lip of stone, disappearing somewhere underneath.

How could that be? Was there gigantic sinkhole down there, draining the ocean?

They had been pulled in from kilometers away. The speed of the water movement, the water depth, the diameter of the vortex—Lagrasse tried to compute how much water was being sucked down every minute and his head pounded.

The island—what was it? It looked man-made. Even the shore looked as if it were chiseled, long ago. How did the island cause the vortex? Was the vortex man-made?

Lagrasse felt his mind become light and his limbs stopped working. His eyes rolled into his skull involuntarily, and he collapsed on his face. He knew his face hit hard, but he didn't feel it.

WHEN HE OPENED his eyes again, the place looked just the same. The twilight gray was no darker or lighter than before, but the crusted blood in his hair told him he had been out long enough for his split face to bleed, clot and dry up. A few hours at least.

The vortex looked unchanged, and it was eerie how quiet it was. Millions of gallons of seawater were getting sucked away with only an unending hush.

Lagrasse had to get inland. He had to find out who was doing this and why. He turned away from the vortex and what he saw hit him like a sucker punch.

Ships. There were ships all over. Where had they come from? When he had passed out, he could swear there were just two wrecks within view—the *Reliant* and the smoldering ash that had been the pleasure yacht. Now the shore was dotted with wrecks, piled up together, bodies strewed everywhere. Lagrasse ran to a nearby fishing boat and found the bodies of the fishermen spilled out of the gashed hull with a few tons of the catch—so fresh that neither the men nor the fish were starting to rot.

He went next to a nearby pile of burning wreckage. There was a rotor blade poking out. A helicopter had crashed here, only to be plowed down by a fishing charter and at least two other small craft. It looked as if one man had survived the series of crashes, but not for long. The bloody trail ended where the body lay in a fetal ball.

Lagrasse heard the scream then. Not a human scream, but the shriek of steel. It started and didn't stop. Lagrasse knew that sound. It was engraved on his brain.

Then he saw the ship, careening over the rock surface as fast as a car, and the friction of the hull made it red-hot. The heat swept onto the deck, which became engulfed in a ball of flame. Human figures moved in the flash-fire and tossed themselves over the side. It was suicide. Their flaming bodies flopped and rolled and crumpled until they finally stopped.

The ship lost momentum quickly, but it was completely ablaze and Lagrasse was forced to run away from the intensity that threatened to burn him, even at twenty meters.

With this many wrecks, there had to be other survivors. He was going to find them. And together, they were going to find out who was responsible for all this horror.

HENRY LAGRASSE PUT his mind to work gathering whatever data was possible to gather. He counted his steps. It was 723 paces from the edge of the basalt lip at the waterline to the low barrier of eroded blocks that designated the limits of the ruined city. He committed the number to memory. The rocky shelf was shaped, above the waterline, like a beach, but Lagrasse couldn't bring himself to call it a beach. Its purpose was to catch ships before they were dragged into the vortex. The Catch, as he decided to call it, was about a third of a mile wide based on his thirty-inch stride.

He got a little dizzy and sat down on one of the low rocks. It was slimy and wet, and it soaked into his slacks. Reality abandoned him for a few more hours.

When he was finally able to think straight again, he pushed against the ground. He was flat on his face. He didn't remember falling.

He had to get himself to work. His intention was to march across the shore and count his steps. Figure out the dimensions of the rock ledge. The Catch. He had already named it the Catch, because it caught boats. Wait—he had already counted it. Now he remembered 723 steps. That's why he was already at the edge of the city.

Something was wrong with him, and when he put his hand to his head he could feel the swelling. Oh, shit. Fluid buildup on the brain. Lagrasse knew what that meant. Disorientation, unconsciousness, then death, unless he relieved the pressure fast.

He had to find other survivors. With luck, he'd find a doctor.

Lagrasse entered a maze of stone monoliths. It was an ancient place, eroded by the ages. Each of the buildings was huge, twenty feet floor-to-ceiling, and the open doorways were made for giants. The walls were yards thick and where they had fallen, which was infrequent, Lagrasse saw that the stones were pieced together with tongue-and-groove construction. No wonder they lasted so long—but who had built them?

The coating of glimmering slime confused Lagrasse. The algae was as thin as a first coating of wet paint. Why was that? Where was the smothering blanket of barnacles and coral and other sea life that would have built up on the surface of the rock during the centuries it was submerged—and Lagrasse knew it had been submerged. This island, these ruins, had not been sitting here on the surface undiscovered.

How old were they? Lagrasse was a diver and he had explored the sunken ruins off Alexandria. Could he use that as a measure? The ruins off Alexandria had been eroded by the passage of two thousand years, but this city looked positively smoothed by the millennia. That implied that their age was four times the age of the Alexandria ruins. Maybe ten times.

Impossible.

There was a smell. Lagrasse followed it to a circular building, where it became an overpowering stench. He forced himself through the gigantic passage and emerged on a narrow ramp above a ring-shaped trough that was forty feet in diameter. In the center, the trough walls rose and blossomed—the opening to a dark tube that disappeared into the floor.

The trough was full of rot and decay. Thousands of fish bones. Masses of seaweed. Sprigs of coral.

Sweepings. This was where the detritus was brought when the city was cleaned. But the coral pieces were tiny and the plants were saplings. The city had not been recently cleaned of thousands of years of accumulation; it had been cleaned on a regular basis throughout the passage of time. The growth of parasites had never been allowed to get out of hand and rip the city apart—this was another clue as to its excellent preservation.

So who had served as the janitorial staff?

Then Lagrasse's question was answered. A limb rose from the murky trough and scooped a mound of detritus into the trash chute.

Lagrasse squinted into the darkness, and something in the trough looked back at him.

It was a giant squid, a monster, a whale fighter. No one had ever seen one of these creatures alive. Modern man had seen only their corpses. But this one was alive, although how it could survive in the polluted cesspool of the trough was beyond Lagrasse.

Lagrasse's presence alarmed the squid, and it reached for him. Lagrasse wasn't afraid, but rather fascinated by the thing, which barely had the strength to lift its tentacle into the heavy air. The creature *was* poisoned by its environment, and dying by degrees. It wouldn't last much longer. The tentacle fell back into the thick sludge, and it seemed to sigh in defeat, then, with a great effort, took another scoop of bones and muck and pushed it up the trough wall, into the trash tube.

Lagrasse walked away from the building, wondering how close he was to madness. What he was seeing couldn't be real. Every moment some new aspect of the nightmare presented itself. He had pieces of many different puzzles.

From the center of the island was a towering shape, rising to a point. He made his way toward it, moving from wall to wall so as to stay hidden. But there was never any sound. Never a hint of movement. He gave up on finding footprints—the surface of the island was the same black rock, but the flowing sheen of water kept the algae off, and any tracks would have been washed away.

There had to be other survivors. It couldn't be just him.

When he felt a wave of vertigo he forced his feet

to propel him inside a boxy stone structure, and he collapsed behind the wall, in the darkness of shadow.

When he awoke again, he heard voices. They weren't real—that's what he thought. But his vision cleared and the voices remained.

He got to his feet, fought off dizziness, and went to find out where the voices were coming from.

THE VOICES WERE beyond the wall that surrounded the pyramid. Lagrasse tried calling to them, but his head exploded with pain when he tried to shout.

He found one of the rare collapsed buildings along the edge of the wall and painstakingly climbed the rubble, from there scrambling atop a neighboring structure. From that roof, he saw over the wall and into the courtyard surrounding the pyramid.

It was a three-sided pyramid. Lagrasse had never heard of such a thing—and it was as massive as the biggest of the Egyptian or South American pyramids.

There were people scaling the structure. They looked like ants to Lagrasse, but he could have sworn a few wore the tattered remnants of Coast Guard uniforms. He tried to shout, pain be damned, but he managed nothing better than a weak gasp that they never heard. All he got for his trouble was excruciating pain.

He could hear them, though. The vast city was so still that their voices travel unnaturally far. Lagrasse searched for anything to make a noise. Two rocks to pound together. Nothing on the rooftop. He should have grabbed some stones from the rubble below.

The people were heading for a crack in the pyramid, and Lagrasse glimpsed a yellow glow inside. The glow was unclean somehow. Lagrasse, too drained of energy to climb down, slumped on the roof to rest and watch.

The climbers would get a few yards up the steep pyramid, then slide back down again. It took another twenty minutes for one of them to finally reach the crack that seemed to be an entrance. He crawled inside. He called for the others, and eventually all but one of them made it up. The one left outside was a tiny woman who didn't have the strength for scaling the moldering rock.

She shouted for her friends to tell her what they saw. Instead, they began to scream.

The tiny woman ran, but she didn't get far.

Something like a rope flopped out of the crack and fell across the woman, knocking her flat.

Lagrasse knew what the thing was. He had just seen one like it in the trash shed. It was a tentacle, but this one was laughably huge. A hundred feet long. His mind was playing tricks.

The tentacle constricted around the small woman and dragged her in. That's what Lagrasse saw, anyway. But he knew it was just an illusion conjured by a sick mind.

The screams of the dying climbers—which had to be another trick of his ailing brain—seemed to last an hour.

## 23

Okyek Meh Thih, the Caretaker of the People, felt sad and helpless. He stood up to stretch his legs, and strolled to the lip of rock. A narrow trail hugged the mountainside, but if one walked directly out of the cave entrance one would fall to the bottom of the mountain.

His plea was still coming from his lips, delivered gently and incessantly; after countless repetitions the words had become ingrained and delivered without thought. His throat was raw. What was the point of this? Chuh Mboi Aku was surely not hearing these words and ignoring them if he did.

He had come to guess why he was supposed to be in this cave, beseeching Chuh Mboi Aku. Maybe he could encourage Chuh Mboi Aku to show the world mercy. It might be a small chance, but it was a chance nevertheless. Taking steps that might help save the People was better than busying himself in vain over their suffering and allowing their annihilation to happen without resistance.

But would that truly come to pass? What evidence

did he have of this? Nothing but an old inscription and the words of an old, dead man.

Ah, but there was another indication of the truth of the legend. There was the bird, Chak. The bird was always attentive to the Caretaker's work, but especially so when there were dreams that appeared to come from Chuh Mboi Aku. It came to pass that the Caretaker would look to the parrot for guidance while listening to the troubles of one of the People, and the bird would show a certain behavior—nodding its great head, excited shifting on its perch—to show when the dreams were of Chuh Mboi Aku. This behavior manifested gradually over the years, for the dreams were infrequent, even for the People, who were sensitive beyond other Peoples.

The Caretaker had a revelation one day: the bird could identify the touch of Chuh Mboi Aku. It wasn't the training of a pet. The bird was sensing the residue of a god's dream in the mind of a man or woman or child, and no bird was known to do such a thing.

But this bird could do it.

The bird's behavior became more obvious, not because the bird was more skilled than before, but because the dreams came more often. The dreams became a darkness in their lives so often the People no longer came to the Caretaker for his advice. Not that he could ease their spirits about these dreams, not since they stopped believing in his tales of phalluses.

Chak became agitated for days and flapped across the village in fits, until finally he woke the Caretaker crying about "The meaning of the cave!"

The huge and brilliant creature winged off over the jungle, toward the mountain, and Okyek Meh Thih was too intrigued to not follow. He arrived at the cave at the end of the day, finding the bird there before the inscription. The bird was trembling from the high-altitude cold and prancing wildly in front of the inscription.

Okyek Meh Thih lit a fire to warm them both. The bird screeched and cried out all night, as if demanding something of the rock wall and its meaningless symbols. When the Caretaker tried to pet and comfort it, the bird wouldn't remain in his hands, but paced and strutted and screeched. When it finally slept, it was a fitful sleep in the Caretaker's hands.

Okyek Meh Thih awoke when the bird screeched in the late morning, jumping out of his hands, staring at Okyek Meh Thih. The bird wobbled to the cave mouth and leaped into the air.

Chak flew away, over the canopy of the jungle, and Okyek Meh Thih saw him no more for two long years.

# 24

"I'm fine, Mrs. M.," Mark Howard insisted to the elderly old woman. "Hi, Dr. Smith."

"Mark? What are you doing here?"

"They just released me from the free clinic," Mark said.

"Why wasn't I informed?" Dr. Smith asked the nurse who was guiding the wheelchair into the office, and fighting Mrs. Mikulka for control.

"I insisted. Thanks, you've been great. Thanks, Mrs. M. I've got it. I've *got it.*"

The nurse took the hint. Mrs. Mikulka steadfastly refused to. She fussed with him until he had stepped out of the wheelchair and slumped into the office chair behind the desk.

"You shouldn't be out of hospital care," Dr. Smith said.

"Yes, I should be."

"That will be all, Mrs. Mikulka."

The old woman left, promising to bring Mark tea. She closed the door behind her.

"How are you feeling?"

"What's happening, Dr. Smith? What's the news?"

"Problems are intensifying globally, but there's nothing new. A worsening of the same. Why?"

"Europe?"

"A mess, but the truly dangerous security threats are under control."

Mark Howard looked dissatisfied and began snapping out commands on his keyboard. "Something's happening."

"Much is happening. Are you all right, Mark?"

"I mean something is really happening. I don't know what it was that I saw. It was something *big*."

Sarah pushed into the office and hurried to Mark, embracing his head against her stomach as he sat.

"Why are you here?" she demanded. "God, you know what I thought? I walked into your hospital room and the bed was *empty*."

"Sorry. Something is happening. I saw it in the dream. That *thing* showed it to me. What it intends to do."

"What thing?" Smith demanded, but he knew perfectly well what thing.

"I was dreaming. I was in the ocean." Mark stood up, clearing his head, trying to see it again. "It was pulling me down deep, into the water, where it was pitch-black. It was pulling me by the leg—Jesus, it hurt even in the dream. It hurts now." He was in baggy sweatpants and he felt the leg, felt the bandage and yanked up the sweatpants to see the bandage.

"That explains the wheelchair."

"What else did you see, Mark?"

"I should take him back to the doctors," Sarah insisted.

"It pulled me down through the earth and into the hollow. I saw the water in the hollow. It was too big—I couldn't make sense of it being something that was inside the earth but so big. Then I was pulled into the water. It was moving fast. I never would have believed it could move so fast. The erosion of the stone walls was visible. Then I was in the water. It was a maelstrom, out of control, chaos. I may never ride a roller coaster again."

He peered into the middle distance.

"Then it got bigger, the space around me, and the water was boiling. I was riding inside a wall of steam and I was falling—up."

Mark looked around the room, as if expecting to find what he was looking for. Harold Smith didn't like the look in his eyes. "I want you under a doctor's care, Mark."

"Where it's cold. My skin was scalded, but when I touched the air, the air was cold."

Mark was trembling. Sarah pierced Smith with a look as she eased him into the desk chair.

"He was laughing at me, Dr. Smith. He was taunting me. He knew there was nothing I could do about it."

"Mark, I need to know more details if I'm to take action."

"There's no action to take. It was too big. Bigger than anything on Earth, ever."

"What was it you saw? Clear your mind. Picture it. Tell me what it was."

Mark nodded and squinted at the desktop. "I saw cold."

Dr. Smith looked disappointed.

"Antarctica," Mark blurted. "What's happening at the South Pole?"

Dr. Smith frowned. "Nothing." He tapped out commands on his desktop and confirmed the news. "No reports of anything out of the ordinary."

Mark Howard shook his head. "Not yet, but it's coming."

## 25

The Caretaker became miserable in the two years after the bird left him.

Nothing was worse than watching one's People suffer, especially when one is the Caretaker charged with alleviating their suffering.

Okyek Meh Thih's dread grew. The legends of Chuh Mboi Aku, the elder god who would destroy this world, appeared to be coming true. Why in his generation? Why now? Countless Caretakers had come and gone and carried the old secret of Chuh Mboi Aku. What evil trick of fate caused the legend to rear its ugly head while he was Caretaker?

Then Chak returned, a bedraggled and emaciated version of its former self. It announced its return by perching outside his hut and shrieking, "Is it come? Have you heard it? Have you heard it?"

The Caretaker felt great joy at seeing the bird, but the bird wasn't interested in any affectionate homecoming.

"Have you heard it in the cave? Have you heard it?"

The Caretaker had never been in the habit of treating the bird as if it could converse, such as a human could converse, but he answered the question. "I have not been to the cave."

"In the cave! In the cave!" The bird took wing, and Okyek Meh Thih set off after it.

The bird was crying in the cave when the Caretaker reached it.

"Hear it?" Chak demanded.

Okyek Meh Thih did hear it—a strange sound like a bird note but never-ending. It simply went on forever, but where did it come from? He moved about the cave until he traced the sound at its loudest to the tiny punctures in the stone that was a part of the inscription.

The sound reminded him of the noise a radio could make. They had a radio now, and the People would turn it on every once in a while. The children enjoyed the novelty of hearing voices coming from far away. But they could find no real purpose for the device.

The parrot looked at him long and hard, and Okyek Meh Thih used the patience he had learned from his grandfather. He said nothing, but waited for the bird to do what it was trying to do.

"I could not prevent it!" the bird screeched finally.

"None expected you to prevent it," the Caretaker said soothingly, but this only inflamed the creature's self-recrimination—if that's what it was. Time and again, hour after hour, it seemed to be trying to speak more words of meaning, but it couldn't break through whatever invisible barriers were hindering it.

Mostly it repeated the old limericks and phrases it had picked up over the years. Sometimes, when it struggled the most, it came up with new fragmented phrases that made little sense.

"Master Lu made bad decisions," the bird exclaimed, in English. "Master Lu ate a parrot."

This told the Caretaker nothing. When he and the bird finally returned to the village, they found the People in a panic. The dreams of Chuh Mboi Aku had suddenly become horrific. Almost every one of the People was having the dream and suffering from it.

"Awake. Awake." The bird's chant was a dirge. "Caretaker, you will carry out your duties."

The Caretaker heard a new intonation in the voice that was as familiar as the words of old. "I will," he answered.

The bird left him again.

The Caretaker wished the bird were with him now. Such good company the bird was, and he was so filled with loneliness and dread. He despised this cold cave in the mountain, his prison, but he wouldn't break his vow.

He would keep making his plea to Chuh Mboi Aku for as long as it took—until he died of starvation, or the world ended around him.

## 26

Remo felt like a soldier coming home from a humiliating defeat. After a night at the Ritz-Carlton, he had hoped there would be something else for him to do before returning empty-handed to Folcroft.

"At least Cho-gye scored somewhere else and brought some gold home with him," he complained.

"You bring success," said Chiun, head craned to look out the window. He was scrutinizing the wing of the British Airways jumbo jet. Chiun didn't trust people who claimed that the wings of modern aircraft almost never fell off.

"I almost brought failure crashing down on everyone."

"And how long will you carry the burden around with you? It is an annoyance."

"Sorry for being annoying."

"Hardly a sufficient apology."

They were in the small business-class section on the top level of the jet, which was somewhat better than coach and still allowed Chiun to watch the wing. The flight attendants were aggressive about attending to Remo's needs, which were nonexistent. He tried making it clear.

"No wine, no meal, no blanket, no lavender-scented hot towel. Just leave me alone."

They weren't dissuaded until he paralyzed one and sat her in the empty seat across the row. She was wide-eyed, silent and smiling for fifteen minutes.

Remo had a way with flight attendants—and most other women. It came from his Sinanju training. Chiun had explained how Sinanju's perfecting of the human body created an allure that the human female could sense. Remo knew it was like pheromones and had something to do with his scent. He could turn it off by eating shark, for example—the shark smell spoiled the Sinanju smell. But he didn't like shark and Chiun told him he smelled like a stagnant aquarium when he ate it.

Remo had learned, by degrees, to control the production of pheromones, but it was one of his less consistent talents. He wasn't exactly sure what he did, but he seemed to be able to make it turn off if he really tried. It took a while before the pheromones actually tapered off, and they might start up again without warning. Chiun knew how to do it well. Stewardesses rarely hassled Chiun.

"If I turn you back on will you promise to leave me alone?" Remo growled to the flight attendant.

She blinked her acquiescence. He adjusted her spinal cord and cured her of total paralysis. She looked a little afraid of him and a little aroused. When another attendant joined her in business class, she apparently relayed the story, but it only suc-

ceeded in intriguing the second attendant. Remo was
shooing them away for the next six hours.

Six hours during which the world began to see its
end in sight.

**27**

The South Pole was remote enough. But when you reached Lake in the Valley, you were *really* out in the middle of nowhere.

People came and went all the time at the geographic South Pole on the Polar Plateau. There was a permanent base there; always somebody was there with the front light on and the coffee hot—like a twenty-four-hour truck stop.

The Ross Sea and the Ross Ice Shelf were hubs of activity compared to this place. The Weddell Sea? Comparatively crowded. Casey was busy with Australians. Leningradskaya bustled with Russians. Showa was inhabited by Japanese. South Africans hung around Sanae. In addition, just about everywhere you went, there were Americans acting as if they owned the entire place.

But in the Lake in the Valley you could truly call yourself alone, like Antarctica ought to be. Eight hundred miles from the South Geomagnetic Pole, six hundred miles from the Russian base called Vostok, and one thousand frigid impassable miles from any other outpost of humanity.

A thousand miles was a hell of a lot of territory. That's what people didn't understand about the South Pole. It wasn't a bunch of ice chunks floating around. It wasn't a large island. Antarctica was a continent. If it were temperate and paved with asphalt, it would take days to drive across.

It offered the kind of extreme loneliness unavailable anywhere else in the world. Stuck in Lake in the Valley with nothing to see in either direction, knowing with utter certainty that you and your companions and your little metal shack were the only people and the only building in a swathe of land the size of Texas.

Karl Yurman got through it okay by not thinking about it. If you think about the solitude too much you go nuts—or you get tired of thinking about it and you worry about something else. You think abut the cold until the cold gets old. You just keep going.

Someday Karl and the others would get their payoff and this would all be worthwhile. They'd be famous, even if they discovered nothing except germs. If they discovered something photogenic, they'd be *really* famous.

The Lake in the Valley had been identified a few years earlier by seismic mapping of the Antarctic ice layer. Here, in the then-unnamed valley, the instruments discovered a pocket of water under the three-mile layer of solid ice.

The concept was almost too much to comprehend. A lake of liquid water inside the Antarctic ice. Trapped there for millions of years. Salty enough to remain liquid at extremely low temperatures.

Now Yurman and his team were determined to get at the water, open her up, see what was in there. Subglacial lakes had yielded some amazing and unique life-forms, specially adapted to perpetual darkness and a hypersaline environment, but none accessed so far was nearly as old as the Lake in the Valley. It had been encased in ice for more than fifteen million years. It was known to be supersaturated with oxygen and nitrogen levels fifty times that of a freshwater lake on the surface.

On long nights like this, when Yurman stayed up alone watching the drill grind through the ice, hour after hour, he daydreamed a little about what might be down there. He let his fancy run away. He knew what kinds of creatures might have lived in the lake when it became ice covered; which of those would have survived in the microcosm? What challenges would the environment have presented and how would those creatures have evolved?

His knowledge and experience told him they would find nothing more amazing than a few superhardy bacteria strains. But wouldn't it be cool if they found some sort of animal, something hideous and aggressive?

Yurman thought it entertaining to draw out monstrous creatures that would be biologically suited for the environment of the lake. The other guys loved his drawings of implausible primates that sifted microscopic particles from the water for food and pooped rock salt.

It was going to take another eighteen months minimum before they knew for sure what was in the lake. Drilling was slow going. They were on their third drill in a year—this one was an improved laser unit that was only slightly more reliable than its predecessors. It superheated the ice with a narrow beam, melting it into vapor and ventilating the steam to the surface in tiny puffs. They were lucky to get through a hundred feet a week, and the deeper they went the slower they went.

Something beeped.

Eighteen months to reach liquid water was a pipe dream, if you asked Yurman. It might be double that, or more.

Something beeped again. Nights like this were all Karl had to look forward to for a long time....

What the hell had beeped at him? The drill seemed okay. No lens to replace. Vent motor was okay. Or was it?

It was stopped. The entire drill was in standby mode. Autoshutdown activated. Why was autoshutdown activated?

Oh. It had stopped because it had reached water.

"Say again?" Karl Yurman asked the monochrome display. Something was really screwed up. Sure enough, the front-end sensor had picked up moisture traces in the bottom of the drill shaft. Hell, the laser must have gone haywire. When it melted way too much ice the fan couldn't ventilate the steam fast enough and it condensed into liquid and shut down the drill for hours.

Yurman would have to run a diagnostic on the drill and hope he could figure out the problem, because if he couldn't, then he'd have to extract it and that would put them out of commission for days.

Something else beeped. Since when did their displays have all these audible alerts? A temperature gauge? Yurman sneered at the screen. Ninety-two degrees Celsius? Yeah, right. Something was truly F.U. He hit the retract button and the large drum began to reverse, rewinding the mile-long umbilical cable to the ice drill.

Another beep said the temperature was now above boiling. Karl Yurman switched on the remote camera and tried to figure out what he was looking at.

The harsh white light on the drill showed him— boiling water.

That couldn't be right. The laser was powerful, sure, but it was pulsed and aimed in a way to melt one penny-sized circle of ice at a time. It would take a total system failure, and the breakdown of various protective fail-safes, to make the laser stay on long enough to melt and boil water in the drill shaft. In fact, why was it boiling if the autoshutdown had been triggered? There wouldn't be that much residual heat.

The internal temperature gauge began sounding an alarm, and Karl was astounded to find the external temperature was still rising. But the laser was off.

There had to be another heat source. A mile under the Antarctic ice, which had been frozen solid since way before man first jumped out of the trees, and now there was a new heat source. Ridiculous.

"What's going on? You woke me up." It was Gerhny, the head engineer, coming in bleary eyed from the dormitory, where others were now stirring. "What's all the racket?"

"I can't figure it out," Karl said. "You won't believe what the temp gauges are trying to tell me."

Linfrey was next to come investigating, in his uniform of paisley-printed boxer shorts. He was the computer whiz. There wasn't anything Gerhny and Linfrey didn't know about the equipment.

"It's really messed up. I'm pulling it in," Yurman reported.

"What's that on the screen?" Linfrey asked. "Steam?"

"I can't even figure out the malfunction," Yurman admitted. "I think the damn laser's still going."

Gerhny made a face. "You'd see the glow on the screen. I don't see anything except the drill light."

"The drill light didn't raise the shaft temp high enough to make steam."

"Neither did the laser," Gerhny snapped. "This ain't a malfunction."

Linfrey guffawed shortly.

"I'm serious."

Yurman was glad somebody else had suggested what he suspected. "What else could it be? A hot spring? We mapped this ice for miles around and never saw a hot spring."

"The laser's gonna crack—look at the temp!" Linfrey shouted. "It's gotta be something in the drill head overheating, Gerhn."

"Explain the steam," Gerhny snapped. "The whole thing couldn't make that much heat under any circumstances."

"Hey, shit. Come see this!" It was Charlie Cho, an optical-engineering doctoral candidate from Columbia University. His promising drill head innovations had earned him a place on the team and a free, six-month-long vacation in beautiful Antarctica.

Yurman ducked out of the control room. Cho was dragging on his thermal gear as the others crowded around the porthole windows, where the drill shed was leaking wisps of vapor.

"She's coming up," Yurman reported. "That's steam from below."

"Gonna cook my laser," Charlie reported.

"Leave it," Linfrey called from the control room. "The temp's going way up. It might cook you, too."

Cho ducked into the control room and shook his head at what he saw on the monitors. "Whatever it is, it's not that hot yet. I'm getting my drill."

Charlie ducked into the vestibule, dragged the door shut behind him, then opened the door to the outside. The draft that leaked through the cold-lock was subzero.

"This is nuts," Gerhny complained from the control room. "It's gotta be a hot spring."

"In the ice?" Yurman asked.

"Why's the drill coming up so damn fast?" Linfrey asked.

"Cho's not stupid. He'll stay clear until the winch stops."

"But why's it going so fast?"

It came to Karl Yurman why it was going so fast. "Call Cho! Tell him to get back. It's gonna burn him!" At the porthole he saw Charlie Cho tromp through knee-deep snow and drag open the door to the drill shed. Clouds of steam came from the vestibule. He was in such a hurry he didn't drag it closed behind him.

"Why?" Linfrey asked.

"Call him!" Yurman insisted.

"Didn't take his radio," Leek growled.

Karl Yurman yanked both doors and battled through the frigid wind without his coat. "Cho, get out of there," he shouted.

Through the open doors of the drill shed, Yurman saw Cho amid the gentle puffs of steam trickling from the umbilical shaft. The man was looking at him quizzically. The big drill spindle was rotating fast, as if the long drill umbilical weighed almost nothing.

"Get out before it blows!"

Cho shouted back, "It can't blow, Yur. It's electric."

"Steam pressure building under the drill," Yurman shouted. Now was not the time for an explanation. "When the drill pops out, the steam's gonna fry everything in the shed."

Cho's stricken expression told Yurman that he understood what the danger was, but it turned out to be too late. There was a clank from below. That was the clank of the drill head entering the steel-reinforced opening channel of the drill shaft. Yurman dove face first into the snow.

Charlie Cho tried to run, but the battered drill head ejected from the drill shaft like a champagne cork, and then the high-pressure steam surge filled the shed. Cho yelled when the exposed skin of his face became scalded. His goggles weren't on and he couldn't open his eyes, so he missed the door and ran into the wall. The steam vent was roaring. Scalding steam entered his lungs when he gasped for breath. He slammed into the wall a few more times, unable to find the way out, but then his rational mind kicked in just long enough to instruct him to follow the escape route of the steam blast. He somehow managed to feel the current and staggered along with it.

Then there was a fresh burst behind him and the steam pressure increased dramatically. Cho was slammed from behind, knocked onto his face, and the urgent fingers of steam slipped through the tiniest gaps in his thermal suit. Trickles of fire burned his skin.

Cho couldn't help it. He screamed, and when his body forced him to inhale, it brought in white-hot vapor that scalded his windpipe and boiled his lungs. His thermal suit became a burning blanket.

Karl Yurman crawled through the snow that was melting into slush under his body while the steam blast heated up his back. The back of his sweatshirt was soaked with sweat. He felt arms grabbing him and dragging him inside the lab building, but he didn't stand up until he heard the doors closed behind him.

"Talk to me, Yur," Gerhny demanded as they dragged the wet clothing off of him.

Yurman swayed on his feet. "I think I'm okay."

"Cho's cooked," Leek was moaning. "He's cooked!"

Yurman allowed the dripping sweatshirt to be removed from his body, then he shouldered Leek out of the porthole window.

Cho was cooked, all right. The young man who

would never get his doctorate had managed to strip off the thermal suit from the waist up, and he got his shirt half off. Then he succumbed. The blast of steam jetting out of the drill shed was as strong as the discharge of a jet engine, and the heat parboiled Cho's front. His face and chest were pink and puffy.

His chest was shaking.

"He's still alive," Yurman said.

"Not for long," Gerhny replied dully. "We can't help him."

"We have to."

"How we gonna get to him?" Gerhny demanded. "We almost got killed dragging you back." Gerhny nodded across the room. Polo, the Argentine scientist with the unpronounceable name, was bandaging Linfrey's bright red forearms.

Yurman couldn't believe that they were helpless. He turned back to the porthole, just in time to witness Cho's swelling eyeballs burst behind their lids, one after another. Sizzling goop spattered out.

Cho's tremulous breathing stopped a few seconds later.

"Yur, if you're okay I want you on the phone with the seismic boys at Aslab," Linfrey said. "I want to know what the fuck this is."

Yurman nodded and returned to the control room. He wondered how everything could have gone to hell so fast. Fifteen minutes ago he'd been sitting there alone, bored and happy while everybody else slept—including Cho.

He slumped in his seat and dialed up the permanent U.S. Amundsen-Scott scientific base at the South Pole.

"What the hell is going on up there, Yurman?" demanded the base commander, a man named Walken. "You guys trying to blast open that damn lake?"

"We broke through into some sort of a steam vent." He gave a brief account of the tragedy, but Walken wasn't in the mood to listen to details.

"Yurman, you guys are in trouble. That's not a steam vent. It's something big."

"Big?"

"We're getting readings on seismic."

"Seismic?" Yurman wasn't following.

"Listen, it's triangulating weird but it's less than a hundred miles from where you're sitting."

Yurman considered that. "We didn't feel any earthquake."

"Earthquakes don't give off a lot of heat. We're thinking volcano."

"Volcano?" Yurman repeated stupidly. He wasn't the only one. The others were standing around, listening on the speaker, and every single one of them said, "Volcano?"

"That's our best guess," Walken said. "We're coming to get you."

There was a large noise outside. Linfrey left and offered an assessment. "The drill shed's gone. The steam shaft's widening itself to two meters already. The collar's disappeared."

Gerhny did some instant calculations. "If it stays constant it'll swallow the lab in two hours."

"It's not staying constant," Linfrey snapped. "Everybody get suited."

Yurman was dragging on dry thermal suit pants

as he relayed the information to Walken and gave him the coordinates of their escape—the overland route that would give them the least resistance to quick travel. He pocketed a satellite phone, which might or might not work....

The front entrance was blocked by sizzling steam, which hadn't dissipated after the drill shed was blown off and was no longer directing the steam flow at the building. The front dorm and cooking areas of their Antarctic home had grown hotter than they had ever been. Sauna temperatures. The steam outside blocked their view of the shaft opening, but the sound had become the thunder of Niagara Falls.

They were ready in minutes, and every one of them took an emergency pack with a GPS beacon.

When they opened the door, water flooded in around their ankles.

"WALKEN, it's Yurman and we're in deep shit!"

The South Pole commander took the phone. "Go ahead."

"The steam's melting everything. Our damn field building is sinking in the ice—we almost didn't get out in time. Both our Sno-Cats are sunk up to the windshield. We're on foot and we're up to our knees in slush."

Walken and his base were prepared for a hundred varieties of South Pole emergencies, but this wasn't one of them. "Our boys are on their way. They'll find you, even without the Cats."

"How long?" Yurman demanded.

Walken scanned the progress of the rescue aircraft. "ETA eighty-seven minutes."

"We'll be dead by then."

Walken pursed his lips, then said, "No. You listen, boy. Get onto solid ground as soon as possible. Don't get wet above the knees. You can do that."

"We're freezing already!"

"Yeah, you're gonna freeze. And you boys can forget about having feet. But you can stay alive. Keep walking. Keep making energy. Keep your bodies working. You keep going until we pick you boys up. You hear me?"

"Yeah."

"You keep moving!"

"We'll keep moving."

"THERE IT GOES!" shouted Polo, the Argentine scientist. Yurman and the others turned to watch.

Their corrugated metal home had never looked more spotlessly clean—free of ice and snow and drenched by the heavy fall of water droplets from the geyser. The metallic roof glinted in the sun as it slid into the deepening slush.

The geyser was five meters in diameter.

Gerhny turned away abruptly. "It's impossible. Walken must have been wrong about the volcano. We're right on top of it. That's the only way there could be so much heat."

Leek mumbled in reply through his face coverings. "No man. No man. Volcanoes are big."

"Not that big," Gerhny said morosely. "No volcano generates so much heat it's going to melt a four-mile-thick ice layer for a hundred miles in every direction."

"It's a frigging volcano," Leek insisted. "They're big."

"It's a matter of calories, Leek. The amount of energy used for that much heat is bigger than a volcano a hundred miles away. It's got to be right under our damn feet."

"No," Leek said to himself.

"We'll get out of here," Linfrey insisted. "Even if there's a volcano down there, it's not gonna erupt in the next two hours."

Yurman wondered what expertise Linfrey was basing his assessment on. "That's not our problem," he said. "Our problem is the lake. Do you people realize that we're now standing on an iceberg? The ice layer was less than a mile thick when everything went to hell, and now it's melting fast."

"A mile of ice is still a lot of ice," Leek shot back. "It can't melt in the next two hours."

Yurman could hear the terror in Leek's voice. He didn't bother pointing out that *everything* today fit into the "can't happen" category.

He was so damn cold. His feet were numb already, but his legs still burned with the cold. What was worse was the trickling of the cold blood coming up from his legs and sucking the warmth from his whole body.

He couldn't dwell on the cold. He couldn't let it get the better of him. He had to think about something else.

"Wonder what it will be like without legs," he suggested. "Walken's right that we'll probably lose them."

Linfrey got the idea at once. "Not so bad considering the alternative."

"Yeah," Leek said. "That ain't so bad."

"The prosthetics they have now are sophisticated," Polo forced himself to say through chattering teeth.

"Right," Linfrey said. "You can race marathons and shit."

"You can run a shrimp boat, like in *Forrest Gump*," Gerhny added, trying to sound unconcerned.

"Yeah. Let's all pool our cash and buy a shrimp boat," Leek said. "In Louisiana. Where it never freezes. You're invited, too, Doc Polo. We'll get you a work visa."

"What worries me is not the losing of my legs but the other parts," the Argentine said. "Do they have prosthetics for those? I do not know."

"You mean the little shrimp? Now, that could be really serious," Gerhny added, so gravely that the others chuckled. "Hey, legs you can do without. But if *that* freezes off, then what?"

Leek was sniggering and shaking from cold, almost uncontrollably. Yurman grasped the man by the arm. If Leek fell—if any of them fell and got wet above the crotch—their body heat would be sucked out of them long before the rescue chopper showed up.

The wet slush was getting shallow, he noted. They had waded almost two miles from the base camp, and the current of warm steam was reduced and the slush went only to their ankles.

They just might make it, Yurman thought. In another hour and fifteen, they'd be on the rescue aircraft getting warmed up.

The ground shook.

Gerhny toppled. He was big and sturdy, and it was like watching a beer-barrel tip. The man landed on his chest in the slush and his suit soaked up the water. Their high-tech outerwear was made for extreme cold, but not for water. In the Antarctic, landlocked a thousand miles in, exposure to standing water was not a factor, so the suits weren't designed for it.

Gerhny got up sputtering on his hands and knees, and Karl Yurman knew he was looking at a dead man.

Gerhny was looking at something else, and his mouth hung open.

Yurman turned to see.

The valley was bulging. A magnificent upheaval occurred and the ground shook more as a slab of ice rose ten, fifteen, twenty feet high before it stopped, and furious plumes of steam hissed from the mile-long seam.

Five miles farther, the ice burst open like a popped pimple, sending a new steam column soaring into the air.

"It's erupting," Gerhny shouted. He scrambled to his feet, ignoring the fact that he was soaked with freezing water, and plodded off as fast as he could move. The others ran after him.

The ground shook repeatedly, and Yurman glanced back to witness the eruption of more steam geysers, some of them miles away. How was this happening? Where did all this heat come from?

There was a tremor that started and would not stop. Gerhny fell down again, and Polo lost his footing. Leek slipped. Yurman tried to hold on to Leek, but the man slipped through his fingers and splashed into the slush.

A thought skipped through Yurman's head. Slush is getting deeper again.

"It must be close!" he shouted, but then he saw he was wrong. The newest eruption was a hundred miles away, beyond the horizon of soggy snow and buckling ice. It burst out of the Antarctic valley like a submarine-fired missile erupting out of the sea, and it went up and up into the clear blue sky.

And it was white. It was water. It was steam.

"Impossible," Gerhny said through stiff jaws.

The tremor died and the smaller steam vents began to droop, losing strength, and Yurman hopelessly helped the others to their feet. He didn't know what to make of all this and he didn't really care anymore.

"We're gonna freeze," Leek moaned. "I don't wanna freeze!"

"Let's keep moving!" Yurman ordered. "That's the only way to stay warm."

"Why are you so special?" Leek cried. "Why ain't you all wet?"

"Come on, Leek, let's march," Yurman commanded.

"Don't give me that. I'm dying. We're all freezing to death except for you. It ain't fair!"

"You can make it for another hour," Yurman said. "Just keep going for one hour and the rescue will be here."

"One hour! I'm freezing to death, Yur. I ain't gonna live twenty more minutes! And you know what—I'm taking you with me!"

Leek charged. His feet were already lifeless and his entire body was becoming stiff, but he managed to lumber through the splashing slush and raise his arms to tackle Karl Yurman.

Let him, Yurman thought. Leek was right. He didn't deserve to escape this any more than the others did, and he sure didn't want to have to live with the guilt of being the only survivor. So let Leek push him into the water, so that he could freeze to death alongside his comrades.

Something else was coming toward Yurman. It was Polo, the little Argentine doctor, who tackled Leek hard. Polo and Leek sprawled in the slush.

"It's not fair," Leek whined. "It's not fair that he gets to live and we don't." He picked himself up, soaking wet and dripping. Polo struggled to his feet.

Gerhny and Linfrey moved alongside Polo to keep him from doing anything else stupid. They all knew they had just minutes of life left in them, and yet they had silently allied to save Yurman. They prodded Leek to walk ahead of them, with Yurman following.

None of this made sense. The numbing cold made the suffering all the more genuine and yet it was surreal. Even Yurman's thoughts were sluggish, as if the blood in his brain were slushy. One voice in his head kept insisting that he must do something to help the others. He couldn't just stand there and watch them freeze. Another part of his brain reminded him that there was nothing he could possibly do.

Another part of his brain kept insisting that *none* of this could really be happening. It just couldn't.

When he looked behind him, he could still see the gigantic steam column. It must be fifty miles away, and unthinkably huge. Something new was there, too—a white sandstorm.

"What's that?" he asked aloud.

Polo stooped and squinted. "Steam. Superheated from below ground."

It was a tornado on its side, rolling across the vast valley at a tremendous speed. It was hundreds of feet tall but shrinking visibly with every passing moment.

"It cools fast on the outside and hot steam churns out from the middle and it goes faster and faster," Polo said. "It will burn itself out quickly."

"How quickly?" Yurman asked.

Polo shrugged slowly. "Maybe before it comes to us. Maybe not. How could I know?"

"Run, Yur," Gerhny said. His feet folded up beneath him, and he sat with a splash in the slush. "Get over the ridge."

Yurman looked at him.

"Yeah. Run. Beat it. Beat it." Linfrey sat down beside Gerhny, then laid himself down. The ice water and slush covered his face. Bubbles trickled from his nose. Gerhny watched him.

Polo raised an arm and pointed. "Run."

Karl Yurman ran—or did his best imitation of a run. He left the others without speaking. He plodded around Leek, who was kneeling in the slush and no longer blinking. He left his companions behind.

He ran for the ridge. It was just a ripple in the landscape, but they knew it was caused by a series of stony spikes in the ice-covered rock, and there was rock beyond it. The ice melt would be slowed by the ridge, they had hoped. That's where they had been headed. Now maybe, beyond the ridge, Yurman would be protected from the steam storm.

What a joke. He was a mile from the ridge. The steam storm was coming too fast.

He felt his body growing weak but becoming warm. That gave him hope. He heard the scream of the wind behind him. His hopes were dashed.

He glanced over his shoulder as the maelstrom bore down on him and engulfed him in bitter cold that instantly transformed into searing heat. His body was tossed by the blow. His goggles and hood and cap were torn off, and he was thrust under the water, which boiled through his layers and cooked his skin.

He fought to the surface, only to feel a sudden gust tear away the water and Yurman was on his stomach on a rock-hard layer of ice. The flesh-cooking heat from the steam cloud was gone.

He experienced fire like he couldn't imagine. Every inch of his skin surface was burned, and continued to burn when the boiling water soaking his clothing refused to cool.

Then came the thunder. The air convulsed in the wake of the violent steam storm, rushing to fill the displacement. It was good, clean Antarctic air, minus 28.3°C and moving along at more than one hundred miles per hour.

The wind chill was unimaginable. In a heartbeat,

Yurman's clothes went from scalding to bone-chilling and seconds later they were frozen on the surface. His drenched face was locked in ice. The shallow water in which he knelt crusted over instantly.

Rain. Hot rain. It ate into the flesh of his exposed face, then froze a moment later. The wind went on and on and Yurman was a statue, locked up solid.

He couldn't move.

The physical suffering would go away soon. He would grow numb or he would die in the next few minutes. Right?

*Right?*

**28**

Had a day passed? Had two? Okyek Meh Thih's limbs were stiff as death and his throat was parched. The water gourd was empty—he must have sipped it away as he sat chanting his endless plea.

Then he felt again the shaking that had awakened him, and he scrambled to his feet. He lumbered to the mouth of the cave. The mountain was shaking under him.

The Caretaker's feet had been folded together for more than twenty-four hours and he stumbled, almost pitching out of the cave mouth to his death, but he managed to grab the wall of the cave and hold on.

Then he saw the fountain of Chuh Mboi Aku erupt from the jungle. It was miles away, just a hiss of steam that darted out of the earth and reached into the sky like a finger pointing out of the treetops. Okyek Meh Thih, the Caretaker of the People, was fascinated, and relieved, too. The plume was small and harmless looking.

But it grew in fits. Part of the earth that it was forcing up through had been blocked, but the blockage broke and the hot column of water roared into the sky.

Twice as tall as the tops of the rain forest canopy. Heavy billows of steam poured off of it. The Caretaker could see the shadow of the scalding rainfall and he witnessed the jungle wilt under the boiling water.

It became bigger again.

The People! At this rate, the column would soon grow huge enough to drench his precious People with its killing rain. He had to get to them! He staggered along the trail on wobbling legs.

Before he'd traveled ten paces, the earth exploded at the base of the column of water, which doubled in size and height, then doubled again, until the top of it was higher than the mountain of the cave.

The rain fell, boiling water that burned the Caretakers's unclothed body. He wept for the pain and crawled back into the shelter of the cave. There he lay in misery as the jungle was scalded in every direction. The agony of the animals was so intense he could hear it, even this high up. The screaming stopped eventually, and the jungle became a limp and soggy landscape. Every plant was dead. Every creature was dead.

The People were dead.

The Caretaker hoped his end would come soon, and he found comfort in the rising sea of burning steam that filled the world to the horizon. The water column had finally stopped growing, it seemed, and the steam stopped rising, and as the world below and the air all around became heated, the steam stopped clinging to the earth. It drifted away into the sky, great clouds of it. The Caretaker gagged on the dank, earthy aroma of the steam when it poured in on him, and he hoped it would kill him quickly.

It didn't kill him at all. The steam dissipated. The steady fall of burning rain no longer allowed it to collect on the jungle floor. The Caretaker wasn't going to die that easily.

He was alive when everything he loved was dead. He was trapped. He would die slowly from hunger. What was he to do until then?

To his amazement, he heard himself speaking. It was the Plea of Enlightenment to Chuh Mboi Aku, coming unbidden from his lips. He let the words come, although he hated Chuh Mboi Aku more than he had ever hated anything in his life.

Chuh Mboi Aku was the one responsible for this. Chuh Mboi Aku deserved no prayer from him.

But the words kept coming.

**29**

Remo and Chiun found out the same way everybody else was finding out. All the TV monitors in the airport were tuned to the news, and people were gathering around to watch the reports.

The video showed a column of steaming water soaring out of the Pacific Ocean, filling the sky with clouds of steam that went on forever. In the foreground was Waikiki beach, which looked as if it had been hit by a typhoon.

"The tsunami came too fast for the people of Honolulu to react. The evacuation order had just been sounded when the first wave broke here an hour ago."

"The Pacific Ocean itself is keeping the steam vent in check. In Colorado, a larger vent burst open twenty-five minutes ago and engulfed the town of High Woods in a steam cloud that apparently wiped out the entire town in seconds. This was followed by a deluge of superheated rain water...."

AT FOLCROFT SANITARIUM, they joined Smith and Mark Howard in Smith's office, where the coverage had taken on a less catastrophic tone.

"...appears the worst of the damage is done and first responders are finding an amazingly small death toll, at least as a result of the U.S. hot springs in Colorado and Hawaii," a new anchor reported.

"They're calling that a hot spring?" Remo demanded. "It's a mile high."

The announcer was almost bouncy. "Two water columns emerged in the Antarctic, where casualties were naturally light. The largest hot spring yet reported is a giant in the Amazon jungle, where again the human population was sparse."

"The man sounds positively pleased with this," Smith complained. Mark Howard glowered silently.

Next on the television was an environmentalist. "...possibly the best thing that could have happened. It won't take long for mankind to learn to harness these new thermal power sources. We may be at the dawn of a new era. As of today, fossil fuels are obsolete!"

"Please turn that off, Emperor," Chiun asked politely.

The news went away. The office was silent until Remo asked, "How bad is it?"

"We don't know. But it's bad," Smith said.

"The Amazon basin is deluged," Howard intoned. "The acreage destroyed by the rain is going to be nothing compared to the flood damage. In the Rockies, the water is channeled naturally into the Colorado River, which is already flooding, but they're controlling it somewhat by opening all the dams."

Remo shrugged. "I guess it really doesn't sound all that bad."

"It is the beginning of the end of the world," Chiun declared flatly, his eyes masked with gloom. "Sa Mangsang is drinking the world dry."

Remo said, "But it's not. In fact, this could solve the water shortages in the Southwest."

"The water is pure," Smith agreed. "It's been distilled by the planet itself. The salinity has been boiled out of it, and any bacterial or viral contamination is killed by the heat."

"This means nothing."

"Master Chiun, I beg to differ. I must point out that the seas are not being dried up. The water is being returned to the world in ways that might be beneficial in the long term."

"No, Dr. Smith," Mark Howard said. "The danger lies in Antarctica. Nobody's had time to think it through yet, but they will."

"Antarctica?" Smith said.

Chiun nodded in understanding. "That is the key to all this. The water that Sa Mangsang releases elsewhere is incidental."

"Incidental?" Remo exclaimed.

"Sa Mangsang's true purpose was to remove the water to Antarctica—the other fountains are side effects or mistakes."

"What are you talking about?" Remo asked. "Junior, give me a clue."

Smith was searching the news feeds from all the world's media organizations, and he found footage from Antarctica. The first to arrive was an Australian documentary team that had been at the Mawson outpost. They were hundreds of miles away, but still the closest media team to the twin South Pole vents. They were feeding back their first video images, and CNN was picking them up for global distribution.

White mountains of ice were building up in the South Pole as the twin fountains sprayed boiling liquid. The steam and rain reached dizzying heights, and cooled as it fell. Eventually it precipitated and froze, and the pinnacles grew.

"Just three hours ago the first of the steam vents erupted here in Antarctica...." the Australian news report began, but Smith switched the sound off.

"That's a lot of ice," Remo noted.

"The great heat propels it above ground and the great cold locks it into ice," Chiun said. "One wonders how much of the oceans is displaced there already?"

There was a knock on the door and Sarah Slate entered. She placed an affectionate arm on the shoulder of Master Chiun, and put the somber macaw on the cracked leather arm of his chair before leaving without a word.

"Bird," said the Master by way of greeting, and by way of asking for a progress report.

It nodded at him and said nothing. Chiun appeared pained by this lack of response.

"Master Chiun," Smith said, "I wish you to tell me more about the legends of Sa Mangsang."

Chiun stroked the fine yellow threads of his beard. "It is not usual for a Master to reveal the knowledge of Sinanju. Especially to an Emperor." Chiun had much more he might say, but he knew how to hold his tongue in the presence of his Emperor. Mad

Harold was wise about many things, but in other ways he was a fool who would not suffer himself to be named one. Chiun had attempted to educate him about Sa Mangsang and had been thanked with insulting disregard.

Smith stood and looked out the window, his hands clasped behind his back, examining the shoreline and the thin, dirty watermark.

"I have come to believe in the truth of your prophecy, Chiun. Forgive me for doubting you."

Chiun inclined his head.

"I am a man of science, but I failed to see the scientific truth in the Moovian legends," Smith explained. "Now it is incontrovertible."

Chiun pursed his lips.

"It is not the first time I have made such a mistake," Smith added. "Regardless, I believe, and I will believe what you tell me you know, if you will tell me. I may translate it into terms I may understand better, but I will believe."

Chiun was silent and still as an ancient edifice, then he said, "Too much does this world rely on its science. Science is destructive. The collection of knowledge is destructive. What if, some day, man learns too much?"

"Knowledge is beneficial. Man cannot learn too much," Mark Howard commented.

"Wrongo," Remo said. "You hear about the mechanical buggies we found in the Land of Golf and Haggis?"

"Developing new weapons is harmful—specifically, advancing the foundation of human knowledge?" Mark asked. "That's what you're talking about, right, Master Chiun?"

"Yes. Too much association of science."

"That is progress," Smith insisted. "But it's not our purpose now. We're here to discuss Sa Mang-sang."

"It may make humanity mad, to find out its place in the universe," Chiun declared. "Nevertheless, I shall tell you of Sa Mangsang."

Smith nodded and sat back in his chair, and he was about to ask how Sa Mangsang and the place of humanity in the universe were linked. But he thought better of it.

Chiun said, "Sa Mangsang is Korean for 'Dream Thing,' for he exerts his will in dreams. He reaches out to the minds that are amenable to his influence. These are the mad and the perceptive and the devout. Also, and especially, the Seers."

Chiun nodded to Mark Howard.

"He is Tako-Ika, the Octopus Squid, to the Japanese, and Khadhulu, Forsaker of Life, to the Arabs. To the Norsemen he was Kraken, but the Vikings never knew Sa Mangsang—only his minions."

"The people of the ancient civilization of Mu knew Sa Mangsang best and feared him as Ru-Taki-Nuhu for what he was destined to do to this world. They tell of an elder god coming from the stars and seeking the comforts of the ocean. He stirs from time to time, rousing from his slumber long enough to test his strength and to stretch his thoughts out to the world for news of its development. Still, he has never truly awakened, until now."

"By Jack Fast?" Remo asked. "Is that what we're assuming?"

"It is no assumption. It is the truth. We deposited the juvenile madman into one of the places of the ancient speaking tubes," Chiun said. "In millennia past, there were cults devoted to the creature. Some worshiped him. Some feared him. They located passages that carried their voices around the world to the sunken city where Sa Mangsang sleeps. Those who worshiped him sought to awaken him. Those who feared him sang songs designed to soothe him into deeper slumber."

"Lullabies for a sea monster?" Mark Howard asked.

"I knew the nature of the place where we had deposited the miscreant, the son of Fastbinder. I knew fear of the place and yet, to my shame, I never considered that one boy, however deviant, was capable of reaching Sa Mangsang with his voice, when once it required the tumult of thousands to reach him."

"Too late. Too late." It was the bird, hanging its head and cawing unhappily.

"You foresaw this, bird?" Chiun asked, without surprise.

"We saw cataclysm for the People. We saw. We saw."

"You sought to pass the message along, that I must be watchful and take care? This is the message you came to convey to me."

The domed purple head seemed to shrink lower as it rocked miserably from side to side. "We tried. We tried."

"Why did you fail?" Chiun demanded.

"Too weak. Too weak."

"To do what?" Remo asked.

"To exert our will."

"On the bird?" Chiun squeaked. "What manner of spirit are you?"

"From far away and long ago came we, sleeping for ages have we."

Chiun frowned.

"Trail mix!" the parrot demanded, leaping up on Chiun's shoulder.

"You're gonna have to do a lot better than that to earn trail mix, Polly," Remo growled.

"He speaks as a collective," Chiun mused. "Some old group of magicians who have been alerted to a new danger. They sought me in hopes of warning me, before the commitment of the act that resulted in this disaster. They took the form of this creature, with the will of an animal, malleable to their influence, but with the voice a human may understand. They hoped it would be an expedient to communicating with me."

"Why not just take over somebody we know, somebody closer to us?" Remo asked. "Smitty. He'd have been perfect."

Smith became visibly alarmed.

"They are weak, Remo. Possessing a human mind was out of the question, and even this bird's will exceeds their capabilities. They must have been desperate to even attempt it."

"But who are they?"

"Someone from long ago and far away," Chiun responded, waving the question away.

"He talks like Yoda."

"You speak nonsense."

"Trail mix trail mix trail mix."

Remo took the macaw out and placed him on the back of the chair in the waiting area. "Mind if Gertrude waits here for a few minutes, Mrs. M?"

"Course not, Romeo," said the elderly Mrs. Mikulka, Smith's longtime secretary. "He's a beautiful creature."

"He likes poetry, too," Remo said with a smile as he slipped back into the office.

"A man from Atlanta named Nick," the macaw began, "was fond of exposing his—"

Remo shut the door fast. "Okay," he said, retaking his seat. "What have we figured out? Anything that we can make use of?"

"There is nothing for us to make use of," Chiun said. "It is too late."

"Can't be, Little Father."

"Accept it."

"I won't accept it."

"Master Chiun, was there any more to the Moovian legend?" Mark asked. "Did the people of Mu know of a way to put Sa Mangsang back to sleep once he was fully awake?"

"The people of Mu never would have considered it to be possible," Chiun sniffed.

"What of those sects you spoke of, who chanted to Sa Mangsang in hopes of calming him into a deeper slumber?" Smith asked, squirming slightly at his discomfort with the concept.

"There were Arab peoples who did this, who burdened themselves with the responsibility of protecting the world from their Khadhulu. The arrival of Islam diluted their faith in Khadhulu until he became only a demon and a lackey of Shatain in their worship. Many in the islands of the Pacific never lost their fear of him until the whites came and polluted their faith with ridiculous fairy tales of carpenter gods. There were others, here and there."

"Their legends are lost now?"

Chiun shrugged.

"You aren't sure?" Smith pressed.

"I know not. Have any people survived spaying by the Christ cult in the last three centuries? Little survived the taint of the Christian missionaries in the Pacific Islands, and that which did survive was warped so that its original beauty is beyond recovery."

"Why do you care about this, Smitty?" Remo said.

Smith's lips were pursed tightly. He wasn't enjoying the taste of what he was about to spit out. "Forgive me, Master Chiun, if I translate your legends into terms more palatable to my mundane mind," Smith began.

Chiun said nothing.

"Sa Mangsang fell from the stars—could that mean he is an alien being?" Smith suggested. "If he does have a tentacled body, he would, of course, be a god to any people who saw him. Could his sleeping under the ocean be, in fact, a recuperative state? He was damaged in the landing on Earth and must heal before attempting to leave again."

"He'd have to have extreme capabilities by our understanding," Mark Howard said. "You're saying he's a space traveler who uses no spacecraft. I suppose an invertebrate body would be best suited to withstand the pressure variations that would be experienced in space. The life span must be tremendous."

Remo made a face. "Chiun's elderly gods sound downright plausible next to that yarn."

"But whatever the nature of Sa Mangsang, there is a possibility that some of the peoples of the Polynesian islands did once know how to speak to him and lull him into a deeper state of unconsciousness," Smith said. "It's a slim hope."

"It is no hope whatsoever," Chiun declared.

"What other option do we have?" Mark Howard asked.

"We can go pay a housecall on the son of a squid," Remo said. "That's what I should have done at the beginning. After all, we're old friends."

This was the part of the story Smith had the most trouble believing. "Remo, it is possible that you met one of the sentinels of Sa Mangsang, not the actual entity? That creature was small enough that you could disable it."

"I punched it in the nose. It was Sa Mangsang, all right, not his people. He was probably shrunken from much sleep and little food."

"Yes, that is it, exactly," Chiun said. "Now he has been feeding voraciously. Think of the human cattle who have been driven to him. He will be ten times the size he was when last you encountered him, when he was barely conscious."

Remo Williams pictured a Sa Mangsang ten times bigger than the Sa Mangsang he had encountered under the ocean, years ago, during his Rite of Attainment. And if that Sa Mangsang had been drunk on sleep, what would a fully awake Sa Mangsang be like?

"You're trying to scare me so I stay away," Remo said when he felt Chiun's eyes on him.

"You would be a fool to deliver yourself into its power."

"On this point I agree," Smith said. "You don't know what could come of that."

"But there's nothing else we can do," Remo said. "Are we just going to sit around and let all this happen?"

"For now, that is the best course of action," Smith said.

"For now? As opposed to later? There is no later, Smitty!"

"For tonight," Smith amended.

Remo shrugged. "Fine. Whatever."

"I shall seek to learn more from the bird," Chiun said. "It may yet have more to tell."

"Yeah, I know what it's going to tell you about," Remo said. When they left the office they found poor old Mrs. Mikulka in a state of shock.

Remo gave her a smile. "You look a little flushed, Mrs. M."

She was wringing her hands.

The bird winged to his shoulder and rode with Remo and Chiun down the stairs to the private wing of Folcroft. "You told that nice Mrs. M. the one about Delores, didn't you?" he asked the macaw.

"She had a great big—"

Remo's fingers clamped the parrot's beak shut. "No, thanks. I've heard it."

# 30

Remo came into the main room of the Folcroft suite in his underwear, and lowered himself into a cross-legged sitting posture on a reed mat. He made less noise than the ladybug walking on the wall.

The old man appeared a moment later.

"Didn't mean to wake you."

Chiun made the smallest motion with his hand that told Remo his apology was unnecessary. Of course, he had hoped Chiun would hear his near-silent footsteps, even over the wild-boar racket of the old man's own snoring. If asked, Chiun would have claimed he did not snore, so what could possibly have kept him from hearing Remo stomping around in the next room? It was the kind of Chiun-like logic that made sense if you would only let it.

Remo wished he could let it. He wanted the comfort of some kind of rationale for what he was experiencing.

"You are troubled." Chiun descended into a sitting pose on a mat across from Remo, and the movement happened with all the disturbance and noise of drifting down.

"Tell me more about Cho-gye."

Chiun considered this. "I do not think there is more to tell. You seek to understand the meaning of the tale of Cho-gye?"

"I seek to believe it," Remo said.

"And to find comfort in that belief," Chiun added.

"Yeah. I'm having a hard time with this, Little Father."

"What this?"

"This failure."

"What failure?"

"You know. My bad judgment call. I can't stop thinking about what might have happened because I did the wrong thing. I know you think there's a lesson in the story of Cho-gye that works for this situation. But I just don't get it."

Chiun nodded with his eyes. "You are a white. You are an American. You lack the ability to have faith."

Remo knew this wasn't Chiun's typical bashing of things Caucasian and Western.

"It is the way of this world now," Chiun continued. "Perhaps it is in inevitable that faith is sacrificed to fact, until faith can no longer be tolerated, even in the absence of fact. The Emperor is a product of this era, old as he is. Despite all his years and all that he has witnessed, he will not allow himself to have faith. He believes in Sa Mangsang, here, in his core." Chiun moved a hand to his abdomen. "But he will not allow himself to believe in Sa Mangsang here, in his mind, because he does not have the facts that make it plausible."

Was Smitty really such a fool that he would allow himself to be blinded to the truth just because the truth was inexplicable by his data? Remo decided that Smitty was just that foolish.

"He lacks faith in himself," Chiun added.

"He has faith in himself. Otherwise he wouldn't be so damn stubborn about sticking to his guns."

"No. What he believes here is a part of him." Chiun motioned toward his stomach again. "That is where his instinct and his intuition are manifest. What he knows of Sa Mangsang in his head is only factious elements of truth that may or may not mean what they pretend to mean."

Remo meditated on this for a moment. "Smitty lacks faith in his own gut feeling. If we all went with our gut feeling, the world would be a mess. We'd be animals."

"We are not animals, and the our instincts are not wholly animal, and our instincts are tempered with wisdom that an animal cannot possess. It is therefore not instinct."

"It's faith," Remo said, feeling a surge of pleasure as he understood the distinction, only to feel downcast again.

After a long moment, Chiun said, "You find no comfort in this. You know what faith is, but you do not know how to achieve faith. This is the symptom of the Western world—atheism or agnosticism. No one *believes*."

"You can't make yourself have faith. Not in Jewish carpenters or elder gods or even in yourself."

"Those who need it turn in desperation to whatever storefront religion is close at hand. This explains the Church of Elvis."

"I'm sort of desperate. Why can't I bring myself to have faith in myself? Am I going to walk around for the rest of my life trying to believe in what I believe in?"

Chiun raised an eyebrow.

"Maybe I'm really just a grunt who'll always need a CO making the decisions. You know, I've always felt like one of those guys who doesn't get paid to think and it ticked me off. Even before CURE, I mean, and all these years with CURE. I finally arranged things so I do get paid to think and, surprise, surprise, I'm not very good at it."

"No," Chiun agreed, "you are not very good at it."

Remo was taken aback. He had been insulted by Chiun a hundred times in just the past week, but somehow this comment came as a genuine slap in the face.

"Why?" he demanded. "What do you mean?"

Chiun raised one finger and his face broke into the smile of a child on a picnic. "There it is, Remo Williams." Then he pointed his bony finger at Remo's stomach.

What? Remo wanted to make the old man tell him what the hell he was talking about, and then he knew. He did have faith. A speck of it, sitting at the bottom of his bucket of self-defense. It was small, but hard as a diamond.

Chiun retired to his room while Remo stayed awake, examining the pebble of faith and wondering, exactly, where it was supposed to go.

**31**

Smith was a scientist, but not the right kind of scientist for this kind of work. He wasn't even sure what the right kind of scientist was.

He needed somebody to tell him that his own calculations were wrong. They must be wrong.

The Folcroft Four, which spent twenty-four hours a day watching television, alerted Smith when an interesting guest appeared on one of the news networks. The giant mainframes watched and listened for certain keywords and phrases in a hundred languages.

The guest was interviewed by the feature anchor, who wore a perpetually amused smile and often reported on the ridiculous behavior of Hollywood celebrities. When he interviewed a scientist, it was a guaranteed nutjob.

The nutjob today had come to the same conclusion as Harold Smith, and Mark Howard, and Master Chiun.

"How much ice will build up, Dr. Dell?"

"I don't know. It's impossible to predict the amount of pressure behind the steam vents. The ice is building in a cone shape, which is structurally strong, but the hollow steam vent in the center will eventually collapse and plug the vent."

"Problem solved," said the features host with a smile.

"If the steam vent is powerful enough, it will simply build up pressure and heat until it opens a new release vent. It's already burned through a four-mile-thick ice covering in the Antarctic Plain. There's no reason to think—"

"But what will stop it, Dr. Dell?" The host looked at the audience and gave them a get-a-load-of-this smile. Time for the punch line.

"Nothing that I know of. The ice will continue collecting on the Antarctic continent indefinitely. The world's oceans will be depleted. Eventually, Antarctica could become so heavily weighted that it will interfere with the gravity of the planet."

"Really? But Antarctica is already at the bottom. Wouldn't the extra weight just keep it at the bottom?"

The scientist explained that there was no "bottom" in space. "I don't know what the displacement of mass would do to the gravitational behavior of Earth, and we might not be around to see it. The shrinking of the oceans on that scale is going to create climactic extremes—"

"Hey, now, don't start talking dirty!" the host interrupted, and he played a *boing* sound effect.

Mark Howard was in his seat well before dawn, trying to find a channel through the activity at various think tanks around the world. It was apparent that

CURE wasn't the only organization taking seriously the buildup of South Pole ice.

"They're acting like they don't even care abut their own security systems. They're e-mailing data. They're using insecure file-sharing sites. They're going crazy."

"They're scared," Smith said. "So far, there seems to be a high level of concurrence with Dr. Dell." Smith frowned at his desktop. "Are we missing something? Nature is a system of checks and balances, Mark. Something like this upsets the way the world works. The earth would react to it."

It was almost a poetic sentiment from the dry Dr. Smith, but he was speaking in scientific terms and Mark Howard knew it. "Eventually, yes. The gravitational pull might cause the buildup of Antarctic mass to shift toward the sun. The Antarctic would then heat up and the ice would melt."

"Maybe it wouldn't even get that far," Smith said. "The climatologists are generating reams of hypotheses about the effects of oceanic depletion on the weather. There are a number of predictions of uncontrolled global warming."

Mark Howard thought about that. "Enough to raise the temperature in Antarctica above freezing, to control the buildup of the cones? It would get pretty hot around here."

Smith nodded. "It would."

Howard said, "You're right, Dr. Smith. No matter what's making this happen, elder god or not, Mother Nature will probably find a way to balance itself out."

"But mankind won't necessarily survive the balancing act," Smith concluded.

"Remember what Chiun said. If people only knew how inconsequential the human race was in the universe..." Howard shrugged.

Smith considered that. It wasn't exactly what Chiun had said, but close enough.

IT TOOK an amazingly short amount of time for scientific lunacy to become accepted scientific fact. By five in the morning, a group of the world's most respected climatologists and geologists was on the news making a dire prediction.

The features host wasn't on the set anymore. It was one of the most senior anchors interviewing a panel of scientists around the world.

"Which one of you is right, gentlemen?" the anchor asked.

"It doesn't matter which one of us is right," shot back a Dutch geologist. "What matters is we must act now to save this planet."

The anchor nodded. "What's your view, Dr. Marteen?"

"Exactly the same as that of my colleague. We must act immediately."

The anchor considered that. "Dr. Benton, your view differed—"

"My theories don't matter because nobody will be alive to prove them," Dr. Benton shot back. "Let us forget the theories and concentrate on the problem of survival. We all agree on that."

"Not everyone here agreed, as I recall," the host

insisted, getting nervous. Conflict was the name of his game.

"Yes, we all agree. Have you not been listening?" Soon the anchor was drowned out by every voice on his distinguished panel.

"We need to deliver one message and one message only—we have to make this stop now," the Dutch geologist shouted finally.

The interview ended when all the panelist feeds were killed.

"Clearly, a contentious issue," the unsettled host said.

SARAH SAT UP to the sound of the bird talking to itself. It had insisted on sleeping in her room the night before, and now it was mumbling.

"Dee-ya dee-ya dee-ya."

She wondered what Mark was doing. What was there to do? She really ought to watch the news, see what had happened overnight.

"Do not feed it, Sarah."

She stiffened.

"The more it eats the more it grows. The more minds it consumes, the more powerful becomes its mind."

The words were clear and sensible and unmistakable.

"Hear us, Sarah. Hear us speak and hear us dream and heed our words. Delay the coming of Mboi Aku. Delay him. Delay him. Dee-ya dee-ya dee-ya."

**32**

When Remo answered the door he found Sarah Slate in a translucent white T-shirt that must qualify as pajamas. The Snoopy decal was almost entirely washed off. She was barefoot, her hair mussed and her face flushed. She couldn't have been more appealing.

She took one look at Remo and her body temperature shot up. Her breathing speeded up noticeably. She parted her lips to speak and got stuck.

Remo didn't mean for this to happen. He just affected women this way and no matter how hard he tried he couldn't seem to turn it off the way Chiun did—not indefinitely. It made for some awkward situations—especially when it came to Sarah Slate. She was affected by his Sinanju male charms, and he was affected by her, too.

She was also gratingly smart and Mark Howard's significant other. Much as Junior annoyed him, Remo actually, almost, liked Mark. He wasn't about to stab the guy in the back just to get a stab at his girlfriend.

It was amazing how easily a crude and off-putting comment came to mind.

"You know I can see all your goodies through that thing?"

She became angry—with herself, as well as Remo—and shot back, "I can, too. At least you've got a nice view."

"Well spoken," Chiun announced, emerging from his room. "Back to your cave, lecherous animal."

"Wait. You may want to hear this, Remo. Master Chiun, the bird spoke in its sleep. I think it has a message for us."

Chiun looked doubtful. "Tell me the message," he commanded.

She repeated the words of the bird, including the odd phrase, "'The more it eats the more it grows. The more minds it consumes, the more powerful becomes its mind.'"

Chiun became thoughtful.

"This mean anything to you, Little Father?" Remo asked.

"It's not the first time he's said this," Sarah added. "Once, days ago when you were away, he spoke similar words. But I thought it was the bird talking. Not—whoever. I thought it was just a phrase he had picked up from his former owner. This time he was more precise."

Remo repeated thoughtfully, "Delay the coming of—"

"Hush!" Chiun snapped.

"Is it one of the names of you-know-who?" Remo asked.

"I know the word. It is on the tongues of a thousand peoples of the Amazon River. It is one of their pantheon of gods."

"Sounds like you-know-who," Remo said.

"For what it's worth, hyacinth macaws come from Brazil," Sarah said.

Remo was weighing the facts. "Seems odd that the bird would mention an unrelated god."

"I cannot know all," Chiun stated flatly. "But it is an assumption we must make. The name spoken is two words. *Mboi* is 'snake' and *aku* is 'big'."

"But you-know-who isn't a snake, Chiun. He's a squid. Or an octopus. A squirmy thing with lots of tentacles. Not a snake."

"Neither is the Kraken in all stories, nor the Hydra, nor the legends of the South Seas islanders. The deity of which the bird spoke is capable of changing shape at will. Maybe it is him. Regardless, the message itself means little."

"It can't mean nothing," Sarah insisted. "What can we do to follow these directives?"

"Stop feeding it?" Remo asked. "I don't see how."

"Stop feeding who?" Mark Howard appeared in the open doorway. He took one look at Sarah in her see-through Snoopy shirt and Remo in his sleeping shorts and snapped, "What's going on?"

"Look, he who we can't name eats seafood," Remo said. "I'll bet he eats squid mostly. There were a lot of squid around when I paid my social call."

"Yes," Chiun agreed. "The waters are channeling through him and carrying the bodies into his maw, to be consumed."

Mark grew pale and Remo saw his skin become cold. "You okay, Junior?"

"I dreamt of that. The first dreams I had were of being in the ocean and being boneless, being swept along helplessly. I was about to be consumed. I knew it. I was one of those squid."

"I'm guessing there's an inexhaustible supply of squid in the oceans," Remo suggested. "We can't stop them from getting carried in by the current."

"No," Chiun agreed. "Perhaps that is not the meaning of the message."

"Then what is?" Remo asked.

**33**

Smith had a wife, who for years saw little of her husband as he dedicated his life to, as far as she knew, running the Rye, New York, sanitarium. As Mark Howard proved himself capable of handling the daily operations of the hospital—and CURE—Smith began spending more time at home.

But not now. Not when the world was in a crisis. He remained at his post and monitored the growing danger of the amassing ice cones on the Antarctic continent. Watch, and wait, was all he could do.

Unexpectedly, the old office was the scene of an impromptu 5:00 a.m. meeting of CURE's entire staff.

Plus one.

"She must stay, Emperor, for she is the fount of this knowledge," Chiun said with an ingratiating smile. "The bird spoke only to her. My efforts to speak to it just now were fruitless."

"She's the one with the intel," Remo explained. "Just accept it, will you?"

Smith nodded sourly. "You wish to be here, Ms. Slate?"

"Yes, Dr. Smith, I do."

Dr. Smith stood, leaned over the desk and extended one hand. "I suppose this makes it official."

"Yes." She smiled seriously and they shook on it.

"Welcome aboard." He offered her the nicest chair in the office.

"What just happened?" Remo asked.

Smith's sour face became a grim smile. "Ms. Slate is now an employee of our organization."

"Really?" Mark Howard asked.

"You didn't even bicker over the salary," Remo said.

"We came to our agreement weeks ago," Smith explained. "It became clear that Ms. Slate was fully knowledgeable of the existence of our organization and the identity of Master Chiun and yourself, Remo. Also, she seemed determined to remain with Mark."

"She is?" Mark asked.

"As far as I can tell," Smith said offhandedly. "She had also become honored in the eyes of Master Chiun, and that sealed her fate. She could not be assassinated so I was forced to hire her."

Remo said, "God, Smitty, you can be so *sweet*...."

"So," Smith interjected loudly, "I discussed it with Ms. Slate and we came to an agreement. She was not certain of her long-term intentions. I extended the offer of employment. By coming here today, she accepts my terms. She has previously given her oath to maintain the anonymity of CURE."

"CURE?" Sarah said.

Smith nodded. "CURE."

"Stands for?"

"Nothing. Ms. Slate is now executive assistant to the assistant director of CURE and Folcroft Sanitarium."

"Welcome, Sarah," Chiun said graciously, apparently entirely without surprise.

"You're Howie's secretary?" Remo asked. "Aren't you worth millions?"

"I didn't take the job for the salary, Remo," Sarah explained.

"She'll obviously be more involved in the CURE operations than my own secretary has ever been," Dr. Smith said. "She knows the risks of being associated with this organization. I have not glossed over the fate of past CURE associates. And that supposes that we have a chance of surviving the dangers the planet faces now. I hope you have something positive to tell me?"

"Perhaps," Chiun said. "Hush. Please speak, Sarah."

Sarah reported again the words of the sleeping parrot, and wrote, rather than said aloud, the name the parrot spoke. Chiun explained the possible interpretation.

"Mark?" Dr. Smith asked. Mark Howard had paid little attention to the momentous events of the past few minutes. He was behind his desk pounding out commands.

"Not much on the name that Chiun hasn't told us already," Mark reported.

"The facts are slim and circumstantial," Dr. Smith decided aloud. "The bird might be from Brazil but just as likely is a pet bred in North America. The deity in question might be an interpretation of the Sa Mangsang myth or not. The suggestion the bird provides is improbable."

"We must heed it, nevertheless, if a way can be found," Chiun said.

"The problem is how," Remo said. "Nobody can get near the vortex where you-know-who is, let alone move in an operation big enough to plug its feeding tube."

Chiun glowered.

"Maybe we can poison the squid." Remo mused. "Kill off the food supply."

"An environmental catastrophe," Smith countered.

"So's Armageddon."

"There's no way," Mark Howard replied. "There's not enough toxin on the planet to kill all the squid in the ocean."

"What about a genetically engineered, species-specific antibody?" Sarah Slate offered. "These do exist."

Smith nodded. "Some do, but they're infamously imprecise." He punched out the commands. "Of those in existence, none target squid or cephalopods in general. Regardless, deploying the toxin would take weeks—and we don't have weeks."

Remo sighed. "Maybe he'll run out of squid."

Mark shook his head. "Cephalopods are thriving like never before. The fishing industry is removing squids' competition for food sources. The oceans are warmer because of climate change and that's making conditions better for squid, as well. They're growing faster than ever because of optimized conditions."

"Ideal for Sa, uh, you-know-who."

"The biomass of cephalopods has eclipsed that of humans," Mark Howard added. "That's not counting the unknown population of the giant and colossal squid, about which very little is known."

"The biomass of humans?" Remo asked. "All the squid in one hand, all the people in the other?"

"The squid hand outweighs the human hand," Smith concluded. "If there is a creature that thrives on the cephalopods, it must be gorging consistently."

"Squid live fast and grow in a hurry. Here's a researcher quoted saying that a single-degree increase in water temperature will cause exponential increases in the growth of the young cephalopod." Mark Howard looked up. "If you-know-who has a metabolism like that, and feeds like we think he's feeding in equatorial water, the results would be obvious."

"Yeah," said Remo. "I guess so. Smitty, you and I both wanted to know how he could grow so big so fast. Now we know."

"Yes," Smith replied. He was still unconvinced that a mad, boneless sea creature was the cause of the problems.

"But what about the second part of the message," Sarah said. "'The more minds it consumes, the more powerful becomes its mind.'"

Mark Howard chewed his lower lip. Dr. Smith looked sour. Chiun was silent.

Remo wished somebody would say something.

"Some cephalopods are thought to be intelligent," Mark said at last. "It's difficult to measure. I guess you can't test a squid like a dolphin or a chimpanzee. It would follow that the bigger-brained squid could be more intelligent—nobody's ever seen a giant squid alive, let alone a colossal squid. Maybe they're much more intelligent than anybody expects."

"The message speaks of humanity," Chiun declared. "It is the brains of humans that he needs. Sarah, you have provided us the key."

"People? Eating smart people makes Sa Mangsang smarter?" Remo asked.

"Say not the name," Chiun chided. "It is not the intelligent minds of this age that are drawn to him—it is the sensitive of mind. The powerful seers have always been the most highly tuned to him, and now it is they who spur the worshipers to take themselves into his realm. His siren song goes out to the world and the people come to him and are devoured by him. This increases his power of mind, and his siren call grows louder. Thus it shall continue to escalate."

Smith nodded. "The creature grows in physical strength as he grows in mental reach. Eventually he'll have the strength to do whatever it is he wishes to do."

"What he wishes to do is end the world," Chiun insisted.

"Master Chiun, I can't accept that. Regardless of the nature of this creature, it must have a goal that is selfish—all goals are selfish. It wouldn't take these steps without a reason."

"Perhaps it will have the physical growth to launch itself from the earth," Mark Howard said.

"You guys still on the space-alien kick?" Remo complained. "Maybe it's just the opposite. Maybe he's going to use his hyper-special-ESP to summon more things like him to Earth."

"Under the circumstances, it makes more sense," Dr. Smith admitted.

"A planet full of Sa Mangsangs," Remo said. "There wouldn't be room for people."

"Remo, you bring his attention closer to you every time you use his name," Chiun said. "Emperor Smith, there is nothing we can do to halt the flow of sea creatures that are being swept into the maw of the beast, but we must halt the flood of human beings who go to him and sacrifice themselves to him."

Smith nodded. "I agree. Even if I can convince the President to commit the resources—and I don't know that I can—I'm not sure if it can be done logistically. The area that will need patrolling is huge. The number of people converging on the vortex is growing each day."

"It is?" Remo asked. "What kind of numbers are we talking about here?"

"Unknown," Smith said. "Many ships, every day."

"How many?"

**34**

Henry Lagrasse couldn't count the number of powered ships coming onto the shore every day, but it was easy to count survivors. Zero here, two here, four here.

They were more headstrong with every passing day, too. They crashed, picked themselves out the wreckage and almost immediately began their trek into the interior of the city.

The small and nonpowered watercraft had a better survival rate, and the South Seas natives were flowing in to the island in ever increasing numbers. Yesterday there was thirty-four. Today the count was a hundred and it wasn't even noon.

Not one of the arrivals, from yesterday or today, was alive. Every last one of them had become food for the thing with the tentacles in the pyramid.

Henry Lagrasse, on the other hand, was still very much alive and having a great time. Life was one rollicking entertainment after another. His head hurt, sure, but the hurt came and went. Right now the pain was ebbing and he was watching the arrival of a sweet-looking yacht with some kick-ass power plants.

"Check it out!" he shouted. "Impact in two, one—now!"

The rushing yacht bottomed out on the stony incline of rock, still in two feet of water, but the friction was so great the hull still let out a screech and shot out a blaze of sparks. Once it cleared the sea it made twin twenty-foot feathers of white friction sparks.

"Look at them go! This is gonna set a record!" Lagrasse shouted.

He had been counting the skid grooves of all the vessels that slammed into the rocky island and knew the record was four hundred paces, set by a fiberglass pleasure crash. This yacht was big, with a metallic hull, but it had come in fast and straight. The pilot looked as if he was steering into the current of the vortex, which meant he sailed neatly up the incline and across the stone beach.

"Oh, no, come on, baby!" Lagrasse shouted as the speeding yacht homed in another pile of wreckage. It was speeding right at the mass of metal. Lagrasse desperately hoped it would miss and he leaned bodily to the right to help the new arrival.

"Yes!" he cried as the yacht slipped past the wreckage with inches to spare—a marvelous stroke of luck. The yacht's inertia finally ran out and it ground to a halt.

Lagrasse was sitting down again. A wave of pain in his head made him want to throw up, but it went away. Shouting made the pain come. He really should try not to shout. But what about that yacht?

He started at the shore, where the fresh groove

marks appeared, and he paced all the way to the yacht.

"Four hundred and twenty-one paces! You guys rock!"

The folks emerging from the yacht were in brown robes with deep hoods that hid their faces. There were several of them regarding Lagrasse somberly as other robed figures were being carried from the wreckage.

"Nice outfits," Lagrasse commented.

"Who are you?" intoned a tall robed man who left the neat new rows of corpses. "Whom do you serve?"

Lagrasse shrugged. "I don't know. Not the Coast Guard anymore, I guess. You know you guys made the best landing of anybody? You set the distance record for sure. I can already tell you set the survivor record, too. The best survivor rate so far was five, I think."

"We are the chosen," the man in the robe said. "What makes you so mirthful?"

"Hey, I'm only having the best time ever," Lagrasse said. "This place is so interesting and now, with you guys here, it's bound to get better. You're a real trip. I like your robes."

"So you have said," the tall one responded, losing some of the deepness of his voice.

"Not exactly tropical wear," Lagrasse added. "But nice. You sail all the way in from Idaho?"

The tall figure wiped his hidden face with his hand and it came back coated with sweat. "We are the Supplicants of Anarchy. We are the ones who have found the truth in the words of Lucre."

Lagrasse's attention wandered. He did a quick head-count and totaled nine survivors. Almost double the previous record.

"We worship the gods of the *Necronomibok*."

That got Lagrasse's attention. "The *Necronomibok?* Come on. You mean H. P. Lucre and all that stuff? I read those stories when I was a kid."

The robed figure nodded as if his head were heavy stone. "We know the truth that is the *Necronomibok*."

Lagrasse laughed. "All right! This is great! You guys really believe in that stuff?"

"It is truth, hidden in fiction."

"Cool!" Lagrasse couldn't be more pleased. Real wackos! What luck! In robes, no less, and trying to talk in real deep voices! This was going to be the most fun ever. "Wasn't the *Necronomibok* just made up?" he teased.

"It is real."

"I love those robes," Lagrasse said. "Must be a lot cooler in Idaho than it is here."

ROB LANDSBURG WAS getting very hot indeed in his Robe of Supplication, and he was distressed by all the deaths that accompanied their landing. He was also very annoyed by the frivolous man with the blood clot that covered half his head. "We are not from Idaho."

"Says Idaho on your robe," the strange man insisted.

"What?" Landsburg demanded, then snatched at the lapels of his robe and saw the words coming through the brown dye. Super Spuds From Friendly Idaho. Dammit, he had paid three bucks for that dye and it was already wearing off.

He couldn't take all the scratching and sweating anymore, anyway. "Let us all disrobe," he announced.

He was expecting resistance. They had all worked hard on their robes. Some were rich, dark velvet. Some were made from the denim of old blue jeans. All were dark brown in color. Somehow, it had never occurred to them that this was not practical worship wear in the equatorial Pacific. Now the robes came off in a flurry.

"You guys aren't nearly so pretty now," said the stranger.

"How we look does not matter," Landsburg insisted.

"Then why'd you have us make these stupid robes!" asked a young woman named Sandy, whose rayon robe was a ball in her hand. Her mascara made black streaks on her cheeks and her T-shirt and gym shorts were drenched with sweat—all of the supplicants had been sweating profusely under their robes for hours. She was also bleeding from a gash that started at her temple and vanished in her bloodied hair.

Lagrasse was delighted to realize that he could see her breasts perfectly.

She burst out laughing. It wasn't a pleasant laugh. "Your dye ran."

Landsburg's eyes flitted in panic. He ran to the wrecked hull and found some brightwork and tried to see his distorted reflection, which was stained with splotches of muddy brown. Cheap-ass dye!

He held back the outburst. He had to remain in control. This was his moment.

"Who the hell are you?" Sandy was asking the stranger. She wavered on her feet like a drunk.

"Henry Lagrasse of the United States Coast Guard at your duty, ma'am," Lagrasse said. "Use to be, anyway. Now I'm just the local lunatic."

"Why are you staring at my chest," Sandy demanded.

"You guys are not in Idaho anymore. This is like some new freaky world and normal rules don't apply," Lagrasse said, looking her in the eye for the first time. "So I do whatever I want. Besides, you have a really nice rack."

Sandy gave him an odd look.

"Let's assemble for our march," proclaimed Rob Landsburg, and rose to assemble his flock. He had rubbed at the brown splotches to spread them out evenly. He looked like he was in poorly applied blackface. "Krac'thlen awaits."

The unrobed supplicants gathered around their leader, and even Landsburg had to admit they were a sorry-looking lot. They were all drenched in sweat and many in blood. "We have survived landfall on the island home of Krac'thlen where most others have perished. This is one of the few survivors." He waved to Lagrasse, who felt like the man of the hour.

"Thank you, thank you. He's right. You guys made the best landing of any boat yet. You did just the right thing, steering in the current and gunning it. Brilliant. I'd like to shake your pilot's hand."

"He was killed in the crash," Sandy said. "How'd you manage to survive?"

"Used my head." Lagrasse beamed and nodded his head forward to display the mass of clotted blood and hair.

"What happened?" Sandy asked.

"Pressure buildup. I started passing out and stuff. So I relieved the pressure with a piece of metal. His name is Sharpy." Lagrasse showed them the sliver of aluminum scrap that he now carried everywhere he went. "You guys must really like H. P. Lucre."

"Whether we like him or not is irrelevant," Landsburg explained. "The fact is, he based his stories on a true but hidden mythology that we, the Suppliants of Anarchy, rediscovered in the *Necronomibok.*"

"I saw that movie a couple of years ago, *Darkness over Sipplewich*," Lagrasse said. "It wasn't nearly as good as the H. P. Lucre story, far as I remember. I haven't read any of that stuff since eighth grade."

"The movie is not relevant," Landsburg insisted.

"You know the story when all those frog people come out of the ocean and mate with the people of Sipplewich. And Johnny Depp was reading from the *Necronomibok* to dispel the sea frogs. Didn't work though. Johnny Depp ended up gettin' frog mated himself."

"I never heard of that one," Sandy said.

"It was a while back. Johnny Depp looked like he

just got out of high school. And man, that flick was a stinker. Must have gone straight to video."

"It is irrelevant!" Landsburg insisted. "What is relevant is not the fiction, but the fact! The *Necronomibok* is fact."

Out of his wallet pocket came the well-worn paperback. The cover said, "The book that H. P. Lucre wanted you to believe was a figment of his imagination is horrifyingly real!"

"This?" Lagrasse asked delightedly. "This is the basis for your whole cult?"

"That's it," said Sandy.

Landsburg was stricken by her tone. "Sandy, you have lost faith?"

Sandy sighed. "The truth is, I never believed a word of it. I just thought it was kind of exciting and all, Rob. So I went along with it. I thought it was all, you know, dramatic. Then, when we crashed, I realized you were taking this mumbo jumbo way too far. People got killed, Rob."

"But it is not mumbo jumbo. This is truth." He held out the *Necronomibok*.

"Rob, it was made up by some college kid in Dayton, Ohio, in 1974. It's just a bunch of old alchemy books and manuals on leeching and stuff that he put together with Lucre gods inserted here and there."

Rob Landsburg said firmly, "I have read his stories. They are there for a reason—to make people think the *Necronomibok* is false. It was repressed for centuries!"

"I went along with the worship ceremonies and the weird orgies and the bad costumes. I even helped them steal this boat," Sandy explained to Lagrasse, who was an enthusiastic audience. "Then, right in the middle of the crash my common sense kicks in again. Guess I look pretty stupid."

"Not as stupid as them," Lagrasse said.

Landsburg could feel the silent worshipers as they weighed these words. God, what if Sandy was right? What if the book wasn't genuine? What if all the others had died in vain?

But wait—

"These arguments are moot. The evidence lies beneath our feet. I and the *Necronomibok* have led you to the island of the great Krac'thlen, and it is just as the *Necronomibok* said it would be. This is the final evidence of the righteousness of our faith!"

The worshipers seemed to stand up straighter and Landsburg rejoiced. His power over them was restored. He was their leader again. They were eager to get going, into the city. Landsburg, too, felt the compulsion to penetrate the ruined city.

Only Sandy wasn't responding. She was biting her lip and staring at the row of dead former friends. Well, she did not have to share in the glory that would be bestowed upon him by Krac'thlen. There would be women a-plenty for the chief priests of Krac'thlen. It was so written in the *Necronomibok*. He was pretty sure of that.

"You want me to show you the way?" asked the man with the hideous head wound.

"I shall lead the way," Landsburg declared. "You may accompany us if you so desire."

LANDSBURG WAS MORTIFIED that Sandy was hanging back with Lagrasse, which put a huge wet blanket over his triumphant march through the streets of the long dead city of Krac'thlen. But Lagrasse was doing him a big favor—Landsburg would have been lost in the maze of stone edifices. Whenever he was unsure of where to turn, he would face his flock of followers, and Lagrasse, at the rear with Sandy, would silently indicate the correct way to go.

They came at last to the lip of a drop-off into a vast, flat amphitheater, where the bones were pale in the perpetual gray of this overheated part of the world.

"Who are all these dead people?" Sandy gasped.

"Oh, that's all the *other* people who found the final evidence of the righteousness of our faith," Lagrasse said.

"Is this where you bring the bodies of the dead from the shipwrecks?" Landsburg asked, projecting his voice for his followers to hear. "Even the non-believers are inspired by the awesome temple where Krac'thlen awaits dreaming!"

"Hey, don't drag me into it," Lagrasse insisted. "They brought themselves."

"Heed not the madman," Landsburg intoned. "Heed the wisdom of the *Necronomibok* and march with me to Krac'thlen."

Landsburg stepped down into the amphitheater, and heard the steps of his followers. He was still their leader, and he felt triumphant. Christ, he hoped he was right abut all this.

Sandy, he saw with a glance back, wasn't coming. She gave him a sad little wave.

With Krac'thlen's power to wield, Landsburg would enslave her and punish her for her duplicity!

Landsburg stopped at the chasm opening of the pyramid and raised his voice to the great god Krac'thlen.

Sure enough, Krac'thlen—or a reasonable facsimile—answered.

"I COULD HAVE saved them. I should have tried harder to stop them." Sandy had tears on her face as the great tentacle tossed another clean bone out of the pyramid. They were watching from Lagrasse's favorite rooftop nearby.

"Don't beat yourself up. I've tried over and over again to keep them from going in there. They never listen. If they came here to go in, they're gonna go in. You can't stop them." He was still staring at her chest.

"Oh, here," she said, and peeled off the still damp T-shirt. "I guess I'm beginning to see what you mean about this place. About normal rules not applying. I should be horrified but I'm just—not."

"It's too freaky a place to act normal in," Lagrasse agreed. "Tell me about those kinky orgies you mentioned before."

Sandy was dumbounded that he would even ask the question, then she was surprised that she wanted to tell him all about the kinky orgies. They ended up having a kinky little orgy of their own, even as Krac'thlen, or whoever it was, spit out more sucked bones.

They heard the rumble of stone on stone, and Lagrasse had a vision of something emerging from the pyramid. Strangely, he didn't want to stop his entertainment with the new arrival, Sandy.

Her eyes were shining. She too was aware of the movement of heavy stone inside the courtyard below, and yet she, too, continued working on their task of mutual satisfaction. The fear injected a fresh thrill into the coupling.

They finished up breathlessly and lay staring at the gray sky for a moment. Finally, Lagrasse got to his feet on the old roof and took in the changed landscape below him.

"There he is. Hey, little fella."

Sandy became curious and she joined her lover on the roof edge. In the courtyard, the walls of the three-sided pyramid had been shoved open, like the petals of a gigantic flower of old stone. The creature with the tentacles was inside.

It had the winged mantle of a squid, but also the bulbous, fleshy torso of an octopus. There were only eight tentacles, Sandy decided after watching it for many long minutes.

The creature had to weigh hundreds of tons. It floated in a crater inside the pyramid, filled with murky green water and bobbing carcasses. The Colossal Squid were fingerlings to the gargantuan Master of the Pyramid. The human corpses were small as crumbs.

"Huh," Sandy said. "It kinda looks like Krac'thlen, after all."

"I'll bet your old boyfriend's pretty pleased with himself," Lagrasse said. "There he is. Hi, Rob!"

"Hey, Robby!" Sandy did jumping jacks to get Landsburg's attention, but Landsburg was too busy being torn apart by the giant beak. A minute later, the flesh was being sucked off his bones, which were tossed away.

Sandy sighed. "This is just what he always wanted."

"I'm sure he's very happy," Lagrasse said, putting his hands on her parts again. "I know I am."

**35**

The President of the United States of America said, "You won't *tell* me?"

"Correct. I won't tell you," replied the voice of the man on the red phone. "It would be counterproductive."

"You want me to deploy the resources of the U.S. Department of Defense on this huge operation without telling me the purpose?"

"The purpose is to put a stop to this crisis."

"How can a bunch of suicidal maniacs have an impact on any of this?" the President demanded.

"Will you do this, Mr. President?"

"Why should I?"

"To save the world."

"Bullshit."

"Maybe. Maybe not. You can spare the resources."

"Are you kidding me, Smith?" the President fumed. "The DOD is stretched thin as a wire. They're watching conflicts in every country on the earth."

"About which you can do little. If we assume that the rise in global tensions is linked somehow to the catastrophe in the equatorial Pacific Ocean, then the

best and only action you can take is to address that
problem. I am asking you to trust that I may know
of a way to slow the growth of the phenomenon."

"You may know of a way? What if you're wrong?"

"Then it is the same as if you fail to act. If I am
right, then we might save ourselves."

The President glared at the clear blue dawn outside the Oval Office. "Fine. What do you want me
to do about it?"

THE PRESIDENT TOOK the first call after issuing his orders, and it just happened to be from the Secretary
of Defense.

"Mr. President, have you gone mad?"

"Not at all."

"What's the purpose of all this?"

"I'm not telling."

"You've gone mad!"

"No, I haven't."

"What's this all about, then?"

"None of your business."

"With all due respect, Mr. President, it's my
business."

"Not this time."

THE ADMIRAL LOOKED stunned when he hung up the
phone with Washington and emerged from his office,
stopping a moment to gaze out the windows to the
view of the vast fleet stationed at Pearl Harbor.

After a moment he shrugged to himself and noticed his staff waiting patiently. They knew something was up.

"Get them ready to sail." The admiral waved at the window. "All of them."

THE U.S. NAVY, Coast Guard and Air Force joined forces in the venture. They moved into the Pacific and deployed in the watch zone, an unaffected buffer area around the no-man's-land of the vortex. Their ships numbered in the hundreds. The French, Japanese and Russian fleets joined the Americans, more out of curiosity than anything else. The Americans weren't explaining why it was now so important to keep people away from the vortex.

The orders were simple: keep anybody and everybody from approaching the vortex. With the benefit of U.S. spy satellites watching the perimeter, this was easy enough.

But what became remarkable was the number of ships actually *trying* to get in. No one had guessed it before. Once it became clear that ships from all over the world were determined to break into the vortex, the urgency of the mission became clear.

In the first twenty-four hours, more than one thousand human beings were dragged kicking and screaming off their suicide ships.

# 36

Henry Lagrasse wasn't feeling so good this morning.

Waking up with a lunatic is a surefire way to start your day badly. Sandy's head injury had grown worse in the night, and she was in convulsions by daybreak. Howard went for a walk while she rode them out.

The air felt different this morning. The sky was quiet. Something was wrong. He started on a patrol of the island, looking for the cause of the wrongness, but nothing had changed since the previous evening.

Nothing had changed. It hit him suddenly. There were no new shipwrecks.

How could that be? There were more every day. The shore was a junkyard of wrecks now. There ought to be some sort of watercraft washing up every half hour at least. But none?

Then he found the wreckage of a new ship. It came in the night, and one survivor was screaming for release. "Help me out!" he pleaded. "I have to go in there!" He pointed at the ruins with his one functional arm.

Lagrasse began pulling on the metal panels that

had collapsed across the survivor, a man in his fifties with white hair and white stubble on his chin. He was in a priest's collar and he was babbling about how lucky he was.

"We slipped through. They tried to stop us, but we gunned it when a bigger boat got their attention. They chased us, but then they stopped when we reached the current."

"Who tried to stop you?" Lagrasse asked.

"Coast Guard. Navy. French and Japanese and even the Australians showed up. They're trying to keep everybody out of here. We were lucky to get through."

Lagrasse felt a sudden dread. The people had to get through! They had to get to the island! Otherwise—well, he didn't know what the consequences would be.

The white-haired priest finally grew impatient with Lagrasse and pushed himself out of the wreckage, tearing himself open on the metal edges. He didn't care. He staggered off into the city to become breakfast for the thing in the pyramid.

Without people, the thing wouldn't feed, Lagrasse realized. That was a disaster! It must feed! It must have human beings to sustain and strengthen it!

Why? He didn't know.

He paced nervously, then it occurred to him that he should go get Sandy and deliver them both to the thing in the pyramid. But that was no good. There was a reason he and Sandy hadn't wanted to go into the pyramid with all the other island arrivals; they were broken in the head. They didn't have the sustenance the thing needed.

The thing needed fresh, healthy human beings, and there were none to be had.

## 37

Mark Howard was in that body again, but now the oceans were his element, not his enemy. He reached into the sea, reached impossibly far, and dragged the sea toward him.

He could feel that the body was incredibly powerful, but also aching from exertion. It was pushing itself harder than it had ever pushed.

The mind was working, but the way in which it worked was alien and he couldn't follow it. He felt his thoughts recoiling and shutting down rather than experiencing the incomprehensible workings of the creature's brain.

There were currents in the mechanics of the thing's thoughts that he could understand. Confusion. Some helplessness. An overpowering aggression.

Once, he saw a shape in the darkness of the ocean—huge as a submarine, but alive. It avoided the creature. The creature's aggressive instinct became a song of bloodlust. It must attack. It must kill. The whale was the enemy and sometimes the food.

But its natural instinct was redirected to something else—something that looked almost familiar when Mark Howard saw it in the dream-mind of the alien being.

He recognized what it was and he woke up in a panic. He was drenched in sweat and Sarah was holding his shoulders, saying his name.

By the time he recovered his wits, the memory was stolen. The noontime sun was coming through the window.

"He's taunting me," Mark said.

"Who?" Sarah asked.

"Sa Mangsang, that son of a bitch."

**38**

Mary Ordonez took the mayor's hand and thanked him profusely in front of the cameras.

"Even in these dark times," she announced, "we can take heart in the joy of scientific discovery."

The crowd offered polite but hardly enthusiastic applause.

"What the world hasn't yet realized is that this is a major discovery. It is a once-in-a-lifetime event. Never before has a specimen of the Colossal Squid been seen alive by human eyes. Now, we have not only seen the creature, we have captured it and brought it to the Chicago Aquarium. I give you the Colossal Squid!"

She pulled the rope, and the curtain plopped to the ground. The crowd made appropriate gasps and murmurs of awe. The creature was truly magnificent and immense.

Just her luck, Mary Ordonez thought. She picked now to make the greatest biological find of the century. Now, when nobody cared.

It had seemed like a miracle when they spotted the thing tangled in a stray fishing net on the surface of the Pacific a hundred miles off Baja. They had been on their annual specimen-restocking trip. Mary had ordered the creature brought aboard and stored in the expandable holding aquariums. Everyone assumed it was dead.

But it started squirming as soon as the hook snagged the net and began to lift. It struggled until it was in the water again, in the holding tank.

Only after it recovered from the relocation did it begin to show its vigor. It lurched around in the narrow tank, looking for a way out. Ordonez knew she had to get it into a decent-sized tank soon in order to keep it alive.

She called the director of the aquarium, who called the director of the City of Chicago promotions and events, who called the mayor. In less than an hour the funds were arranged for the horribly expensive transportation of the Colossal Squid. There was just one aircraft in North America that was outfitted for the job—a whale carrier used for freeing trendy marine mammals. The specialty cargo jet met them in San Diego, where the custom aircraft bay was opened to allow the squid, again in its net, to be hoisted inside.

It was amazing, but here she was showing it off in Chicago, twenty-four hours after she'd first spotted the creature.

"This young specimen will be placed in the aquarium's largest holding tanks, where it will continue to grow. Nobody knows how large it will be when it reaches adulthood. But it will be huge, and will be the only one of its kind in the world!"

More polite clapping. "If there is a world," they were all saying to themselves. Impending Armageddon could be a real wet blanket.

Ordonez felt dejected as the crowd shuffled out.

"Cheer up, toots," said the mayor of Chicago. "This weather thing will blow over and everybody will wake up and smell the roses." His hand accidentally bumped into the bulge of her bottom.

"They don't realize how big this is," she said, mostly to herself. "It's not even a Giant Squid. It's a Colossal Squid. Nobody has ever seen one alive. Nobody. Ever."

"Lying female dog!" It was the director of promotions and events, stomping across the aquarium exhibition hall. "You ripped us off for 1.5 million."

Ordonez was taken aback by the woman's ferocity. "What?"

"What's this about, Colleen?" the mayor demanded.

"She told us it was a one of a kind."

"It is!" Ordonez insisted.

"It's not?" the mayor asked.

"She just said that to get the money to move the thing," the director said. "They're a dime a dozen. You're gonna pay for this, Dr. Ordonez."

"Colleen, relax," the mayor soothed. "There's got to be some mistake."

"There is a mistake, and it was not Dr. Ordonez's," said the director of the aquarium, coming over to defend the star of his team. "Any marine biologist will tell you there has never been a Colossal Squid seen alive until now."

"Maybe you marine biologists ought to get out of your museum and watch some TV every once in a while," sneered the Chicago director of promotions and events.

**39**

"I was dreaming of being one of Sa Mangsang's squid," Howard explained. "Only I was swimming *away* from the vortex. Swimming hard. He showed me what I was searching for, then he snatched it away again."

"Maybe you were the Chicago squid," Remo said. "I heard they caught one yesterday and flew it to the city aquarium for an unveiling today."

Smith nodded. "It's said to be a Colossal Squid. The first one ever captured alive—or even seen alive, as far as is known." He began flipping through the news feeds on the crisp computer display mounted under his desktop.

Sarah and Remo had accompanied Mark to Dr. Smith's office. Mark had only taken two of the four hours he was allotted for a nap.

"Here it is." Smith tapped on the screen. They gathered around the desk to watch the live feed from the press conference in Chicago. The beast in the aquarium looked oddly fake, like something too big to be genuine.

"What's this, then?" Remo asked as another news

feed showed another—in fact, two other big squids, thrashing in a canal in California.

"Oh, my God," Sarah said. "Are those Giants? Or Colossals?"

"They're twice as big as that houseboat, I'd say," Remo estimated. "That's colossal by my standards."

"Oh, God," Sarah repeated as a red-faced man bobbed to the surface amid the flailing tentacles and screamed, then vanished under the water again.

"They're everywhere, Smitty," Remo said as the news feeds and the live transmissions switched over, one by one, to giant squid footage. Washed up on the beaches of Washington State. Swarming in the waters of central California and wiping out most of the sea lion population in just minutes.

An Oregon news reporter was filing a live report from the open-air dining tables of a restaurant on a pier in Lincoln City. Half-finished meals were still on the tables. The floor was knee-deep in the slimy tentacles and mantle of a squid. Lincoln City police officers were covering the obviously dead creature with a half-dozen shotguns, as paramedics dragged a mottled human body from the slime.

"What are they after, Junior?" Remo demanded.

"I don't know."

"You saw it. What are they trying to do?"

"I don't remember, Remo," Mark insisted.

"Well, remember! People are getting killed. Why?"

"Dammit, you think I want it to happen?" Mark retorted. "I saw something. Not people. Some *thing*."

"Figure it out," Remo ordered. "I'm going to see Chiun."

He burst in on Chiun seconds later in their suite in the private wing of Folcroft. Chiun hadn't been watching television much in recent weeks, but it was on now. Chiun was flipping channels, which one after another showed the mayhem of the swarming squid. The macaw's perch was near the screen, and it cocked its head angrily at the images.

"Little Father, let's stop pussyfooting around."

"You have come to demand that we go at once to confront this thing," Chiun said dispassionately.

"You better believe it."

"So you will make yourself the lackey of him before even being in his presence."

"What do you mean?"

Chiun rose from the reed mat and faced his protégé. "My son, why do you think that Prince Howard is being played with? It is to draw you out. It is to pull you in. Why would you change our direction now—when our enemy is weakening?"

"Weakening?" Remo waved at the television. "This looks like his weakening? He's on the offensive!"

The bird squawked derisively.

"He is taking desperate measures. I believe that we have begun to weaken him. Remo, consider what he is doing—sending his food supply away on errands. He must need something else more than physical power. He seeks the human minds that expand his mental capacity. We are weakening him."

Remo shook his head. "What if he's had enough squid meat? What if he's full? Maybe he's at full strength."

Chiun considered it. "Unlikely. Whatever size he must want to achieve, he has not reached it yet. But we do know that his mental powers are not peaked, and maybe they have stopped expanding because of us. Maybe Emperor Harold's armies have served a purpose for once."

"So what?"

"If the god grows less able to influence the minds of men, he ceases to be a god. If his intelligence wanes, he becomes only a big beast. A big beast can be defeated more easily than an intelligent god."

Remo fumed. He glared at the bird, who looked hastily away. "I hate this, sitting around staring at these ugly freaking walls, Chiun. I want to do something. I want to go there and kick some octo-butt."

"And this is exactly what he hopes you will do," Chiun said harshly. "What if he makes use of you as I have foreseen, and you—Remo Williams—become the tool of Ru-Taki-Nuhu? At his disposal will be the man who possesses unsurpassed skills. He will send you out *hunting*."

"Urk," agreed the parrot.

"I hadn't thought of that," Remo said.

"You will be dispatched on sustenance-gathering excursions into the world—and no one will be able to stop you," Chiun hissed angrily. "You will seek them out, the unbalanced minds of the seers and the sensitives, and bring these sweetmeats to your master. You'll stalk the most powerful unbalanced minds. Prince Howard shall be one of your first victims. Maybe you will not even be permitted to feel remorse as you transport him to his death. He will be alive and fully aware, so that his mind sings its song of life as Tako-Ika drains him of it and absorbs his very essence and becomes stronger."

The bird bobbed its head and squawked raucously like a churchgoer enjoying Reverend Chiun's fire-and-brimstone sermon.

"And when Prince Howard is devoured, then our enemy will be more powerful and his hold on you will be stronger. You will go out into the world again, and even I will be forced to stand against you and I will fall, for who can stand against *the* Master of Sinanju? Sa Mangsang will strengthen, his hold on you will be stronger and there will be nothing that can stop either of you."

Remo was shaken. "You have foreseen this, Little Father?"

Chiun pursed his lips. "Not foreseen."

"Not foreseen, exactly," the parrot agreed.

"But you believe this is what's going to happen?" Remo asked.

"I predict that this will happen," Chiun replied. "Is that not reason enough to heed my warnings?"

**40**

The Japanese fishing trawlers should have steered around the perimeter that was being guarded by the international fleet. The trawler ignored the radioed warning and entered the off-limits watch zone around the vortex.

"Here they come—it's a U.S. Coast Guard ship," announced Chad, peering through his binoculars. "It's a little cutter." He read off the numbers on the bow.

Dr. Williamson punched it up on his laptop computer. He had loaded a database of all Coast Guard vessels—as well as U.S., Japanese and French navy ships—just for this eventuality. They knew they'd run into resistance from somebody.

"She's a quick one," Williamson announced. He fed the specifications on the ship into a little piece of software he had improvised this morning. It took their current position and the position of any potential pursuit craft and came up with an estimate of their ability to reach safety, once the pursuit started.

The laptop gave them a yellow-flag warning. "We'll make it to the inside border of the watch zone ahead of them, but only if they don't fire on us," Williamson announced. "That's too risky. We need one more kilometer of clearance between us and them."

"Maybe they won't fire," Mick Chad said. "Let's try it."

"They will fire. They've been firing on any vessel that tries to get in," Williamson said. "They'll disable us and take away the *Flying Fish.*"

The radio beeped. It was Tom Bomi, captain of the fishing trawler.

They could see him. He was on the bridge of the trawler, smiling and waving to them. Mick Chad and Dr. Williamson were on the bridge of the *Flying Fish,* the vessel that was in tow behind the trawler.

"You need a little extra space, right? I get it for you?"

Chad perked up. Williamson frowned. "How?" he asked.

"I cut you free, then make a run for the vortex, see?" Bomi explained on the speaker. "They chase me, and when they out of range you go like hell."

"You'll get fined," Williamson pointed out.

"And arrested," Bomi said. "That's why it cost you five thousand dollars more."

Williamson choked. "Does he think I'm rich? I'm a professor."

Mick Chad shrugged. Not even a professor, Chad thought. Professors teach in colleges and work in labs. Williamson didn't do that. He lived off of grants from freaks with too much money and too little common sense.

Mick Chad had been on more than one silly "expedition" with Dr. Williamson. Once they were looking for gargantuan earthworms in Siberia. Big as diesel locomotives, miles long. They didn't find any. Another time they went to Tibet to find a yeti. All they found were yaks and Tibetans.

What they were looking for this time, Mick Chad had no idea. He was just along for the ride. He knew how to drive the vessel—more or less—so once again Williamson had hired him. Chad was a good guide who could pilot just about anything and who knew how to cut a path through any international red tape.

This time, Williamson had paid Chad in advance. He had put up the funds to lease this vessel, which wasn't cheap. The so-called professor had a staff of eight researchers with him—a crew of thinkers that was twice as big as any other expedition. Williamson was seriously determined to find *something*. Who knew what? Mick didn't care. He just liked being along for the ride—and he liked the cash, most of it under the table.

"We go in or we go home," Chad said. "Your call, Professor."

"Fine. Tell him we have a deal." Miserably, Williamson used his laptop to transfer the funds into the accounts of the Japanese trawler captain.

The captain waved again when he got the confirmation on his own satellite computer, and his fishermen scrambled to the winch to release the *Flying Fish*'s tow cable. It drifted away from the trawler and bobbed gently in the Pacific water.

Mick Chad started the dock maneuvering engines and began chugging slowly away from the vortex. "The Coast Guard will think we're heading away under our own power. They'll leave us alone to chase the Japs."

"Let's hope so," Williamson said.

Captain Bomi's trawler revved away, across the current but generally toward the vortex. The cutter issued orders over the radio, then gave chase as the trawler increased speed. Within a minute the cutter was just a dot.

"Let's go, Chad," Williamson said.

"You got it." Chad hit the lifter power switches and the vessel rumbled. Giant fans spun up to speed and built pressure until a cushion of air was created, hoisting the *Flying Fish* on it and extracting the maneuvering propellers right out of the water. Then the big propulsion fans, protruding from either side of the hull like open car doors, started to spin.

Mick Chad worked the joysticks carefully. Hovercraft control wasn't easy. Most of them had computerized navigation systems, but the *Flying Fish* wasn't exactly state-of-the-art.

The *Flying Fish* rotated in a circle, to face back into the vortex.

But Chad rotated too fast. Dr. Williamson tipped off his feet with a cry of alarm. Chad pushed hard on the joystick—the wrong joystick. He made the big hovercraft spin faster, like a thrill-seeker's carousel. Chad gulped and hit the other joystick, full throttle.

The alternate fan roared to life and brought the spinning to a sudden halt. Anybody who was still on his feet was thrown off balance and slammed to the deck. Chad realized he was giving it too much power in the other direction....

"Sorry," he announced ten seconds later when he finally had the *Flying Fish* under control.

"Where'd you learn to drive a hovercraft, idiot!" Williamson said shakily, still on his hands and knees.

"I didn't."

"What?"

"I never said I did."

"So why'd you take the job?"

"I can drive a hovercraft as well as any other pilot," Chad stated. "For what you're paying, I'm as good as you're gonna get." He had no idea if it was true, but it sounded good. He locked the joysticks together and accelerated the *Flying Fish* toward the vortex.

The others stormed into the wheelhouse to make their protest. They didn't get far before Mick announced, "Coast Guard's coming."

"How fast?" Williamson asked.

"Unknown. The vortex is starting to affect our systems. Radar's no good. Satellite's crapping out and so's the GPS. Radio's still working and I got a message to stop and be boarded."

Williamson's staffers grew nervous. "Will they get close enough to fire on us?" asked a young woman who had recently joined the doctor from Minnesota State University.

"Depends on the boat that's coming after us—but I doubt it," Chad said with every drop of charm he could muster. He was always suave around Missy

Juk from MSU. "This baby'll outrun almost any ship on the ocean."

One of the older men laughed derisively as he blotted the vomit stains from his peach-colored golf shirt. "This hunk of junk?"

"It's old but quick."

"We know it goes around in circles pretty fast, anyway."

Chad colored. That kind of embarrassing statement was not going to make him look any better in the eyes of Missy Juk.

"We'll outrun 'em," Chad said, and floored it.

He kept the joysticks pressed all the way to their stops, palms sweating from the intense concentration. The slightest drop or rise in thrust on either side could be catastrophic, and at this speed the antiquated auto-align system might not adjust the thrust fast enough. Chad had to be ready to make emergency manual compensation. And he had to admit that his recent performance at the controls wasn't stellar.

The waters were flattening out under them as they reached the growing vortex current. They lost the waves that had been splashing against the air-apron, making the hovercraft ride smoother and faster. Williamson was tense and the others were silent, feeling the danger.

The radio conked out, silencing the low-volume demands of the Coast Guard cutter. The cutter had vanished behind them; they were beyond the watch zone.

"We've gotta be inside the vortex now," Chad announced. "Look at that sea!"

The water was rushing visibly along with them—
like a flat, fast river that stretched into the gray horizon.

"I'm powering down. We're safe," Chad announced.
"The Coast Guard's not coming after us now."

"'Safe' is a funny choice of words," said Goodall,
the man in the foul-smelling golf shirt.

The others were cheering and the girl from MSU
was actually doing jubilant cheerleader hops. Even
that couldn't distract Chad from the ominous note in
Goodall's words.

"What did you mean by that, buddy?" he asked
the man quietly.

"We slipped past the Coast Guard and that means
we're in *real* danger. You know, from the vortex?"

"Oh." Chad felt relieved. "That's why we've got
this. It'll ride out as easy as it rides in. It doesn't care
about ocean currents."

"I hope so. We'll see."

"Believe me, bub, it's a monster. It was made for
hauling icebergs. The engines are huge. Why d'you
think they charged so damn much to rent her out?"

"How much?" Goodall asked.

Chad said, "Quarter-million," and then he remembered that he was absolutely not supposed to talk
money with anybody. It was in his contract with
Williamson. He added hastily, "But you didn't hear
it from—"

"Williamson, is that right?" Goodall exclaimed.
"You paid 250 grand to lease this tub?"

Williamson was floored. "What? Who told you
that?"

"Slick Mick. Is he lying?"

Dr. Williamson tried to think of something to say.

"Spill it, Willy. What's going on here? Did you or didn't you?"

"I did."

"Where in the hell did you get that kind of money?" Goodall asked. "That much cash will operate the entire organization for six months."

Dr. Williamson nodded seriously, then straightened his spine. "I have an announcement to make. Now is a good enough time."

The bridge full of staffers grew quiet.

"The organization you once worked for no longer exists," Williamson said.

He ignored Goodall's "What?" and continued. "I have disbanded the legal entity that was the Association of Cryptozoological Investigations and Studies. You are now all a part of Cryptozoological Investigations and Studies, Inc."

Goodall was the only one who seemed to get it. "You son of a bitch. You went commercial."

"I made us rich."

"He shut down the nonprofit organization and turned us into a corporation!" Goodall explained indignantly to the others. "What'd you do, get private funding?"

"Exactly," Williamson said.

"We're not scientists anymore," Goodall lamented. "We're sellouts!"

"What was that about being rich?" Melissa Juk piped up.

Williamson smiled benevolently. "Every one of

you is now an employee of the new corporation and you all have a guaranteed share of the profits of this venture."

"Hey, Willy, we don't even know if we're going to find land inside of this black hole," Goodall said. "Let alone some great new species. What if we come home empty-handed?"

"Then we'll be the only living human beings who have entered the vortex and emerged again alive," Williamson said. "With or without new scientific samples to show for ourselves, it won't be a loss. The story alone will be worth millions."

There was a wave of excitement among the researchers. "Wait. Wait. I thought we were crypto-zoologists," Goodall said. "I know I am. I dedicated my career to the discovery of new species. I made my-self a promise that I would prove the existence of at least one so-called legendary creature before I re-tired. That's what I'm in it for. What are *you* all in it for?"

"Right, Goodall, and think about what you can do with your share of the money," Williamson said. "It'll be more than you've made in the past ten years. You can mount your own expeditions if you want to. The new Cryptozoological Investigations and Studies, Inc., will have money in the bank. Our new reputation will mean all kinds of new funding, as well. We'll mount expeditions every year! Maybe twice a year!"

"Really?" Goodall said.

"Our funding partner is a well-known media con-glomerate. They have already agreed to develop a television miniseries based on this trip. Everybody on board will get the opportunity to audition to play themselves."

The bridge was filled with excitement.

"What do you say, Good?" Williamson asked.

"I guess it sounds okay. Wish you would have asked me first."

"The studio wouldn't let me," Williamson said, still smiling. "This way, your credibility is intact. You didn't know you were part of a studio deal until it was too late to turn back. Adds an element of drama to the story."

"I always wanted to act," Goodall admitted. "I hope we actually get out of here."

Mick Chad was bothered by that. Why was Goodall so glum about their prospects of surviving this trip? They had a hovercraft, after all. She was performing beautifully, gliding as fast and smooth as a puck on an air-hockey table.

"Hi," whispered Missy Juk, close to Mick Chad's elbow.

"Hi."

"Everybody is really excited," she said in a hush.

"Yeah." Now Mick was getting butterflies in his stomach. Goodall was a smart cookie. Maybe the smartest one of them all. What made him worried about their survival?

"This is what I'm thinking," Missy said. "There's gotta be some love interest in this TV program for it to work. Right? A little sex and romance?"

The word *sex* got his attention.

"D'you see what I'm saying?" Missy asked.

"Not exactly," Chad said. "But I like the direction it's headed."

"You and me, Mick. We hook up. We have a torrid love affair. We flirt in front of the others, we have sex where they can see us, we have a few big fights. We'll be the stars of the miniseries!"

Mick nodded. "Good plan. I'm game."

Missy smirked. "I know a rare opportunity when I see one and I'm going to make the most of it. I'm not opposed to a little whoring. But I say what goes and what doesn't go. Got it?"

"Sure. When do we start the show?"

"Keep bowser in your trousers for now. You'll get your piece at the most dramatic moment and I promise you'll enjoy it."

"Cool."

"Meanwhile, you'll have to settle for a little public display of affection, just to get the rest of them talking."

She wrapped her arms around his neck and pushed her tongue in this mouth while he tried to keep an eye on the dark and dismal vortex.

**41**

You paid for luxury and that's what you got aboard the cruise yacht *Moorea Explorer*. She was 232 feet of sparkling white hull, containing thirty-five richly appointed cabins, all with bay windows and king-size beds. The public areas contained a small fortune in artworks, hot tubs, several small swimming pools, a jungle of lush potted greenery and three restaurants. There were more staff than there were passengers.

One of the key features of the *Moorea Explorer* was its four circular deck lounges, one at the very apex of the ship, resting above the bridge, and one at sea level. "Don't get your shoes wet," the staff joked every night as they welcomed their guests to the Sea Level Viewing Lounge.

Tonight the sommelier was pouring a rare New Zealand Pinot Gris as the perfect accompaniment to the pre-dinner hors d'oeuvres. The chef was displaying an impressive cold platter of antipasti alla noemi—light on the mussels and crab, heavy on the squid. "Today we made a catch of the freshest, plumpest squid and I knew I must make this perfect cold tray for my guests," the chef was explaining as he wandered among the guests. "Try with a little lemon. It is scrumptious."

The night was crisp and the island of Hiva Oa hovered a mile off the deck, her evening lights glinting in the vast South Pacific ocean.

All the polite talk was about the disturbance to the north. The papers were calling it the vortex. It seemed unreal that such a grand and big storm could be so close, while their weather was quiet and lovely.

It was agreed among the passengers that they were quite brave for continuing with their cruise so close to the anomaly.

"Why?" asked a matronly, nervous woman in her seventies. "Do you think there is any danger here?"

"Course not," announced her husband. "You see any sign of them clouds?"

The woman looked anxiously at the sky. The blanket of stars showed her there wasn't a cloud in the sky for miles.

They were safe.

*Splash.*

Everyone looked around. For a moment there was no alarm whatsoever. Then a purser walked quickly to the rail next to a table with half-eaten plates of antipasti—but no one sitting there. The porter called out a name, leaning over the brass rail. His legs went up and he went over.

*Splash.*

"Man overboard," called the chef. He ran to the rail with the sommelier, snatching at life preservers. They stood at the rail and peered into the waters, trying to figure out where to throw them.

There were flickers of movement, and then the chef and sommelier went in, too, seemingly dragged in by their extended arms.

Guests began to fall to the ground, and only then did they become aware of the slimy, boneless limbs that were coming out of the ocean and snaking under the deck rail, grabbing ankles. The guests were yanked into the rail, but they wouldn't go through.

The squid hauled themselves aboard, wrapping their tentacles around every limb and torso they could reach. They were monsters. Their tentacles were powerful and weighty, and bore down each person they captured.

THE CAPTAIN WATCHED the attack on the security monitors, amazed and shocked. He unlocked the weapons cabinet and dispatched his first mate to the Sea Level Viewing Lounge with eight armed men. On the monitors, he saw them blast the invading creatures. He saw the things die with great craters in their mantles, but for every squid that collapsed in a pile of mush, another one dragged itself laboriously onto the deck. In minutes, the squid had overcome their attackers.

The captain grabbed the throttle controls and turned on the power. The engines struggled and the ship vibrated. The captain could feel the screws turning sluggishly, then they churned to life with a lurch. The captain knew what the problem was. He could picture the giant, boneless squids tangled in his propellers.

He had to keep the props turning hard, to plow

through any further jamming. He increased the power, but then came the thick and sickening feeling of the screws tangling again and coming to a halt. The engines struggled to make them turn but couldn't budge them.

How was this happening? Where had they come from? He'd never heard of anything like this happening. The squid on the deck below were bigger than any squid he knew of except for the half-mythical giants that showed up in the stomachs of whales every once and a while.

He felt the ship move in the gentle waves, against the incoming tide. What was moving the ship?

He released the anchors and felt the clanking of the chains as they plummeted to the sea floor.

He felt alone on the bridge. The only other person in the room was the communications man, who was trying hard to reach anyone who would listen.

"Help's not coming—there are fifteen ships under attack in this vicinity," the communications man said.

"Does anybody know what's going on?"

"Squid attacks everywhere," the communications man blurted.

"Ridiculous," the captain declared.

"Tell the squid," the communications man replied.

The anchor chains were grinding against the hull in an unfamiliar way. The captain realized his mistake as the ship moved away from the Marquesas island of Hiva Oa. The squid were using the anchor chains to tow the *Moorea Explorer*.

He tried to retract the anchors, but they only moved a few feet before they were jammed to a halt.

There were squid in the anchor bays. Squid were flopping in through the glass doors of the Sea Level Viewing Lounge and into the halls. They were gasping and heaving and dying in the public parts of the ship. They were water breathers, on suicide missions to incapacitate those aboard the ship. The struggling, screaming passengers in the lounge were imprisoned in the tentacles that refused to yield even after the squid had asphyxiated. More squid had given up their lives to foul the props and jam the anchors.

"What's making them do it?" the communications man asked. "Somebody has to be controlling them, right?"

"Somebody, yeah," the captain agreed. "Somebody I don't want to meet. What's the rescue status?"

"There is no rescue."

"What about the Navy?"

"A couple of Navy ships responded to the first report of attacks and now they're disabled just like us. They can't move."

The captain nodded, picturing mangled squid remains in the props of a powerful U.S. Navy vessel.

"Air rescue?"

"Under way on the other ships. We're one of ten ships being towed northeast in these waters. We're the farthest away and the last on the list for air rescue. More Navy ships are en route."

En route, the captain thought, didn't sound very definite.

THE MOOREA EXPLORER passengers and crew watched in horror as a flotilla of Hiva Oa islanders came to their rescue, only to be overtaken by the swarming mass of cephalopods that turned the ocean to jelly. The luckiest rescuers were marooned on the water with their engines jammed with squid carcasses. The less lucky were attacked and pulled off their small boats by the giant tentacles. A hundred islanders were dragged below the surface of the ocean.

The others could only watch as the *Moorea Explorer* was pulled away.

The pace picked up slowly, and by morning they were bobbing in the waves with the other ships, all heading north into the vortex. The buzz of rescue choppers was ceaseless.

The passengers demanded that the captain bring the rescue to them. He laughed. "I've begged. I've threatened. I tried to bribe them. They say we have to wait in line. There are a thousand people that have to be rescued from the other ships before they get to us. But they won't get to us. We're dead meat. We'll be in the vortex by lunchtime."

The captain was right. There were still five fully loaded passenger ships in the flotilla when they reached the vortex. Every patrol ship within a hundred miles was befouled before it could move to intercept. A fleet of helicopter gunships arrived with depth charges, and the Pacific Ocean rocked with the thunder of the charges. The squid died by the thousands, their slimy bodies turning the ocean to the consistency of egg drop soup. The flotilla came to a stop, and still the depth charges continued to thunder, until the gunships had used them all. The gunships raced away to get resupplied at their base ships.

Minutes later, the ships started moving again. More squid had arrived, ignoring the countless dead brethren and taking up the towlines.

Five empty ships, and five ships full of human beings, were pulled inexorably into the vortex, where no rescue could follow them.

# 42

The seizures were just a part of her existence now. Everything else in the world was new and changed, too, and the seizures were just another novelty. She rode them out and carried on. Sandy knew they were a sign that her head wound had caused something to go terribly wrong. She might die from it. But there wasn't anything she could do about it, so why bother worrying?

She spent the night in a lean-to of collapsed, ancient stone, and she wandered out the next morning feeling groggy. Hungover. Her lover was standing on the beach looking intently at the sea. She stood in front of him.

"I don't like the looks of this," he commented.

"Hey, spend the night squirming on the ground and see how good you look."

"Oh. Hi, Sandy. Glad to see you made it. I meant *that*." He speared the horizon with a finger.

There was a ship offshore, gliding smoothly across the current and raising a cloud of mist from under her curiously flat hull. It took Sandy a minute to figure out that it was a hovercraft.

"It's looking for a clear landing place, I think," Lagrasse said. "Free of wrecks."

The vessel came to the shore at a point nearby, drifting onto the beach as easily as it had moved over the ocean, then settled with a winding down of the engines.

"Let's check 'em out," Lagrasse said. "Act friendly."

Sandy didn't know why she wouldn't act friendly. Her lover was sort of a suspicious jerk sometimes.

The hovercraft looked alien and huge—the one intact and upright vessel in a field of scorched wreckage. People came down the retractable gangway, looking stunned.

"Hi!" Sandy called.

They spotted her. A man pushed through the others and jogged over to meet her. "Let me help you!"

"Help me what?" Sandy asked. "That's a cool boat."

"You'd better lay down," the young man asked, putting a gentle hand on her shoulder. "I'll give you my shirt."

"Why?"

"You're naked," he pointed out.

"I'm not cold. It's always warm here, even with no sun."

"Who are you people?" Lagrasse demanded.

The young man took one look at him and exclaimed, "Oh, my God! What happened to you people?"

"Shipwreck. You're the first un-crash-landing so far," Sandy said.

"Why'd you come?" Lagrasse asked.

Sandy thought her lover, what's-his-name, was showing his moody side. She didn't quite understand it—unless he was jealous. Did he think she was going to start giving up her goodies to every other warm body that showed up? Well, yeah, sure she would.

That was the strange thing—all the chains were gone. Fear. Doubt. Inhibitions. All the mental insecurities that had governed her words and actions had dispersed when she landed on the rock island. The old Sandy had never touched alcohol, never smoked, and remained celibate until she was twenty. She thought she had freed herself when she joined up with her old boyfriend and his loony sex cult. But now she was really, truly *free*.

"You guys have any booze on that tub?" she asked brightly.

MICK CHAD POWERED DOWN the *Flying Fish* and locked the bridge, then emerged to find Melissa Juk glaring over the rail.

She wasn't looking at the countless shipwrecks, the rotting corpses or the vast monolithic ruins of the interior.

There was a naked woman on the shore, and Missy wasn't happy about it.

"Whoever she is, she'll steal the attention away from us."

"Oh," Chad said.

"No, no, everybody goes naked here," said the naked woman to the others on the expedition team.

"There you go," Chad said. "Everybody goes naked here. So you go naked, too, then all the attention will be back on you."

She scowled at him.

"You're way hotter than she is," he elaborated.

"Yeah, well, half her head's caved in," Missy shot back.

"Head wound or no head wound, you're hotter," Chad said sincerely. "As far as the audience can tell."

She considered that, then stripped naked.

Chad thought Missy Juk was the best woman he had ever met.

Henry Lagrasse was getting more agitated all the time. "The specimens are in the city. Don't you want to go into the city?"

Dr. Williamson recovered remarkably well when his newest intern scampered down the gangway in her birthday suit. "This is more incredible than I expected," he commented. "The island, I mean. What's your take, Good?"

Goodall's eyes were dancing in their sockets. "There's all kind of theories about volcanic activity raising land inside the vortex, but not reraising land that has sunk previously. This is incredible."

"But where do you think we'll find specimens?" Williamson asked.

"In the city," insisted the young shipwreck survivor, who was a pushy sort of a man.

"You don't even know what we're looking for."

"If this land emerged from the sea floor with living creatures on it, they'll be long dead," Goodall suggested. "There's a chance that we'll find samples washed up on the shore that could still be alive."

"Or less decayed—my thoughts exactly," Williamson said. He then turned and called out, "We'll start by scouting the island on foot."

"I'm going to get these people recuperating in bunks on the *Flying Fish*," announced the young man with the biomedical background.

But the shipwreck survivors, the naked woman and her moody boyfriend, had no intention of getting into bunks. The entire group set off on a march around the island, spaced out to cover the entire beach from waterline to the edge of the ruins.

They didn't get far.

"Things are looking up," Lagrasse exclaimed aloud, but to himself. There were ships coming in from the south, carried like derelicts in the current.

The team of researchers began panicking. Shipwreck virgins, Lagrasse thought disdainfully. "They're gonna crash!" exclaimed one of the older men over and over.

Lagrasse had to admit it was an awesome sight. Even he had never seen so many ships coming in together. All big ones, too. As the current flung them onto the shore one after another, the spectacle was breathtaking.

"Now, that was cool," Sandy commented.

"Your pals don't think so," Lagrasse grumbled. The researchers were crying and praying as the last of the giants settled noisily on the basalt slope.

Lagrasse approached the nearest gigantic crushed V of a cruise-ship hull, investigating the grotesque clots of mush and gore that seemed to be hanging from every protrusion on the ship, at and below the water level. One big clot dangled on a side of the hull that was now raised twenty feet into the air, and a strand of tissue separated. The clot fell and landed with a thump.

It was a squid, bigger than any squid Lagrasse had ever seen. It had to be one of those giants that were found in the stomachs of whales.

He inspected the pulpy remnants that clung to the hull. There was even a mass of them shoved into the cage around the main props. The creatures had sacrificed themselves to disable the ship.

Lagrasse felt a curious satisfaction. This was as it should be.

THE TEAM of cryptozoologists helped the survivors free themselves of the grounded ships, and the population of the island ballooned. Soon there were hundreds of able-bodied men and women joining in the rescue effort. They told stories that couldn't be believed—about giant squid that attacked as a group to disable the ships.

"It couldn't have been deliberate," Williamson protested to one of the cruise-ship captains.

"It was," the man said. "I'm not saying they came up with the plan on their own, mind you. I bet it was people controlling them with subsurface ultrasound or something. Maybe a new kind of terrorist threat."

"We're a few days too late to discover these," Goodall said, nudging a squid carcass with his foot. "They just displayed a Colossal in Chicago."

Lagrasse overheard the comment, and he found his opening. "That? That's nothing."

Goodall and Williamson looked at him.

"You want a big octopus, I can show you one ten times as big as that."

"It's a squid," Williamson pointed out.

"The one I'm talking about is an octopus, kind of. I think it has eight arms, anyway, but its head has wings like a squid."

"You sure you didn't hallucinate it?" Williamson asked.

Lagrasse knew the man didn't like him. "Ask Sandy. She's seen it. You wanna know the strangest part? It's amphibious."

"Ridiculous!" Williamson said.

"Lives in a shallow water pool in the center of the island."

"That's absurd!"

Lagrasse shrugged. "Want to see it for yourself?"

They followed Lagrasse inland. A constant trickle of cruise-ship survivors was already heading for the three-sided pyramid, lured by the song in their heads. The cryptozoologists questioned the marchers, but the answers they received were vague. The closer they came to the pyramid, the less communicative the marchers became.

"They're like zombies," Missy Juk said, adjusting the straps of her supply pack.

Mick Chad didn't answer.

When they reached the lip of the courtyard, they found the stream of silent human beings filing into the pyramid. There was a silent queue of a hundred people waiting to enter. Above their heads the bones were ejected, tossed by the tentacle of something that was out of sight inside. A hill of human bones and skulls had collected against the base of the pyramid and formed an entrance ramp.

They were stunned into silence until Missy Juk began crying for help.

"It's Mick! He's going in!"

They bustled after Mick Chad, who was heading for the pyramid without noticing Missy dragging on his arm. The researchers huddled around the hover-craft pilot and brought him to a standstill. Mick didn't even look at them. It was as if his mind were already dead.

Something like a growl came from inside. The queued victims waiting to get inside the pyramid turned on the research team and wordlessly grabbed at them. The researchers were outnumbered twenty to one, and they were battered with fists until they became pliant—then they were pulled into the pyramid.

Melissa Juk felt the compacted human bones under her bare feet. She felt the iron grip of Mick Chad on her wrist. She was going to die and she was helpless to stop it. Her head was ringing from the beating and her vision was tunneling.

It occurred to her she was still naked. What a cinematic way to die! A naked young college girl with great boobs gets hauled into the mouth of the monster. If they ever made a movie of this, it would be spectacular.

"There it is, God," she heard Dr. Williamson

wheeze as they were pulled inside the pyramid to face the leviathan.

"A creature no man has ever seen before," Goodall agreed from bloody lips.

"I suppose you'll be retiring now," Dr. Williamson slurred.

Goodall didn't answer. He was constricted in the tentacles of the thing and lifted skyward. Williamson went next, then a few of the other researchers. Finally it was Missy's turn. The tentacles took her. The suckers were painful against her skin. She saw the beak come closer until it was as big as a VW Beetle.

In she went.

Missy Juk felt her mind being eviscerated. A little strand of something was being absorbed from her brain and she suffered incredible agony for a long, long half minute. Then, with a sloppy crunch, all agony ended.

LAGRASSE OBSERVED as the two older men and the naked college girl were dragged into the pyramid. He felt satisfaction and pride. He had done a good job. And the thing in the pyramid was pleased. And it was eating better than ever.

That was just the beginning. The other survivors began to respond to the same invisible lure. There was a perpetual train of human beings marching from the shore to the pyramid. Lagrasse monitored the progress from his rooftop lookout.

Sandy joined him there in the early evening, looking tousled. He knew what she had been doing, and he didn't care. "It's not feeding anymore," he explained worriedly.

"He's full," she said.

"No. It's the people. They're not right. The ones who responded early were good, but the rest of them are not correct," he said.

Sandy watched the thing in the pyramid scoop up human beings in one tentacle after another and bring them to its massive beak. It was tasting them.

But they must have tasted bad. They were released and they dropped into the pool of algae-thickened water. Some of them struggled then, as if some of their free will was restored by the fall. A few tried to scale the slime-coated walls of the pool, but other tentacles emerged to drag them down.

"What can you do?" Sandy said with a shrug. "Come on." She took his hand and pulled him onto the rooftop, where they did their favorite thing, although Lagrasse for once found it hard to enjoy himself.

## 43

He was dreaming of being ten years old.

"You did it, boy!"

It was his dad, standing on the far side of the Crying River, where the brook evaporated to leave a thin crust of sand in the dry months. Walking on it made a sound like walking on potato chips, but in ancient days they came up with a more poetic comparison. They said it sounded like maidens crying, so it became the Crying River.

Crossing it without making it cry was something that only Remo's people could do. Remo's heart swelled. His father sounded so happy at what Remo had done.

"Come on home now, son," called Sunny Joe Roam. He waved to Remo. "Your mother is waiting. Come home."

Remo wanted nothing more than to go home and be with his proud father and his mother. He hadn't seen her in so long. He missed her so much. Yes, go home, now—be with them.

"I'm going home." That's what he was saying as he woke up.

Chiun was looking at him. The tires squeaked as the aircraft touched down in Honolulu, and Remo saw palm trees and high-rise hotels zipping by the window. He was going home—the urge was strong. He would be surrounded by so much pleasure and love when he reached his home. He must go.

He was nearly there.

Chiun watched him, and said nothing.

Home was—where? The Native reservation? He was in Hawaii, not Arizona. He was nowhere near *that* home.

And the dream was a lie. He hadn't grown up on the res. He grew up in a home for orphans in New Jersey. He never experienced the intense joy of seeing his father's great pride in him as a kid. He didn't meet Sunny Joe until he was an adult.

Remo never met his mother, who had died when he was an infant.

Remo Williams had never known what it was like to grow up in a family, but in his dream it felt so real. The urge to go home was so strong. It was still there, nagging him. When he came home the joy would return.

But the home that was calling to him was in the middle of the Pacific Ocean.

The urge went away, replaced by anger. "That was a cheap shot," Remo said, but not to Chiun. "Son of a bitch."

Chiun, thank God, for once, said nothing.

THEY RENTED a sailing craft. Prices were sky-high in Honolulu as the city cleaned up from the devastation of the tidal wave.

"Kinda steep, isn't it?" Remo asked the wharf rat who was renting sailboats.

"Time of crisis." The man shrugged and ate another French fry. He had two more orders of "Bigger Fries" on the counter in front of him.

"Profiteering, you mean," Remo said.

"Look, asshole, you wanna rent your boat somewhere else?"

Chiun said nothing as Remo paid full price, leaving the money on the counter in the tiny shack. The wharf rat was left sitting on his stool, eyes bugging open. He whimpered.

"This one looks good," Chiun suggested.

"Fine." Remo lifted the shack door off its hinges and dropped it into the water. A gaggle of seagulls was already converging on the shack, lured by the aroma of French fries, which were now dumped inside the wharf rat's greasy shirt. The wharf rat was going to be paralyzed for an hour or two. The seagulls began pecking.

The somber Masters of Sinanju stepped into the boat and Remo hoisted the sails. He wasn't a great sailor, but he had done it enough to know how to make things work, and he had an instinct for the balance of the craft and the ocean and the wind that surpassed the skills of any old salt who spent a lifetime on the sea.

They had left the islands of Hawaii behind them.

CHIUN GUIDED them out and around the guarded tract of the Pacific Ocean that was now known as the watch zone. They headed for the area known as the Corridor.

The military vessels wouldn't get near the Corridor. It was too dangerous. It was an extension of the vortex that had sprung up thirty-six hours previously, penetrating the watch zone to the open water of the Pacific. The Corridor didn't have the strong current of the vortex, but it did create the same local level of communication blackout.

Three vessels had entered the Corridor and become so disoriented they had sailed the wrong way. Without GPS, radio, compass or even stars to guide them, who could blame them? The irony was that the satellites could see what was happening. They watched the ships go in circles, then chug into the vortex. Several other ships managed to blunder into and out of the Corridor before it was declared off-limits.

The entrance to the Corridor seemed to shift, and guard vessels had been unable to catch up to it for long. Those who did find the entrance were the worshipers. Mostly third-world spiritualists and their flock, who paddled or sailed into the Corridor in search of their god. After just thirty-six hours, the Corridor had swallowed a hundred victims.

Remo and Chiun were in the open ocean when they saw the paddle canoes coming toward them.

"We shall not follow them into this dark place," Chiun reminded Remo.

"I promise. We just stop *them* from going in. Come on."

Chiun slipped into the water without causing a noticeable ripple, gliding with Remo under the surface until the canoes were overhead. Chiun swam to the surface and began removing paddles.

Remo was being touched by Sa Mangsang, and this worried Chiun greatly. How much power was there in the old god of Mu? What influence would he have on Remo from so close a distance?

Chiun knew this was the best thing that they could do—put a cork in the pipeline that brought Sa Mangsang his nourishment. If Sa Mangsang became weak enough he might descend into slumber again. Chiun, however, doubted this.

As he snatched the paddles from the canoes above he bent them in his ancient hands until they cracked apart. Soon the canoes drifted idly on a surface carpeted with wood splinters. Chiun surfaced alongside Remo, some distance from the befuddled islanders.

On the largest of the canoes was a small tent. Brightly colored fabrics hung from it and created a shady place inside. From this honored shelter stepped an islander with a worn wooden staff that had been carved generations ago. The man raised the staff and addressed his followers.

"He tells them to ignore this trickery of the jealous gods—they will soon bask in the powerful presence of the most powerful god, who is Hunundra."

"Not without paddles they won't," Remo replied. "They won't catch the Sa Mangsang current for another twenty miles."

"They have sails," Chiun said.

The sails started to go up and Chiun began working again on disabling them. He approached one of the canoes from below and ejected himself from the water. Quickly his bare feet would touch down on the deck of the craft, he would slash the sail into slivers of reed and fabric and he would slip into the ocean again. Chiun did more than his fair share of this work, while Remo paused to abuse the cult leader with some of his white wisdom. Whatever Remo had to say was so unbearable to the cult leader that, when Chiun next stopped to look, he saw the man had lobotomized himself with some sharp instrument.

"Everybody, rope together," Remo called. "I'm saving your sorry butts."

Chiun, who now stood midstern on one of the rear canoes, relayed the message in the paddlers' own dialect, and yet they were still disinclined to cooperate.

"We go to our god! We will row with our hands if we must!" shouted a ritually painted man in Chiun's canoe, who then rushed at the ancient Korean intruder.

Chiun extended one finger and slashed the attacker across the throat.

"What's the matter, Chiun?" Remo asked across the distance.

"Nothing," Chiun replied. His attacker's head bounced off the side of the canoe and plopped into the ocean. "They are overcoming their hesitation."

The torso slumped onto the other side, leaked blood into the water, and then splashed overboard.

The canoes were roped together, one after another, until they formed a large raft. Remo took a tow rope as Chiun settled in the shady little pavilion of the now deceased holy leader. It was a smelly place. Chiun dismantled it and dropped the malodorous scraps into the ocean. Thereupon he suffered the blazing and merciless rays of the sun as Remo dallied in the cool, refreshing ocean, dragging the flotilla to Anuki Atoll.

The canoes were smashed to kindling when the would-be worshipers were safe on dry land. They wouldn't be leaving again soon.

"More coming, Little Father," Remo announced.

Chiun scowled at the ocean. More boats were going to bypass the Anuki at a distance that would have made them invisible specks to the average human being.

"We'll have to hoof it," Remo declared.

"I do not hoof it, Remo," Chiun stated, but the headstrong Reigning Master was already running across the ocean.

CHIUN RAN UP alongside Remo. Their feet were barely touching the water's surface, and they rose and fell with the breathlike rising and falling of the surface.

The method of running on the surface of the water was simple enough to understand. Did one not see insects in streams who stood on the water and flitted from place to place? And yet, such a thing is the ignorant mind of most men that they don't believe a human being can do what a simple insect can do.

The principle was quite the same. One must simply detect the pressure limit of the surface of the water and not exceed it. Thus, one does not sink into the water. Chiun knew that anyone could be taught to perform such a feat of novelty—even ancient carpenters.

They found just a small and weary band of travelers who had sailed and rowed all the way from Tahuata in the Marquesas. Their passion to reach the vortex wasn't as strong as their bodies. Still, they attempted to put up a fight that ended when their cackling old crone of a priest got broken and jettisoned over the side.

"This will become tiresome quickly, Remo," Chiun admitted finally.

"What?" Remo asked. The young Master ceased his stroking. He had the tow rope for the Tahuatian boats tied around his waist. "You're tired? Maybe you could try some of this and we'll see if you get tired."

"I think not. Continue, or the outgoing tide will carry us away from the atoll."

Soon the Tahuatians were stranded on the small atoll, which had already been stripped of the few edible fruits that grew there. Remo left their few supplies and smashed their boats, leaving only one canoe for him and Chiun to take back to their rented sailboat. Remo was actually sitting inside the canoe and looking from side to side before he realized that all the paddles had been destroyed. Chiun sighed, embarrassed for him under the eyes of the islanders, and whittled a new paddle from the trunk of a strong palm tree.

The stranded islanders eyed the stripped palm foliage as if it were a buffet.

Chiun handed the paddle to the Reigning Master, who began rowing them out to sea while the rabble tussled over their meal of leaves.

"If you're really bored..." Remo held up the paddle.

"No, thank you," Chiun answered.

Chiun wondered how long this would go on. Would it take them days to starve Sa Mangsang? Weeks? Or would it never happen? Surely, Sa Mangsang had capabilities that were yet to be revealed.

Would this end, ever?

**44**

Finally, the end was coming. It had been an eternity, this waiting without hope of release.

They were the Faithful of Saraswati, and they had existed for a thousand generations, or so their tradition claimed. For a thousand generations they had been *waiting*.

When he was a child, Urik had believed in the doctrine of his father and mother. When he was beginning to become a man, he questioned their teachings.

"How can you trust in this tradition, if it had existed for twenty thousand or thirty thousand years?" he demanded of his father. "Legends alter in a single generation—how could our worship be pure since the beginning?"

"The One comes to our dreams and reminds us," his father explained.

"When? When will I have the dream?"

"Never," his father said, "for I have had it. It comes only once in many generations. That is all that is needed."

Urik disputed that. He didn't wish to carry on the

tradition. His family told him, "It is simply what you must do."

"And if I do not?" he demanded.

"Then the Faithful of Saraswati grow fewer in number." His father waved at the village.

Saraswati was the name of the town and had been for all time. Once it was huge, as the Faithful numbered in the thousands. Today, most of the unneeded structures were crumbling ruins that the villagers kept buried and hidden. There was much that would stir international attention should those ruins become known. Saraswati was just a small enclave now, a hundred or less.

"The One asks too much!" Urik protested when the time came for him to take his vow. "It is inhumane that we are forced to live our lives in expectation of this thing that will never come."

"One day, it will come," his mother promised.

"Father wasted his lifetime and you ask me to waste mine!"

His mother was always tolerant, even of this insult of her recently deceased husband. "He did not think so."

Urik prayed to the One to send him the dream—he needed something to give him the will to carry on the tradition. The dream, however, never came.

Urik took his vows, despite his lack of belief. He had no choice. Generations of the Faithful had come before him. He couldn't break their lineage of service to the One—this was his prison.

Then, afterward, came the dream—to Urik and to all the people. They felt it long before the rest of the world. After all, this was what they were bred for.

The dictates of the One, passed down through the generations, told just how to seek the best bloodlines. For centuries the men of Saraswati had journeyed throughout the Indian subcontinent searching for the brides with the best attributes—then they went to great lengths to obtain them. All this was done to make the Faithful highly sensitive to the call of the One, if he should ever call.

When he did, his call was only a whisper, but it grew louder every day.

They prepared their journey. All the true Faithful would go, leaving the non-Saraswati wives and the children and the very few of the Faithful who weren't sensitive—there were always some in every generation. Their disappointment was bad enough before the call—after the call, these unfortunate nonsensitives were driven to suicide.

Urik and his people left behind the village and the tradition of a thousand generations. They were finally fulfilling their purpose.

Urik was ecstatic. The dreams proved the One was real. His life wouldn't be wasted, and soon he would sit at the right hand of the One.

Then—he wasn't sure what came after that. Surely, it could only be eternal paradise.

They had accumulated much money, saved just for this purpose. They took plane after plane to get to a small island in the far reaches of the South Pacific Ocean, and then they purchased large ocean canoes. Not one of the Faithful had ever been on the ocean, but their will was so strong that they dug into the water and paddled out to sea, guided by the siren song that was always present in their specially attuned minds. They could almost hear the sibilant call. It led them into a passage that would take them through the patrol ships.

Then the servants of the One gathered around their boats. It was difficult for the Faithful of Saraswati to look at these huge and tentacled monsters as their brethren.

The ways of the One were indeed strange and wondrous.

**45**

"What are they?" Remo asked.

"They are the Faithful of Saraswati. Can you not read the inscription upon their lead craft?"

Remo could see the characters on the sash that was draped around the stern of the canoe, but he didn't know what they said. "They Hindu?"

"Of a type," Chiun said shortly. "They have existed for long years and married among those they felt best suited to increasing their people's sensitivity to the call of their unnamed master."

"I guess we know his name now," Remo said.

"Never have they deviated from their purpose, until all who knew them assumed they were but one more dynasty of dedicated acolytes," Chiun said. "They are ignorant of their own purpose. Think of what the unnameable one has bred them for."

Remo thought about it. "Nutritional supplements."

"Exactly. Concentrated with the substance he needs to expand his mental abilities."

"Let's make sure that doesn't happen."

With powerful strokes, Remo dragged the ocean

behind him and had their little canoe skimming across the ocean. The Faithful patiently watched them coming. Their paddles were brought inside and placed in the bottom of their craft.

"Don't like the looks of this," Remo said. "Could they have something up their sleeves?"

Chiun shook his head. "I know not."

"Stay frosty."

"What?" Chiun demanded. "Frosty? In this heat and searing sun?"

"I meant be careful and alert," Remo sighed.

"I am always careful and alert. Or was it yourself you were speaking to?"

"Yeah, it was me. Come on."

Remo slipped into the ocean, submerging thirty feet to examine the boats from below. There was nothing unusual. What could they have up there that would be a problem, anyway? Electric eels to toss overboard? Kryptonite?

Chiun caught his eye and gestured down. Remo looked between his feet, and he saw something moving. Hundreds of feet below, it was as if the ocean floor was a squirming, living, undulating entity, rising up to engulf them.

Remo knew. Of course he knew what they were. He was ready for them.

But, man, there was a lot of them. Squid after squid after squid, and their questing tentacles were reaching out for the Masters of Sinanju a full fifty, seventy, ninety feet ahead of their winged mantles, and the folks in the canoes on the surface began to paddle quickly away.

Remo cursed and used his extended fingernail against the questing tentacles, slicing into them with the speed of flashing lightning. Remo saw the sections of the tentacles drifting in the water and for a moment he was terrified that he might see them spontaneously rejoin with their stumps. Sa Mangsang had performed such acts of regeneration....

But these squid did not, and Remo realized it didn't matter. As he sent one crippled squid after another flitting away, others would come to take his place. The sea was thick with the fleshy giants.

Chiun was more than holding his own. Unlike Remo, *all* his fingernails were long and honed, and his Knives of Eternity were making mincemeat out of any squid limb that came within reach. The two human beings were floating in a murk of shredded flesh, and still the giant squids crowded around them.

Chiun nodded at the surface, and he and Remo shot up with such speed it confused their attackers. Remo and Chiun sprang onto their canoe.

"Let's make a run for it," Remo called.

Chiun was already on the move. With Remo alongside, the old Korean Master stepped across the water's surface in fast pursuit of the boats of the Faithful of Saraswati.

But Chiun was tired.

The battle under the sea had taken much from him, and propelling his water-sodden robes across the ocean was taxing. He felt a niggling of weariness in his body. It wouldn't undo him soon, but it was there, and that was bad enough.

He was getting old.

Chiun found his mind wandering. Would he survive this journey? Would he have the opportunity to once again serve tea to his son, the Reigning Master, who must live on?

"Stay frosty!" Remo called, running close at Chiun's side.

Chiun saw the squid. The water was thickening with them in every direction and they must have been waiting here by the thousands. Of course they were here to protect Sa Mangsang's precious Faithful, who would amplify his born-again mental powers.

The squid raised themselves out of the sea and snatched at the ankles of the Masters of Sinanju, but came up empty.

"They'll never get us that way," Remo declared. "We're way faster than any octo-reflexes."

"They'll try another way," Chiun declared.

Sure enough, the squid began to flail their giant tentacles out of the water in all directions, without regard to the location of their prey. Remo and Chiun sidestepped the dark, boneless arms, which lost their strength when they were out of their native element.

They stepped aboard the last canoe of the Faithful of Saraswati, and the squid charged at the bottom of the canoe and struck hard.

They came from the water on all sides, rose from the depths at great speed and propelled themselves into the air, grasping with a hundred tentacles at the canoe containing the Masters of Sinanju. Remo and Chiun allowed the tentacles to slip around them, until a second attacking formation flung themselves bodily at the canoe, plowing it up as other squid leaped and pounded it down, and in a heartbeat the canoe was destroyed. The Faithful who were aboard were mashed out of existence by the suicidal collision of the multiton cephalopods, and only Chiun and Remo were still intact. But the density of the airborne squid in that moment was impassable, and they allowed themselves to be borne under the surface, where they skirted the grasping tentacles.

Chiun saw the brilliance in the scheme. The Masters of Sinanju were overwhelmed.

The squid at the periphery encased them in their bodies and more squid came to surround them, crushing and suffocating the squid within and in turn being suffocated and crushed by the next layer of giants. In seconds, a hundred of the creatures had tangled themselves together and embraced each other. A hundred tons of squid meat constricted upon the Masters of Sinanju, who were trapped in the very middle.

Chiun's breath was forced out of his chest in tiny spurts. The pressure increased. He was encased in the rubber bodies of the squid without a millimeter of room to maneuver. His fingers sliced into the squid flesh and opened up some space, but immediately it was filled again by the growing pressure.

The pressure was killing the inner squid just as surely as it would kill Chiun and Remo, and abruptly Chiun became aware that the inner squid were dead already. The pressure was too much for them. Even though they lived at great depths, they must require slow acclimation to changes in depth.

"Chiun!" It was Remo, shouting through the sluicing water. "Think like a boulder!"

Chiun had been about to suggest the same thing. He did. He allowed his mind to think as if he, Chiun, were a heavy thing of solid stone that had no business in the ocean. The power of the Sinanju-trained mind made thinking about such a thing into a kind of reality. Real enough for the squid.

Instead of a buoyant, hundred-pound Korean gentlemen, the squid were suddenly trying to hold on to a rock that weighed as much as each of them. The weight ripped through the muscles and the tentacles. The squid tried squeezing tighter, but that only crushed to death more of the inner squid, and loosened up the passage of the boulder. Chiun's body tore through the squid bodies, and Remo emerged beside him.

They faced an angry school of giant squid that made a wall in the ocean, and Chiun and Remo could do nothing except swim away—the other way.

Away from the Faithful of Saraswati.

**46**

"Holy mother of God, look at that thing." The pilot was flying by eye. His radar was going berserk. His compass was spewing nonsense. His GPS signal was inoperative, with one of the satellite feeds continually blocked by the massive cone.

They were joking back home about the "ice cone." It sounded too much like ice-cream cone, and how could an ice-cream cone hurt anybody?

They didn't understand the problem. Even the pilot didn't understand the problem until he laid eyes on the thing.

It was more than a mountain and it was still growing fast. It spewed steam at twenty thousand feet and sent tons of water down to the Antarctic surface every second. Far beyond it was a second cone, just as huge.

"Jockey, you think this'll work?" the pilot radioed.

"Don't know, Jay," his buddy called from the second fighter jet. "I didn't expect it to be so big."

Jockey was amazingly calm. He always got calm when the stress was high, and right now he sounded like he might nod off.

"Let's intercourse those cold bitches," Captain Jerome "Jay" White said, and he headed for Cone Alpha.

"Affirmative." Jockey zeroed in on Cone Beta.

They were armed with something new—nuclear bunker busters, which made all previous bunker busters look like firecrackers. These babies were designed to create a narrow percussive shock like nothing ever witnessed before. Theoretically, it would turn carbon into consommé.

That was the idea anyway. They had only been monkey-rigged into existence within the past forty-eight hours and nobody knew what they would actually do.

White leveled off at thirty thousand feet and approached the cone. Luckily the gap at the top was open like a funnel, a mile across. It wouldn't be a tough target. The steam pressure—Jay had been told—would slow the bomb during its descent, so it shouldn't impact hard enough to disable it. The fins would shear off at a certain pressure level and allow it to penetrate even deeper through the steam until it reached the correct altitude for detonation. The correct altitude was three or four miles below the visible surface, where a vent of rock allowed the release of all that superheated water.

It would blow, collapse the vent and the cone, and that hole would be corked. For how long, nobody knew.

"I'm dropping my package," White announced, and hit the button sequence that sent the bomb down into the billowing steam shaft.

"Mine's going now," Jockey replied a moment later.

Jay sped away and banked steeply, and witnessed the collapse of the cone. It was too big to be real. It was like watching the Rocky Mountains collapse into rubble.

"Christ, the tremor is unbelievable," announced the commander at base, thousands of miles away.

"You seeing this?" Jay asked.

"On video it looks like the steam is stopped," the base commander said.

"Yeah, it's stopped. Jockey?"

A hundred miles away, at the remains of Cone Beta, Jockey whooped. "She's plugged up tight!"

"Keep an eye on those bitches," the commander ordered.

JAY AND JOCKEY traded jokes for a half an hour as they each made wide, lazy circles over the fields of crumbled ice where the cones had been. Jay descended to two thousand feet, eyes on the alert for traces of steam.

AT THE GEOGRAPHIC South Pole, the seismic team had been watching the needles. They had jumped all over the paper when the cones crumbled, and then there were just a few shivers.

Twenty-two minutes after the bombs, the shivers became substantial tremors.

"Just more settling," the seismologist said dismissively.

"Not pressure?" asked the Department of Defense liaison on the open radio channel.

"Too big, too soon. It'll take a while for pressure to start building."

Another series of shakes sent the needles flying. The seismologist eyed the black marks suspiciously. "Man, that's steady."

"For settling?" his liaison demanded.

"It has to be settling."

"Why?"

"Because pressure can't build up that fast. I've crunched the numbers. The pressure coming out of those vents was something we could estimate and account for."

"What if the pressure increases?" his DOD liaison asked.

"Enough to break through again? Can't happen— not that fast."

The needle clicked against the sides of the paper feed.

"I'm calling my men out of there," the DOD liaison declared.

JAY ANSWERED the call. "Yeah, base?"

"You boys increase your altitude right away. I mean now."

"Understood."

"Acknowledge, Jockey," their base commander demanded.

"Understood. I'm—" Jockey shouted something wordless.

Jay banked hard, just in time to see the distant, tiny bomber intersect with the mile-wide steam shaft that had just spewed from the crumbled ice. The force of the shaft must have been tremendous—it sent Jockey's jet tumbling up into the sky. The G-forces were unthinkable. Jockey would already be dead.

Jay yanked the stick and fed fuel to the engines, and began climbing steeply. Below him, where there had been nothing just seconds ago, the Antarctic exploded open and ten thousand tons of ice fragments were hurled skyward. It was ice dust by the time it buffeted the aircraft. Jay knew what would come next.

A fraction of a second later, the bomber was engulfed in superheated steam. The impact killed Jay White before the heat could even reach him.

**47**

Remo paddled the little canoe slowly across the empty surface of the sunny tropical ocean.

"I feel like a guy on the front of a vacation brochure," he growled. "Not some idiot squid chaser."

"You are not chasing the squid. It is the other way around," Chiun reminded him.

"Instead of you, I ought to have a blond babe in a bikini," Remo observed. "If this were a vacation brochure, I mean."

"Do not ever think of asking me to wear a bikini."

Remo glared at the horizon unhappily. "I'm going in."

"You will not!"

Remo paddled them for another ten minutes. There was no sign of the squid.

"Little Father, I'm going in."

Chiun sighed. "I know."

"It's the right thing to do," Remo said.

"It will be your death," Chiun said simply.

Remo glowered. "You told me to find my instinct and then honor it with faith. I have faith in this decision."

"That does not mean it is the correct decision."

Remo knew he had a good reason all ready, but he didn't know just how to put it into words. "Chiun, I looked back at what happened at that castle in Scotland and I was filled with all this regret for something that didn't happen. Now I'm acting on faith, and maybe preventing something worse from happening. If I fail, so what?"

Chiun's eyes flashed. "I have explained to you just what may occur if you are enslaved by the thing that awaits you in there."

"But so what? In the end, Sa Mangsang wins, right? With me as his gofer or without me. Maybe if I go there I can do something about this whole mess."

"You cannot," Chiun declared. "I will allow this only if I accompany you."

Remo nodded. "I know."

THEY MADE IT to the sailboat without being attacked. They set sail and headed into the Corridor. No squid.

"Of course not. They want you to come," Chiun pointed out. "When they attacked us it was only to protect their precious Faithful."

The squid showed themselves again as the current began to pick up under the sailboat. A ring of colossal creatures bobbed just under the surface behind the boat.

"Don't worry. We're not changing our minds," he shouted.

The squid were taken by the current just as surely as the sailboat. Remo collapsed the sails and he and Chiun stood on either side of the small craft, shifting their own weight to compensate for the gyrations of the craft in the current.

"There's land," Remo announced finally. "What a mess," he added minutes later, as they began to make out the jungle of shipwrecks that lined the shore.

"Our boat shall join the others," Chiun said.

"Hey, I gave that nice man a security deposit," Remo said.

But there was nothing that could be done. As the current slung the tiny craft at the dark basalt slope, Chiun and Remo stepped out on either side and ran up the shore. The sailboat skidded over the rock and bellied up against the hull of a Coast Guard cutter that had been there for days.

The stench of death was thick. How many cadavers were crushed and decaying inside all these wrecks was something Remo didn't want to think about.

"This one is still alive," Chiun remarked.

"But he doesn't smell any better," Remo noted. "Who're you?"

The grimy young man was sitting on the ancient rock perimeter wall. He was filthy, and his head was a mass of blackening scabrous tissue. His personality was as pleasant as his physical presence. "I ask the questions around here. Who are you jokers?"

Remo shrugged. "Just a couple of jokers."

"You pulled a neat little trick coming ashore. Nobody's made landfall like that before."

"Who's that?" Remo nodded at the naked girl lying nearby, head pillowed on one extended arm. She, too, had a crusted head wound.

"I told you. You don't ask questions. I ask the questions. For your information, that's my girlfriend, Sandy. She's the hottest babe on the island and she's mine. You don't touch."

"We do not practice necrophilia," Chiun sniffed.

The young man stared at the little old Korean. "Huh?"

"We don't do it with dead people," Remo said. "Your girlfriend bought the farm a few minutes ago."

The young man stood up, squinted at them, then put his hand on the girl's neck. He gave her a shake, then felt for a pulse.

"Huh. How'd you know?"

"The smell," Remo said. "She's already starting to decay."

"Yeah. Well, I'm surprised she lasted as long as she did. You guys want to see the city?"

Remo didn't know what it was specifically, but the young man repulsed him. Everything about the man was disgusting. His wound, his filth, his nakedness, but mostly his mental state. This man was broken. He was something so devoid of humanity, he couldn't even be said to be evil.

They followed him into the ruined city.

"He who we shall not name has taken him as a servant," Chiun observed, speaking too quietly for their guide to hear.

Remo was horrified. "Could he make me into something like that?" The young man stopped to look at them, trying to understand their words. His eyes were dull.

And the rock was dull, crusted with a patina of

algae desiccated during the days since it had emerged from the ocean. The stones piled upon one another to make the shapes of walls and buildings. Remo felt his mind recoiling from the familiarity of the shapes. The city repulsed him just as the loathsome young man repulsed him.

More abhorrent was the familiar shape of the three-sided pyramid, which was resolving itself out of the gray surroundings of the island. Remo had seen the pyramid before, as he swam down into it years ago to introduce himself to Sa Mangsang. That was during his Rite of Attainment, when he set about performing the series of tasks that made up the ritual that made him a Master of Sinanju.

He hadn't felt like a Master of anything when he encountered Sa Mangsang. He felt afraid. And he felt afraid now.

Chiun was quiet. Remo looked at him, and it occurred to him that Chiun had seen the thing for himself when he, too, went through his Rite of Attainment. That was decades and decades ago.

"The pyramid has opened," Remo noted.

The young man stopped short and whirled on the Masters. "How do you know that?"

"We've been here before."

"Who are you? What are you doing here?"

"Cleaning up," Remo said. "We're garbage collectors. This place is a mess."

The dam seemed to burst inside the young man. He charged Remo, screeching.

Remo honestly didn't want to lay his hands on that unclean flesh. He stepped back, allowed the man to charge by him, then Remo snagged him with a single expensive Italian shoe. The young man swallowed his anger and flew into the solid stone wall of a nearby structure. The thick crust of scabrous tissue didn't cushion the impact enough to save Henry Lagrasse. He rolled on his back and his eyes went blank, his feet kicking at the air. They left him, still kicking.

Remo and Chiun stopped at the gap in the wall. Before them, the ground descended into a courtyard that covered thousands of acres, and in every direction the paved floor was covered in the sucked bones of human beings.

The base was stone and raised above the courtyard, but the skewed angles of the pyramid walls were made to appear even more asynchronous by their partially opened state. They had opened enough to expose the interior—but from where they stood, they saw nothing.

"I go alone," Remo declared.

"You certainly shall not."

There was no arguing with that. They went together. They descended into the courtyard and felt themselves engulfed by the putrid air, filled with the decomposition of countless humans.

They mounted the hill of human bones, compacted by the marching feet of even more victims.

At the top of the hill they stood on the lip of the pyramid and regarded the great bulk of the Dream Thing.

REMO WASN'T a man who frightened easily, but Sa Mangsang terrified him, and the Octopus Squid was indeed far more huge than the monster Remo had faced years ago. Its flabby body, bulbous like an octopus but also winged like the mantle of a squid, pulsated atop a submerged platform in the green, slime-filled lake. Its twin, oily eyes glistened on either side of the mantle, and the huge beak snapped at them.

At their appearance, the great beast Sa Mangsang bunched itself out of the water, elevating its face over the Masters of Sinanju. It reproached them with a baleful look, then the beak fell open and a long hiss emerged. A single tentacle reached out of the water.

Remo knew what it was saying.

*Ah, you have arrived at last!*

The words manifested themselves in his head. Chiun heard them, too.

*You have much to account for, Masters of Sinanju.*

"You first," Remo said.

The great tentacle slapped at the surface of the water, and Sa Mangsang regarded them balefully. It shifted its great torso—reminding Remo of seeing a plastic sack full of semisolid filth being moved around. Underneath its great bulk was a crushed and mangled starfish—Sa Mangsang's seat cushion, as large as an aircraft. The thing had two of its five vast arms remaining, until Sa Mangsang wrapped a tentacle around one of them and dragged it off the starfish body. Black liquid spurted from the wound and the starfish trembled.

The starfish arm went into Sa Mangsang's beak, and it crunched the arm. Its body trembled, as well, as if the agony of its victim instilled a new trickle of vitality.

*Why have you broken your pact, Master of Sinanju?*

"I'm here, aren't I?" Remo answered. He felt terror bubbling in his very core, but the anger was bigger, and the anger glowed hot and orange.

The answer didn't satisfy Sa Mangsang. It dipped into the waters again with one tentacle after another, scooping up human beings—limp, but alive. Sa Mangsang snapped their heads off with its beak and gagged on the taste, but swallowed them.

He's starving, Remo thought. He's growing weak from lack of human sustenance.

"Take me!" It was the young man who had escorted them into the city. He was staggering into the courtyard, blinded by his head wound, but he managed to blunder up the ramp of bones, and down again, into the pyramid, where he trembled into the steep-sided lake. He splashed into the thick water and was instantly snatched up by a monstrous tentacle. Sa Mangsang snapped off Henry Lagrasse's head, sucked the sour juice from his brain and let the cadaver tumble into the water again carelessly.

*Master of Sinanju, send me that sweet sustenance.*

Remo looked at Chiun and smiled a shallow smile. Chiun appraised Remo emotionlessly.

"He means me," Chiun stated.

"I know. He can go hungry."

*I require nourishment for my brain—it does not keep pace with this body.*

"Forget it. You're not getting him. You're not getting anybody else. You might as well go back to sleep."

*You are required to fulfill your oath.*

"Who do you think cut off the food supply?"

Remo demanded. "We were the ones who arranged to have this piece of real estate isolated from the rest of the world."

This was news to Sa Mangsang, and not good news. An enraged scream issued from its beak and it thrashed at the waters. *This is in violation of what was promised!*

Remo forced himself to stand his ground. "I don't know who you made your deal with, but you ought to know that Sinanju contracts don't carry over from one generation to the next."

Sa Mangsang screeched and slapped the water, and near the shore many of the Colossal Squids— gnats compared to their master—bubbled to the surface with more living human beings in their tentacles. Five of them were shoved up onto the ledge.

They wore the ceremonial sashes of the Faithful of Saraswati, but their eyes were white, soulless orbs in their skulls. They came sightless up to Remo and to Chiun.

No, to Chiun. They encircled him and approached him with their arms raised. Remo took one of them by the shoulder and crushed it, but the man moved with preternatural speed, spinning and clasping Remo's hand in his own.

Remo Williams felt the hand sucking something out of his body and it hurt. It leaked from his mind and into his arm and out through the hand of the Faithful. Remo slashed the elbow and severed the arm from the body of the man, then he lashed out at the man's foot with a singe brutal kick that crushed his rib cage as it sent him flying, then tumbling down into the water. By then, Remo had moved in on the others, slashing at them, cutting through the muscles and ligaments that made their arms function. They fell away, but one of them was left and he moved faster than any man had a right to move, faster than the Master of Sinanju Emeritus. He stepped around Chiun's flashing arms and grasped the old Korean by the face, then pulled. For an instant, Remo imagined he could see the dark, phantom shadows of essence being leeched out of the strong and precious soul of Chiun.

Chiun hung, knees bent, arms loose, and through the grasping fingers Remo saw the child-like green eyes roll up, up, into the ancient, graceful head.

"No, Chiun, hang on!" Remo slashed vigorously at the Faithful of Saraswati, who turned on him and struck back with his amazing and unnatural speed.

Remo couldn't move faster than that. He was human, but the Faithful of Saraswati were imbued with something beyond human. Even a Master of Sinanju couldn't defend himself—

But Remo did. His hands clapped together with such ferocity and speed that even he hadn't seen them coming together, and his opponent's skull splattered. His fingers slipped off the face of the old Korean and Chiun staggered backward, falling to his knees and staring blindly at the heavens.

Sa Mangsang trumpeted angrily and a questing tentacle slithered onto the rocky shelf, feeling among the remnants of the last attacker. *Nothing left!*

Remo knew what that meant. The head was destroyed, and so was the essence that Sa Mangsang fed upon. Remo drifted up to the two Faithful whose arms no longer worked, and he bashed their brains into paste in two heartbeats while Sa Mangsang bellowed for him to desist.

Another one was in the water. Remo ran to the edge of the rock and sailed into open space.

*Cease, mongrel!*

Sa Mangsang snatched the Master of Sinanju midleap, and Remo felt the embrace of the great tentacle squeeze his chest—but it was removed. It didn't alarm him. Remo collapsed his chest faster than Sa Mangsang could tighten. He slipped free of the tentacle and came down atop the Faithful of Saraswati who tread the water in a stupor. Remo snatched the man by the hair, severed his neck with a vicious slash of his hand and flung the head at the rock sides of the lake. It hit hard and spattered brain tissue in every direction.

Remo flew out of the water in the clutches of a great tentacle, the island resounding with the enraged trumpets of the great elder god. Remo felt his own hatred erupt hotter than his human body could contain, more intense than his human body could endure.

When the great beak opened to devour him, Remo ripped apart the tentacle that held him, dropped onto the face of the elder god and snagged the rubbery flesh. He kicked violently, an unpretty spasm of his entire human body, and the massive beak shattered.

The colossus roared and snatched at the Master of Sinanju.

Remo gripped the flesh and dragged himself to a great, black and oily eye. He was the size of an ant compared to the monstrous Sa Mangsang, but Remo bellowed, "You are as a mongrel to Shiva the Destroyer."

His eyes were blazing red and somewhere, far away, Remo Williams witnessed his own hideous reflection. He saw the smoke rising from where his blazing hands seared the Dream Thing's flesh.

Sa Mangsang quaked. Sa Mangsang was afraid. The huge, wheezing ruin of its beak moved and croaked out human words.

"But I will become as a wolf to Shiva's flock."

"Fah!" Remo placed his blazing hand on the bulb of the huge black eye and it burst.

Sa Mangsang shuddered.

Remo clawed across the massive body. Sa Mangsang fought to keep the other eye inside the rubbery folds of flesh. Shiva batted the tentacles away and ripped through the flesh until the eye was exposed and then he burned it with his hand until it burst.

The colossal creature tensed and reared up, filled with one last burst of vitality, but then it hit the wall.

From the rock around it, it heard the sound of a human voice, speaking quiet and low. It was an old man, but not the old man on the rocks above.

Shiva heard it, too, and stood in silence absorbing the sound.

An old man, sobbing somewhere on the other side of the world, was speaking the magic words that carried all the way to the realm of Sa Mangsang.

"Dee-ya, dee-ya, dee-ya. Dee-ya, dee-ya, dee-ya."

Sa Mangsang sagged. Its body submerged into the green slime of the lake.

Remo jumped across to the shore and watched as water bubbled up in the lake. He said nothing.

Chiun felt his strength returning, although his head bled with pain. He went to the lake edge, and saw that the thing had collapsed into slumber. Remo had rendered it unconscious.

Or the thing in Remo's body had done it. Chiun faced the statuesque figure of the man he called his son, and Chiun bowed to those glowing red eyes.

"All honor to you, great Shiva."

"Chiun!" the Destroyer growled. "Chiun. Stop it. It's me."

His voice demodulated with each word. When Chiun raised his eyes, the eyes no longer blazed with fire. They were the eyes again of his son.

"All honor to you, great Master of Sinanju," Chiun said, a trace of a smile on his old lips. "You have bested Ru-Taki-Nuhu."

Remo nodded and turned away.

He landed on his knees and put a hand to his mouth to hold in the bile that threatened to retch out of him. His body was suffering in ways he didn't understand.

He felt the gentle, strong hands of his father guiding him through the city. The smell of the decomposing bodies made him gag.

"Too much human rot," Remo tried to explain. "This place is too unclean."

But that wasn't the whole of it. It wasn't just the putrefaction around him that made him ill, but the fragment of filth that had placed inside of him.

How had it gotten there? Just by association with Sa Mangsang, or had Sa Mangsang thrust it upon him? What was it and what did it mean?

All he knew at the moment was that it was making him want to throw up.

They were ankle deep in water when they reached the shore.

"The island sinks. We must hurry, Remo," Chiun urged. Remo couldn't even stand up straight to walk. He clenched his abdomen and felt himself be steered aboard one of the vessels on the shore. "This one is sound. It will be our safe house for the time being."

Remo didn't care anymore. He wanted to sleep. He wanted to have dreams about real, undecayed, clean things.

He wanted to dream about the desert.

Chiun put him on a soft mat on a carpet floor, and Remo Williams was aware of the movement of the ship. They were adrift. The island had sunk beneath them.

He envisioned, as sleep claimed him, that all the sickness and decay on Sa Mangsang's island would be enough to pollute the oceans of the entire world.

# DEATH LANDS®

## Vengeance Trail

*Available June 2005
at your favorite retail outlet*

Ryan Cawdor is gunned down and left for dead by the new Provisional U.S. Army, commanded by a brilliant general with a propensity for casual mass murder and a vision to rebuild America. Waging war from his pre-Dark, fusion-powered, armored locomotive, he's poised to unlock the secrets of the Gateways—as the rest of Ryan's group stand powerless. All except one. Hope may be lost for Krysty Wroth. But revenge is enough.

In the Deathlands, vengeance is the only justice.

---

Or order your copy now by sending your name, address, zip or postal code, along with a check or money order (please do not send cash) for $6.50 for each book ordered ($7.99 in Canada), plus 75¢ postage and handling ($1.00 in Canada), payable to Gold Eagle Books, to:

| In the U.S. | In Canada |
|---|---|
| Gold Eagle Books | Gold Eagle Books |
| 3010 Walden Avenue | P.O. Box 636 |
| P.O. Box 9077 | Fort Erie, Ontario |
| Buffalo, NY 14269-9077 | L2A 5X3 |

Please specify book title with your order.
Canadian residents add applicable federal and provincial taxes.

**GOLD EAGLE**®

GDL70